T

Haskell went back to his own world. He walked in the new part of town, the shopping precinct, among the bright neon signs and the neon-coloured clothes. He saw mothers who couldn't handle young kids, teenagers who couldn't handle pavements, and old men who couldn't handle the whole blasted world.

And he needed that, all of that. Needed to see if he was making any kind of sense.

And he was, he told himself. Nothing had changed. It had always been a straight line, he'd gone after the key and he'd got it. He was going to watch this kid coming into the cathedral tonight, see where he took the key from, and where he put it back. Which meant two separate chances. Nothing could go wrong.

By the same author
**available from Mandarin Paperbacks*

Bandersnatch
The Boondocks
*Bellman and True
Boudapesti 3
Sunspot
Cry Havoc

DESMOND LOWDEN

THE SHADOW RUN

Mandarin

A Mandarin Paperback

THE SHADOW RUN

First published 1989
by André Deutsch Limited
This edition published 1990
by Mandarin Paperbacks
Michelin House, 81 Fulham Road, London SW3 6RB

Mandarin is an imprint of the Octopus Publishing Group

A CIP catalogue record for this book
is available from the British Library
ISBN 0 7493 0297 6

Printed in Great Britain
by Cox & Wyman Ltd, Reading

For Matt

PART ONE

ONE

The line of cathedral choristers came down the steps and on to the square. Towards their rear was a boy who walked with the rolling, scuff-heeled walk of the fat boy. His name was Joffrey, and idly he looked out at the traffic in the square. Then he saw it, the red blood coming from the white van. And he said, 'That's red blood coming from that white van.'

The boys around him turned.

'Oh, what?'

'Is Joffrey telling those crashing lies of his again?'

'No, I'm not,' Joffrey said. 'And why d'you always say I tell lies?'

'Because you do.'

'Crashing lies.'

'Rancid lies.'

'*Fat boy* lies.'

Joffrey flushed. 'Look,' he said. 'Will you *look* at that van out there? The white one? Ahead of the motorbike?'

'I see it.'

'And can you see the stuff at the back dripping out? The dark red stuff? . . . Blood?'

'I can't see anything,' a boy called Morpurgo said.

'There's something,' a boy called Hallam said. 'And, all right, it's dark and red, but why's it have to be blood?'

'Because it is blood,' Joffrey said.

'Lies,' Morpurgo told him.

'We'll see,' Joffrey said.

The cars in the square were hardly moving, caught in the

usual mid-morning jam. And Joffrey hurried forward, overtaking other boys ahead.

Until there was a shout from behind him. 'Joffrey. *Joffrey.*' The tall figure of Sorley the sub-organist came up, flapping in his black gown. 'What's the hurry, boy? Why are you getting out of line?'

'It's his trousers, Sir. Been invaded by deadly driver-ants,' Morpurgo said. 'Precipitating him towards a rancid death.'

'Please,' Sorley said.

He laid a hand on Joffrey's shoulder, pulling him back. The line of boys moved on down the pavement. To their right the traffic slowed, came almost to a halt. The white van was much closer, and Joffrey couldn't take his eyes from it. The white door at the rear. The thin film of red trickling from it. The drops of red on the black tarmac.

'*Viz*, blood,' he said softly.

'*Viz*, an overturned tin of paint,' Hallam said. 'Or a broken box of tomato ketchup.'

'*Viz*, two dozen illegal immigrants in there,' Morpurgo said. 'Eating beetroot and peeing red.'

'Blood,' Joffrey said.

They drew level with the back of the van, moving exactly at its pace. 'All right, Joffrey,' Hallam said, 'let's test your theory, shall we?'

'How?'

'Well, I'll bet you. I'll bet you 10p you don't go out there and stick your finger in that so-called blood, and lick it.'

'And catch Aids, you mean?'

Hallam turned to Morpurgo. 'Always some way out, isn't there?' he asked. 'Always some excuse with the fat boy.'

But then they both turned back. Because Joffrey had moved. He was out in the road, running to the back of the van, dipping his finger in the red stuff there. And sniffing at it.

From behind them Sorley's voice came again. 'Joffrey, what are you *doing*, boy?'

Joffrey looked round in triumph. 'Smelling blood, Sir.'

'*What*?' Sorley raised his hands in disbelief.

* * *

It was five minutes later. The others were down in the changing-rooms, fighting with water around the basins. But Joffrey had left them to it, and come up alone to Middle School.

It was a long dim room. Honours boards of faded oak looked down from three of the four walls. Under the windows a ping-pong table stood without shine. The polished floor was pale and scarred. The rows of desks were dark and scarred. And there was that smell that Joffrey hated at the beginning of each term, old wood, old polish . . . and old scars.

Crashing lies.

Rancid lies.

Fat boy lies.

Angrily he crossed over to Armstrong's desk and got out Armstrong's radio-cassette. He knew he wasn't meant to. He knew radios were only meant to be played for half an hour after prep, and then only with headphones. But he didn't care. He left the headphones on one side, extended the aerial, and walked over to the window, jiggling to Radio 1.

He leaned against the sill and looked out. The narrow city street below was still blocked by traffic. It seemed the usual mid-morning jam was worse than usual.

And all at once he saw the van again. The white van from the Cathedral Square, with the red dripping from its rear door. The red he'd said was blood, then known it was when he'd smelt it. And the chill he'd felt only afterwards.

So why the same chill now? Because the front of the van showed no sign of blood. There was just the cab with the dark tinted windows, and the bodywork behind that had no lettering or firm's name. Just white-painted metal. Strange.

And suddenly it happened.

Radio 1 was blotted out, and huge sounds filled the schoolroom. First a metallic *drrrt*. Then a high-speed jingly noise like bells. And then a man's voice. Only it wasn't so much a voice as a scream, bubbling and terrible.

'Fucking carnage in here,' it went. 'Carnage, every fucking where.'

Joffrey stared at the radio in his hands.

'Fucking Woodsy lost half a fucking arm. And I got it in the hip. There's all this fucking blood. This blood.'

Joffrey saw the radio-aerial was pointing directly at the van. He threw the thing away and ran from the room, shouting for help.

But it was Sorley he bumped into outside, and Sorley was no help. Not when he heard about four-letter words and blood. He kept trying to stop Joffrey. Kept telling him he was in trouble.

And he was. Because a minute or two later he was told the headmaster wanted to see him.

TWO

The green baize of the door was just in front of Joffrey's face. He heard a voice from inside shouting, 'Come'.

He went in. There were two men over by the desk, Sorley, and the large shambling figure of Melchior the headmaster, with his mane of white hair and his massive red-pitted face.

And it was trouble all right, Joffrey saw, big trouble. Because Melchior wasn't his usual gruff self. Wasn't just in from a class and throwing his gown over a chair. Wasn't taking the essay marked See Headmaster, and saying, 'Oh, Lord, Joffrey, what kind of flannel is this?'

No, Melchior was still, unusually still. He was leaning back in his chair, lining up one cigarette-stained finger with another, and speaking very quietly.

'Come in, Joffrey. Close the door. Tell me exactly what happened.'

Joffrey stood just his side of the carpet. He cleared his throat and found a voice. 'Well, Sir,' he began, 'we missed last period before break because of choir.'

'Yes?'

'And we came back across the Cathedral Square.'

'Yes?'

'And it was in the square, Sir, I mean, I saw this white van . . . with blood coming from it.'

'Blood, headmaster,' Sorley cut in. 'At least, he said it was blood. One minute he was walking on the pavement. And the next he was out in the road, dipping his finger in this blood, and, for Heaven's sake . . . *sniffing* at it.'

Melchior nodded. Then he turned back to Joffrey. 'You agree with all this?'

'Yes, Sir.'

'But why on earth sniff at it?'

'To see if it was, Sir. Blood, Sir.'

'And was it?'

'Yes.'

Melchior sighed. 'And what happened next?'

Joffrey hesitated. And Sorley cut in again. 'I don't want to get the boy into trouble, headmaster. As I see it, he's going through a sticky patch at the moment. I mean, the others do seem to be, well, picking on him just a little. But . . .' His voice rose excitedly. 'But, for Heaven's sake, the next thing *I* knew, back at school, was Joffrey rushing at me and shouting out all these . . . *four-letter* words.'

'The swearing, yes,' Melchior said. There was a long pause, then he glanced at his watch. 'Mr Sorley, break-time is now almost over. Would you do me the kindness of going along to my class and telling them I'll be along presently?'

Sorley went out. Joffrey and the headmaster were left alone. And Melchior sat in silence. He seemed to be genuinely upset, seemed to be waiting for some kind of clue. 'Joffrey,' he said then, 'would you say we were treating you all right at the moment?'

'Yes, Sir.'

'You're not, as Mr Sorley said, going through a sticky patch?'

'No.'

'And the others aren't picking on you?'

'No.'

Melchior still seemed to be waiting. He turned in his chair and looked out of the window at the great bone-white nave of the cathedral, and the green grass of the court. 'God knows, it's a difficult enough job looking after boys in this day and age,' he said. 'And God knows, this is an old-fashioned school. But I try to do my best. I've put in modern kitchens. I've allowed transistor radios after prep. Even television in the case of national emergencies, such as the Test match.'

It was a joke, Joffrey knew, a joke Melchior often used on parents. And for a crazy moment he thought things were going to go his way.

But they weren't.

Because Melchior gave up waiting. He got to his feet. And his voice changed, it became harder. 'Let's get it over with, shall we?' he asked. 'This story of yours, this incredible story of a white van with blood coming from it.'

Joffrey nodded.

'I mean, d'you think, d'you *really* think that if there were blood inside that van? If there were carnage? If there were men in there communicating through some kind of radio-link? That the police wouldn't come? Restore order? Alleviate suffering?'

'Yes, Sir, but . . .'

'But what?'

'Well, the police couldn't come, could they? I mean, the traffic jam blocking up the streets? Every street around?'

'What about policemen on foot? Or sirens clearing a path?'

'Yes, Sir.'

'But nothing of the kind happened,' Melchior said. 'All that happened was that a white van crawled through the city in this famous traffic jam. Later the jam cleared, and the van drove away. No sirens. Nothing.'

Joffrey was silent.

And Melchior began to shift uncomfortably. 'I have to mention this,' he said then. 'There are things one can punish a boy for, and things one cannot punish a boy for. Things one hopes will sort themselves out on their own.'

Joffrey didn't understand.

'Not to put too fine a point on it,' Melchior said. 'I hear you tell a great many stories. Let us say there's a vivid imagination at work here.'

Joffrey felt the sweat prick out under his arms, felt the flush beginning.

And Melchior looked down at him. 'I want to make a couple of things quite clear to you, young man,' he said curtly. 'There's a world of difference between a vivid imagination and downright lying. And a world of difference between the odd swearword, out of earshot of a master, and the four-letter word shouted smack in that master's face.'

The flush spread up from Joffrey's chest to his neck.

But the voice went on. 'I have to impress upon you the seriousness of your offence,' it said. 'Rushing down a corridor, shouting out those things, spreading alarm throughout the school. It's tantamount to a boy shouting Fire.'

His face burning, Joffrey nodded. But then he realised that Melchior had moved away.

'I told you this was an old-fashioned school,' the man said with his back turned. 'It still canes for serious offences.'

And suddenly a stab of alarm went through Joffrey. He saw that Melchior had reached the cupboard to the left of the window. Where the school cane was kept.

'Caning is a punishment that has no dignity for the boy, and absolutely no dignity for the master,' the man said. 'I dislike caning.'

'Yes, Sir.'

And slowly Melchior turned back. 'So, what I want you to tell me now is this. Is there any truth in this rigmarole? Any single part of it? The white van? The blood? Or the voice coming over the radio?'

There was a long pause.

'No, Sir,' Joffrey said then.

'Good.' Melchior moved away from the cupboard. 'And d'you give me your word there'll be no repetition? No more lies? Otherwise it *will* be a caning offence.'

'Yes, Sir,' Joffrey said.

Melchior breathed out a sigh of relief. 'We'll leave it at that then, shall we?' he said. 'And get back to lessons?'

THREE

It was a quarter to six. There was the intimacy of evensong in the huge cathedral. The lights of the choirstalls were close in the growing darkness, the choristers and lay-clerks were close, and all that was far away was the light high up in the organ-loft.

There was movement up there. The opening bars of the magnificat wound softly around the massive arches. Like silk being rubbed over old stonework, Melchior thought. Until, that was, the longer sixteen and thirty-two foot pipes came into play, producing a sound that touched him to the core. Not a sound but a trembling, making the vast building come alive. My soul doth *magnify*, he thought.

He sat in his stall behind the cantoris choristers and watched them get to their feet. Among them, Morpurgo, the small clever boy. He heard Morpurgo whisper something to the chorister next to him, heard the boy snigger and then fluff his entry in the difficult Howells setting. While Morpurgo got it right. As he would do for the rest of his life, Melchior thought, complete with that dark clever smile of his.

Melchior looked on to where Sorley was conducting from the aisle. Sorley who had turned towards the fluffed entry, but couldn't see the culprit. As he never would, Melchior thought. Sorley who was no schoolmaster but a very good musician. Quite often nowadays he took evensong. While his superior, Maunder the organist, sat at the manuals in the loft.

The choir settled, sang on, *floated* as Maunder would have it. Every voice with a mind, as he would also have it, which thought of the middle of the note before singing it. And ears which heard the other voices around. And then without effort became the single sound that floated.

It was happening now, Melchior knew, as it did happen on the good evenings. Sorley was smiling as he conducted, his fingers catching at the ends of phrases like loops in a cloth. And Melchior looked on past him to the shadowy stalls across the aisle. Past the canons wrapped in their cloaks, past the Precentor and the Dean. Coming finally to the decani choristers, and the one boy in particular he needed to think about . . . Joffrey.

In cassock and surplice, Joffrey looked little different from the other boys around. Perhaps there was a deeper flush to his face, perhaps a gleam of sweat on his upper lip. Certainly there was the necessary constant smile of the fat boy. But, behind that smile?

Turmoil.

Melchior's heart went out to the boy. There'd been the lying and the swearing, of course, but also the threat of the cane. And this last Melchior regretted. He hadn't used the cane in, what, ten years? And the threat of it no more than a dozen times? But this morning it had been necessary. He'd conferred with Gerald Fraser, the deputy head, and they'd both agreed.

Melchior scrubbed his fingers through his hair. He'd had boys who'd lied before, had boys who'd sworn. And in his experience the reason was always the same. Trouble at home.

Certainly it was true in Joffrey's case. And certainly, too, Melchior could do very little about it.

Because there was a problem he was meeting more and more often the older he got. And put quite simply, it was this . . . His own path through the world could be measured in a matter of yards. Forty-five years ago he'd sat with the boys on the cantoris bench, and now he sat in the headmaster's stall. He'd left the school only for university and national service. And, as he'd be the first to admit, he understood very little about present-day trouble at home.

School, though, was a different matter. *Had* to be a different matter. Because if the boy persisted with his lying, his way was going to become very rocky indeed.

How to make that way smoother? Melchior asked himself. How to break the chain?

Sighing, he turned back to the music in his hands, the Howells setting of the magnificat. And the words leapt at him, 'He, remembering his mercy, hath holpen his servant . . .'

Because suddenly he remembered.

The man Sorley coming to him recently, in some excitement as usual. Talking about Joffrey. Saying that incredible things were happening. That after years of slouching his way through choir practices, Joffrey was developing a *voice*. A small one as yet, but it would be *real*, a voice of *character*.

Again Melchior looked at the small flushed face. It could happen, he told himself. It had happened before. That moment when a boy discovered he had talent, something of his own. When he found himself.

And it would happen again, Melchior was sure. Just as he was sure, looking above him to the vaulting of the cathedral, that there were years and years of God up there, piled on top of each other in the shadow.

FOUR

The doorman of the Soho restaurant put Haskell down as a builder who'd made good. He was hard, and he was all hard edges. Maybe it was the dark suit and tie against the white shirt. Or maybe it was the way he'd dyed the grey from his hair. That too-black colour that brought him sharply in from the light of the street.

Though inside the restaurant it was dim. There was the green light of ferns, and there was the smell of good lamb cooking in rosemary. Haskell found his way over to the table where Landon-Higgins was waiting. He said he'd have the lamb, and the same Cote Rotie he'd had last time, and he'd skip the starter.

'You sure?' Landon-Higgins asked. 'It means you'll have to watch me fight with my langoustines.'

'Don't worry about it,' Haskell said.

The waiter took their order and left. Landon-Higgins settled himself in his chair. And even though they were sitting at one of the alcove-tables, he spoke softly.

'I heard there was blood,' he said.

'Yes.'

'I heard all kinds of damfool things. I heard that when the police finally got the van off the road, they found these two fellers inside half-dead.'

'Yes.'

'So why was that?'

'Because it all went wrong,' Haskell said. 'All of it, from the beginning.'

'What?'

'Listen,' Haskell said, 'we set up where we said. Just short of this place called Whycliffe, where there's the cathedral.'

'Yes?'

'The van came. We jammed its radio. But then we got nowhere at all trying to bust our way in.'

'What?' Landon-Higgins stared at him. 'I don't understand. What about all that information we had?'

Haskell didn't answer.

And Landon-Higgins leaned forward, tapping his fingers. 'All right, tell me about the blood.'

'That, yes. That's another story.'

'What d'you mean?'

'Well,' Haskell paused. 'What you got to remember is you don't just take two or three people with you on a thing like this. You take more.'

'And?'

'Well, one of them swore blind he was coming with me on the day. But then he let me down.'

'So you had to take somebody else?'

Haskell nodded. 'And this somebody else, he was all mouth, throwing himself about. And then at the end, when he saw we weren't going to get at the shipment, he suddenly upped on the van and lugged explosive down through the ventilator.'

'Dear God,' Landon-Higgins said.

'Dear God is right. I only heard afterwards he'd pulled the same stunt once before, on a Securicor crew.'

Landon-Higgins was silent, chewing on his lip. 'Wait a moment,' he said then. 'You said you stopped the van just *short* of Whycliffe. And yet my reports said—'

'That was the whole thing,' Haskell told him. 'I mean, after the bang there wasn't anything we could do. We just had to sit there and watch the vehicle drive off.'

'Drive off? How could it do that?'

'Easy. The motor was all right, the driver was all right, and the wheels went round,' Haskell said. 'The explosion was just back with the shipment. And you know how much steel there is around that. You know if anyone does.'

And Landon-Higgins looked around him cautiously. 'Yes,' he said. 'Yes, I do.'

'Anyway, like I said, the van drove off. On through this town.'

'Through it?'

'Well, the Law had to let it go through, didn't they?' Haskell said. 'I mean, nobody was going to open up its doors in the middle of those streets. All that blood? Those two guys? The publicity?'

'Publicity is exactly the last word I'd use,' Landon-Higgins said. 'Dear God, how many people in England know about that white van? How many people in the world, come to . . . ?' He tailed away as the waiter came back.

Langoustines, bread, and a fingerbowl were placed in front of Landon-Higgins. And Haskell watched him tuck his napkin into his shirt collar and spread it out to cover his suit.

It was big and tent-like, the suit, with broad city stripes. Years ago the man's tailor had stopped trying to make him look slim, and settled for power. Landon-Higgins had a massive face that hung forward from eyesacks to jowl, a belly that hung forward between his thighs. And Haskell still couldn't work it out, even after three months, why he was doing business with the man.

Except he knew, the way money was getting itself about nowadays.

Landon-Higgins bit on a langoustine, squirting the juices down his chin. 'It's a bloody mess,' he said.

'It is.'

'So how're you going to sort it out?'

'I'm getting out of London this afternoon.'

'And going where?'

'Back to Bristol, where I started.'

'You reckon that'll help?'

'It will,' Haskell said. 'I'm going to see a mate of mine called John Daltrey. Good mate. We go back a long way.'

FIVE

It was a fine autumn afternoon as Haskell drove westwards. About an hour out of London he came to a section of motorway where maples were planted, their leaves coming at him like flames, and where there was good shooting country beyond. Shooting was something Haskell knew about. He had a gun in a syndicate of smart restaurant kiddies out Henley way. And he admired the order there was in the land, the stubble fields drawing away to the copses, and the patches of roots planted out of the wind.

He admired the order there was in Bristol too when he reached it. The motorway coming right into the centre of the city, and the steady movement of the rush-hour in the darkness. He headed for the Unicorn Hotel where he'd stayed before. It was big and modern and used by businessmen, which meant men eating on their own. And it had a multi-storey built onto one side, which meant he could park outside his room, and come and go without being seen.

The room was on the fourth floor, looking down on to the dark waterfront and tne empty cobbles of the quays. Haskell dumped his case on the bed. He hung his two suits in the wardrobe. He put his underclothes, shirts, socks and handkerchieves into different drawers. Each in its separate compartment.

Then he rang home.

'Hello,' he said, 'how are you?'

'Fine,' his wife replied. 'The same as when you left me this morning.'

'You sound a bit tired.'

'Do I?' she asked. 'No, not tired. Just watching Wogan and thinking about supper.'

'What are you going to have?'

'I don't know. Maybe the rest of the beef we had the other night.'

'The beef with the shallots and garlic? I liked that.'

'Yes, I put a couple of portions in the freezer.'

He glanced at his watch. 'I know what I meant to ask. Did Arthur get those geraniums out of the beds and bring them into the greenhouse?'

'I'm not sure,' she said. 'He was working on the pool this afternoon. I didn't see him when he left.'

'Doesn't matter,' he said. 'There isn't going to be a frost tonight, is there? Going to be very mild for a bit.'

They talked a few minutes longer, then Haskell put the phone down. He got out his diary, found a local number, and dialled it.

'Hello?' he asked. 'Is that Lena?'

'Speaking.'

'Lena. Great, well, listen, it's Haskell here. Remember me from last month?'

'Haskell?'

'You remember. The one who showed you Sumo wrestling in that smart Chinky restaurant.'

'Haskell.' She laughed. 'Yes.'

'All right, then. Tell you why I'm ringing. I was wondering what you were doing tonight.'

'Tonight?' she asked. 'Haskell, I'm sorry, it's kind of short notice. Tonight it's washing the old hair.'

'You sure?'

'Really. Yes, I am.'

'Oh.'

'Look,' she said then, 'something could be arranged. A lady-friend of mine who might like a night out.'

'A nice ladyfriend, Lena? Warm and caring, like yourself?'

'Yes.'

'And one of your Magic Circle? You know what I'm talking about?'

'If you mean Aids,' she said, 'I can assure you—'

'No, not that,' he said quickly. 'What I mean is, I was first put on to you, wasn't I, by my good friend Maxie? Up in the Smoke?'

'Maxie, yes, I know him.'

'And Maxie, he made a big point out of how discreet you were.'

'All my ladyfriends,' Lena said, 'are discreet.'

Her name was Julie, and he met her in a wine bar just up from the quays. She was a woman of about twenty-five, dark, and maybe a little heavy. She wasn't used to waiting on a barstool alone, and he liked that. Her grey costume was simple, you passed over it looking at the leggy creatures around, and he liked that too. But what he liked most of all came later when he paid the bill. Because it was only then when she stood up that she decided she was going on with him.

They went to a flat. It wasn't hers, Haskell knew, when she fumbled for a second set of keys. And later, when she opened the wrong sideboard door looking for the brandy. They sat close together, drinking, and watching a late-night movie. And she made it easy for him, admiring one of his gold cufflinks, then laying her cheek against his.

He gave her ten minutes to undress, and then walked quietly into the bedroom. Too quietly. Because he saw her face, the tiredness there, the anxiety, and the strange room. It only lasted a moment before she saw him and clamped on the professional smile.

He went towards her. And he told himself to forget it, told

himself not to get into any kind of stupid competition. For Christ's sake, he'd had a long day, and he was forty-nine years old.

But his hands moved to the back of her neck, smoothing out the muscles there. Then working their way down her spine to the muscles around her hips. Turning her over, spilling her breasts and stomach, smoothing her deeper and deeper into the mattress. Until she was no longer relaxed, was moving faster than his hands, was grabbing him. And finally hissing out her breath in a jagged sigh.

Acting, he thought. Had to be.

But later, when she sat up, he knew it wasn't. Because there was a look she gave him, a look that came straight out of one of his wife's historical novels. What was the word they used?

Reproach.

'You all right?' he asked.

'Yes.'

'Sure?'

She shrugged. 'Well, it's only – only I sometimes wonder what a person like you expects.'

'What I expect?'

'Yes. When you're in a strange town, and you ring up someone like Lena.'

'I don't know,' he said. 'I just want to go out and meet nice women.'

'You mean, women with big boobs.'

'I mean, nice women.'

'They start out nice,' she said.

'Hey, what's the matter?' He touched her arm.

'Well,' she said. 'You're a bit of a goer, aren't you? In that direction?'

'What d'you mean?'

'In bed.'

'No,' he said, 'I don't look at things like that.'

* * *

And he didn't, he thought later as he sat in the bathroom. He truly didn't. And there'd been only one girl in his life who'd known that.

It had been years and years ago. She'd been one of the few touches of real class ever to have crossed his path. There'd been that gleam of skin about her, and that wickedness of mouth that had made her the territory of the rich man. And there'd been a rich man too. Only he'd been five hundred miles away, and she'd been avoiding his cables and getting him on heat.

Which was why Haskell had found himself with her in the Dorchester, locked up in a room for three days. And at the end of that time she'd perched on the bed and watched him while he'd dressed. 'You know, I've got the answer,' she'd said. 'The thing about you is you wait.'

'What?'

'You watch and you wait. And you do that because you have to see all there is of a person. *Have* to. And then you break them. That's what your kick is, to have control.'

Haskell didn't answer.

'I know because I'm the same,' she said.

And then she said something strange. 'When we first met, three days ago, you smelt of cheap aftershave. You smelt of nylon shirts and nylon vests and pants. But now you smell hard and clean.'

'What?' Haskell asked.

'Do yourself a favour. Throw away those trashy clothes and that trashy shaving gear. Buy cotton and wool things, good quality things. And good quality soap.'

And she hadn't said it but Haskell knew what she meant, he smelt like a workman.

As it happened, he'd taken her advice. And as it happened too, he'd given up work at around the same time.

He sat on in the bathroom now, thinking maybe he was going to have trouble sleeping. The answer was a bath, he thought. So he leaned over, fitted the plug, and turned on the hot tap.

‘What are you doing in there?’ Julie called sleepily from the bedroom.

‘Taking a bath.’

‘Well, watch out for the hot.’

‘What?’ He didn’t understand.

But a moment later, feeling the temperature of the water, he swore loudly and clutched a hand that was red and blistering.

Julie appeared in the doorway. ‘I told you about the hot tap.’

‘Yes, you did,’ he said, ‘but I didn’t quite hear.’

‘Let me look at it.’ She came over, took his hand, and held it under the cold.

Gradually the pain eased.

‘The thing is, it’s an old block of flats with one of those very fierce old hot water systems,’ she said. ‘It comes out nearly boiling.’

‘You’re right there.’ Haskell looked at the massive brass tap, and the steam rising up to fill the bathroom.

SIX

The next morning was grey. And from his hotel room Haskell looked down at the windswept quayside. Then he went down to the restaurant, had a light lunch, and looked out at it again.

He was thinking about John Daltrey, mate of his, mate for many a long year, as he’d told Landon-Higgins. And he was thinking how, even so, he’d have to go careful.

He went back to his room and rang Daltrey’s office.

‘Hask,’ the man shouted. ‘Haskell, my son, you’re back in town.’

‘That’s right, Johnno. Got in last night.’

‘So, what are you doing? You want to meet up? Want to make it tonight?’

‘That’d be great,’ Haskell said, ‘if you’re free.’

'Free for you any time, my son. So, where shall we go? There's a new Italian opened round King Street way.'

'I'm easy, Johnno.'

'No, tell you what,' Daltrey said, 'my old lady's out tonight. You could come out to my place. I mean, you know I cook. And you know *how* I cook. Half a bottle for the pot, and a bottle and a half for the chef. What d'you think about that?'

'Sounds all boys together, Johnno. Sounds nice. What time d'you want me to come?'

'Sixish. No, call it six-thirty,' Daltrey said. 'Give me time to leave the office at five and get to the superstore . . . You like veal, Hask? Some people don't like veal. You know, moral grounds.'

'No, I like veal,' Haskell said.

'Right. See you at six-thirty.'

Haskell lay on his bed till four o'clock. Then he showered and put on a clean shirt. At a quarter to five he went out to the carpark. He got a screwdriver out of his toolkit and unscrewed the window winder-handles from his car.

Half an hour later he was in the carpark of the superstore, out on the ring-road. He was parked three spaces up from Daltrey's Jaguar. Three spaces, that was, between the Jaguar and the superstore exit.

He didn't have long to wait. Daltrey's roly-poly figure showed up in the exit. Haskell got out of his car. He opened the passenger door and left it open. Then he stood, bent forward so he was in shadow.

Daltrey came up, carrying two superstore bags. They dropped as Haskell swung him off balance and smacked his head hard against the car-bonnet. Then he got him in through the passenger door and pressed it shut. On his way round to the driver's door, Haskell stepped over one of the bags. A package of meat had fallen out. The veal, Haskell remembered. Moral grounds.

At first as they drove back into the city, Daltrey was dazed. Then he began scrabbling at the door-handles around him. To find they were locked by child-locks. Then he found the window winder-handles were missing.

'Just sit quiet,' Haskell said. And Daltrey did so. All the time it took them to get across Bristol and reach a certain block of flats.

Haskell parked outside the entrance. He turned to Daltrey. 'What's going to happen is this,' he said. 'I'm going to walk you across the pavement. And I'm going to be holding on to your arm like we're mates. But what you should remember is, I'm going to get you in there.'

He did get him in there. He got him up the stairs to the second floor. Then from his pocket he got out a small set of keys. The woman Julie's keys. He'd taken them from her handbag after they'd left the flat.

By now he had hold of Daltrey's tie and was pulling him through to the bathroom. He kicked the door shut and locked it. He went over to the bath, fitted the plug, and turned on the hot tap. Then he waited, not looking at Daltrey, and not talking to him.

The bath was a quarter full. Steam hung under the high ceiling. 'Get your clothes off,' Haskell said.

'What? What are you talking about?'

'The clothes off.'

Daltrey made no move. Haskell went for him, ripping coat buttons off, shirt buttons off, then his vest and shorts. He kicked him over suddenly, and pulled off his shoes.

Daltrey sat there stunned, covering himself with his hands. Steam hung like a curtain over his head. The noise of the bath-tap was loud.

Haskell moved one way. Daltrey moved with him. Which let Haskell come in the other way and grab him. He got his arm, swung it up and around, and stuffed his hand in the bathwater.

There was a scream. Haskell covered his mouth. One of Daltrey's hands tried to fight him off. The other was prawn red, with blisters beginning to form.

Daltrey stopped screaming. He twisted away, sat in rolls of skin in the corner. The tiles around him were dull. Steam came down almost to the floor, almost hiding him.

Haskell went for him again.

'Jesus! Jesus Christ, Hask!'

There was a crazy time. Haskell's hands slipping on wet steamy skin, his feet slipping on the wet floor. But then he had purchase, had his feet braced against the bath, had the man levered up and over the bathwater.

Suddenly Daltrey gave in. 'Okay, Hask,' he shouted. 'Okay, I'll tell you. You *understand*?'

SEVEN

It was lunchtime at Whycliffe Cathedral School. In the long eating hall the racket of a hundred and twenty boys rose up from the tables. From all except one table, that was. Because, sitting among the choristers, Sorley the sub-organist wasn't saying much. He was staring down at his plate, at the stew and the overcooked cabbage there, and wondering if he'd have to finish them.

But Morpurgo, sitting on his right, was watching. 'Better do it, Sir,' he said, 'or you'll be in trouble with the Black Dwarf.'

'Black Dwarf?' Sorley asked.

'Yes, Sir. Headmaster's wife, Sir. She supervises the cooking, after all.'

'What?'

'Better finish it, Sir, if you'll take my advice.'

Sorley reddened. He found himself spearing another piece of meat. Then he turned to the boy on his left. 'I was wondering, Hallam,' he said, 'what kind of stew this was.'

'Can't be sure, Sir,' Hallam said.

'Mole, Sir,' Morpurgo said. 'Mole stew.'

'Yes, that's it,' Hallam said. 'You can tell from the pipes.'

'Pipes?' Sorley asked. 'What are you talking about?'

'The pipey bits, guts, entrails. Look at them.' Hallam pointed to his plate.

'Please,' Sorley said.

'Yes, and this heart-bit I've got here,' Morpurgo said, 'with blood spurting out.'

'Better give it to Joffrey then,' Hallam said. 'He'd like that. He's the expert on blood.'

'That's right.' Morpurgo turned to where Joffrey was sitting on his right. 'Joffrey sees blood in the Cathedral Square, coming out of white vans.'

Sorley raised a hand quickly. 'Morpurgo, will you stop that. That little episode's quite finished with.'

'Yes, Sir, but Joffrey was the only one who said it was blood. Who said he had proof.'

'Stop it. I won't tell you again.'

Morpurgo looked from Joffrey back to Sorley. He saw he'd pushed the man far enough, and reckoned it was time to change the subject. Sport, he reckoned. Sport was surefire with masters, even the wimpy ones like Sorley.

'Sir?' he asked. 'D'you know what happened at Sunningdale yesterday?'

'Sunningdale?'

'The golf, Sir. D'you know how Ballesteros did in the second round?'

'I don't follow golf,' Sorley said.

'But it'll be in your paper, Sir.' Morpurgo pointed to *The Times* by the man's plate.

Sorley nodded. He picked up the paper and turned to the sports page. 'Golf . . . Ah, yes, here we are. Ballesteros appears to be in the lead. His score is 138, whatever that means.'

Then he looked round. He saw that Hallam was reading something on the back page. 'What is it, Hallam?' he asked. 'Something there that interests you?'

'Yes, Sir. I mean, d'you think I could have this paper when you've finished with it?'

'Of course. Delighted to see you're interested in the news,' Sorley said. 'What is it? This article here?'

'Yes, Sir. Only it's not so much the article. More a bit of it, really. More one word.'

'One word?'

'"Belched", yes, Sir. The word, "belched". I want to cut it out for Jackson. He collects words like that.'

Sorley stared at him.

'Jackson can belch up carrots and eat them again,' Hallam said.

Sorley nodded slowly. He folded up *The Times* and then looked down at his plate. He pushed it away. It was a moment before he spoke again. 'I hope you boys remember,' he said, 'that it's rather a special choir practice this evening.'

'Oh, yes, Sir,' Hallam said.

'Unbelievably exciting, Sir,' Morpurgo said.

Sorley looked at them tiredly. 'Well, it might just be a little more exciting than you imagine. Because of course this evening's when we'll be choosing soloists for the carol service at the end of term.'

Morpurgo shrugged. 'I know, Sir. But it's going to be a bit of a formality, isn't it? This year?'

'How d'you mean?'

'Well, let's face it, most of the solos recently have gone either to Ralston who's head chorister, or Gavaine who's leader of decani. And besides them there's Felstead and Avery . . . I mean, we're a bit of a strong team at the moment, aren't we? At least, that's what Mr Maunder says.'

'Yes, you could be right. But maybe we should look at other boys too.'

'Like who, Sir?'

In answer, Sorley looked past Morpurgo to the boy sitting next to him. 'Maybe I'll surprise you,' he said, 'and mention the name Joffrey.'

'*Joffrey*, Sir?'

'You cannot be *serious*.'

'Quite serious,' Sorley said. 'In my opinion that boy's beginning to show a great deal of talent.'

'The only talent that boy has,' Morpurgo said later, 'is for telling lies.'

'Exactly,' Hallam said.

'Lies about anything and everything. All the rancid time.'

It was after lunch. The two of them were in the changing-rooms, getting ready for football.

'*Viz*,' Morpurgo went on, 'when he said he went on Concorde.'

'Said his father took him on Concorde.' Hallam nodded. 'On a business trip to Manchester.'

'And Concorde doesn't fly to Manchester.'

'Exactly,' Hallam said.

'And *viz*,' Morpurgo continued, 'the time he said his father took him to Lord's. And he got Botham's autograph.'

'Never showed it to anyone, did he?'

'And if you had Botham's autograph, you'd show it around.'

'Exactly,' Hallam said.

Morpurgo took his football vest and his shorts down from his peg. 'Why's he have to pretend to be so flash and jet-setty?' he asked. 'I mean, his family's well off. He gets good pocket-money. Always got money for cigarettes.'

'It's his act,' Hallam said. 'Wants to be Mr Big, kind of mysterious. Like that rubbish about gangsters attacking a white van.'

'And like that other act he had once, remember?' Morpurgo said. 'When he went round like some oiky rockstar. His coat collar turned up and his sleeves pushed back in that oiky way.'

'And those folded-up bits of paper he carried around with him.'

'God, yes,' Morpurgo said. 'And when people were looking, he unfolded one of these papers, and licked up the white powder inside.'

'Which turned out to be crushed-up aspirin,' Hallam said.

'Spasmo,' Morpurgo said. He reached up and got his sweater down. And then he saw, in the gap where it had been, Joffrey sitting in the next bay of the changing-room. Listening.

But it didn't stop him. 'Absolutely *spasmo*,' he said.

EIGHT

Before the full choir practice in the evening there was, as usual, a trebles' practice. It was held in the music school, the choristers standing in a semi-circle around Sorley at the piano. And the last piece they came to was an introit that Sorley himself had written.

They made a mess of it, and he stopped them.

'I can see where the trouble is,' he said. 'It's this one particular interval that recurs – the augmented fourth, the tri-tone.'

He played it on the piano.

'Can't seem to get the hang of that, Sir,' Ralston said.

'I know it's difficult.' Sorley nodded. 'But, tell you what, just think about it another way. Think about that tune from *West Side Story* . . . "Maria".'

'Ma-who-er?' Gavaine asked.

'"Maria". Don't you know *West Side Story*?'

'No, Sir,' Morpurgo said. 'Try UB40.'

'Or Dire Straits,' Hallam said.

'Please,' Sorley said. 'Please.'

He waited for silence. 'Now, the first three notes of "Maria" go like this . . .' He played them. 'And of course the first *two* notes form a tri-tone. So, let's try them, shall we? All together? With the piano . . . Ma-*ri*-a . . . Ma-*ri*-a . . .'

They managed it.

But when he asked them, each in turn, to sing a tri-tone above a note he played on the piano, they failed.

All except Joffrey.

Sorley beamed at him. 'Well sung,' he said. 'Very well sung.'

'It's his new act,' Morpurgo whispered, 'greasing up Sorley.'

But Joffrey didn't turn round. He didn't say anything. Because it *was* his new act. Just until the end of practice.

And, five minutes later, when the others went out for drinks and biscuits, he stayed behind.

'Sir?' he said.

'What is it, Joffrey?'

'Well, you know the carols? The carols we're singing in the full practice? You know you said I could put them out in folders?'

'Yes,' Sorley said.

'Well, I haven't quite finished, Sir. I mean, it's a long job. Nine carols, all in order, put into thirty-two different folders.'

'Doesn't matter. I'll finish it,' Sorley said. 'You go along with the others.'

'I'd . . . I'd rather do it myself, Sir.'

'What? Why's that?'

'I don't know, Sir. I quite like doing it.'

And Sorley looked down at him a moment. 'Yes, young Joffrey, I believe you do,' he said. 'I believe you're really getting quite keen on choir work. Making up for past mistakes.'

'That's it, Sir.'

Sorley ruffled his hair and went out. But Joffrey made no move towards the table where the carols were. He didn't have to. He'd lied to Sorley. He'd already finished sorting them, nine carols, in order, in each of the thirty-two folders.

Instead he went over to the door of the music school, or rather to the keys hanging just by the door. Big old-fashioned keys, the cathedral keys, on a massive ring.

He undid the ring and removed one of them. It seemed even larger in his hand, old pitted metal, and a big intricately-carved part, all whorls and patterns, where it fitted into the lock.

More than that, it was a key Sorley would never miss. He never went up to the bellchamber.

Joffrey stood in the cold stone shadows of the cathedral, the south transept, with its torn military flags high above him, and its darkness hanging down like a curtain. He looked up at the three great tiers of Norman arches, one above the other, and the old dust colour of the pillars. Then he listened. But there were no sounds other than the thrum of the heating and the flap of a verger's gown, far away.

He walked the length of the transept until he came to an iron-studded oak door. And for the first time he hesitated. But a glance at his watch told him there were only twenty-five minutes left before the full practice began.

Quickly he crossed to the door, unlocked it, and then locked it again behind him. He switched on the light. Stone steps went up and around in a spiral staircase. They were each about a foot high, and he'd counted fifty of them by the time he reached the top.

He was above the first layer of arches, standing in a long gallery with a balustrade. To his left was space. And to his right dark bays that had timbers and beams. He walked past three bays. Then came to another flight of steps.

There were thirty of these, which meant he was now eighty feet up, and above the second tier of arches. The *clerestory*, he knew it was called. The clear storey, with plain leaded windows to his right.

It was more tricky here because the gallery was narrow, very narrow. And the floor was no longer smooth but rough flints and rubble. Some of it was crumbling and wet, and there were wet streaks in the archways. Worse, to his left was just a single iron rail.

Then it happened. His heel skidded on wet rock. He flung himself away from the rail, in towards an archway, and lay there trembling. Below him the black and white floor of the chancel seemed tiny. And his place in the choirstalls no more than a fingerprint.

He took a deep breath. Then picked himself up and walked on. In a book once he'd read about a fat boy moving with surprising agility. A fat boy didn't move with surprising agility. He moved with unsurprising fear, sometimes along the only path he could follow. Sometimes with quite a lot of fear.

At the end of the clerestory he came to the bellchamber door. There was a passage that led on past it, and then another spiral staircase. And then finally, at the top, a door leading outside.

Wind hit him as he moved slowly to the parapet at the edge of the tower. Wind, and a huge grey day. The great louvres of the bellchamber were clattering below him. And above him raced the sky.

Joffrey ducked down below the parapet, got cigarettes from his pocket, and lit one. He took two or three deep puffs.

Along the only path he could follow. Ahead of him an iron ladder went up and over the parapet. It had eight steps. He went up four of them.

The cigarette was in his left hand. His right clutched tightly onto the ladder-rail. And he looked down. One hundred and twenty feet below him was the dark shadow of the cloisters, and the lit windows of the music school. There were faces there, the choristers with their drinks and biscuits.

He waved. Waved for a long time until one of them saw him. Then others, crowding against the window. Joffrey went up another step. He held his cigarette out at arm's length. He brought it back and took a big exaggerated puff. And he shouted.

'*Viz*, *viz*, *viz*,' he shouted, '*the fat boy*!'

NINE

The full practice was due to begin. Sorley sat at the piano in the centre of the aisle and looked round at the boy-choristers. They were already in their places. Including Joffrey, he noticed, who had been the last to appear, bringing the carol-folders.

A boy who was turning over a new leaf, Sorley thought. A boy who was perhaps going to surprise them all.

The lay-clerks arrived, the men who sang tenor, bass, and alto. With heavier tread they climbed into the stalls and sat behind the boys. There was the creak of wood and the rattle of throat-pastilles. Then the smell of the pastilles and the old damp smell of music from the cathedral library. Things that brought a great deal of calm to Sorley. He'd lived with them for twenty-two of his twenty-nine years.

He opened the piano and took the choir through a couple of scales. He took them through the tricky chants for Friday evening. And then he asked them to open the carol folders.

'Numbers 3, 7, and 8,' he said. 'In The Bleak Midwinter,' arranged Darke. '*In Dulci Jubilo*', arranged Pearsall. And Britten's 'Hymn To The Virgin' . . . And, as you can see, they all have treble solos.'

Sorley turned to the piece of paper he had on his music-stand. It was a shortlist of boys for each solo, drawn up jointly by himself and Maunder the organist.

And Maunder, a dark silhouette down by the rood-screen, was to listen to the boys from the far end of the chancel. He was to raise an arm when he'd chosen.

During the next twenty minutes the arm came up three times. For Ralston the head chorister in 'In The Bleak', for Gavaine in '*In Dulci*', and for Felstead as the quartet soloist in the Britten.

Which was all rather depressing, Sorley thought, because it was exactly as that dreadful boy Morpurgo had predicted.

But there was still one solo left, the solo that had given Sorley a growing sense of excitement over the past few days. Because it didn't depend on musical experience but voice, pure voice.

He got up from the piano and went down the aisle towards Maunder. The dark silhouette became a man in his fifties, a man unlike the tweedy pipe-smelling organists of Sorley's youth, a man who was shiny. Maunder wore expensive suits, he had sleek hair, gold-rimmed glasses. And against him Sorley felt himself to be exactly what he was, a young schoolmaster in bicycle clips.

'Mr Sorley?' Maunder asked in his thin clipped voice.

'Ah, yes,' Sorley said. 'About this last solo . . . We agreed we'd try a young voice, didn't we? A small voice even, given the acoustic of the cathedral?'

'We did.' Maunder nodded. 'And I suppose the obvious choice would be young Morpurgo.'

'No, I don't think Morpurgo,' Sorley said, perhaps a shade too quickly.

'What about Hallam then?'

'Not him either.'

'Why?' Maunder asked, surprised. 'Have you anything against those two?'

'No, of course not,' Sorley said.

Maunder's voice became thinner. 'Who have you got in mind then, from your researches into the depths of the choir?'

Sorley hesitated. 'How about Joffrey?'

'Joffrey? Isn't he rather the . . . sluggard at the back?'

'He was, but he's improved enormously,' Sorley said. 'I told you about him last week.'

'Did you now?'

'There's just beginning to be a fine voice there. A voice of character even.'

'Bit high-flown that, isn't it?'

And Sorley fell silent. He always fell silent in front of Maunder. The man was, after all, organist of one of the top cathedrals in the country. And it was rumoured he was moving on. Rumoured he'd set his sights on Westminster or Canterbury, where a knighthood went with the job.

There was a moment's silence. 'All right,' Maunder said then, 'Joffrey, if you must. But don't take up too much time.'

Sorley went back up the aisle. He stopped in front of Joffrey, picked up an *Ancient and Modern*, and found a page. 'We're trying you for this,' he said. 'First verse, hymn 329. "Once in Royal".'

Joffrey was amazed. But he didn't show it. And he hardly listened as Sorley went on.

'Now it's just a verse in a hymn-book. It's very easy, and you know it like the back of your hand,' Sorley said. 'So just let the tone come out, build on the upward line, and make something of the higher notes. All right?'

Joffrey nodded.

'Good luck then.'

He watched Sorley go away to the piano, heard him play the first three notes of 'Once in Royal'. Then there was silence. And a strange thing happened. The choirstalls around Joffrey slid away. He was surrounded by yards of empty space.

He began. His voice was tiny, *tiny* in the huge cathedral, and all he could hear was his breath. He was very afraid . . . Until, that was, he looked round and saw Sorley, all delicate, all artsy-fartsy, bent like some daft wimp over the piano . . . Let the tone come out, the man had said . . . But, why? Joffrey thought. Why bother to go through the whole number, the bizzo? He didn't want the job anyway.

The music rose higher. Build on the upward line, Sorley had said. Oh, *sure* . . . Joffrey looked up at the darkness below the tower, where he'd been not half an hour ago, smoking, shouting down at the rest of the choir. *Viz, viz, viz – the fat boy.*

He almost giggled.

Then he was reaching the high notes Sorley had talked about. *Mary was* . . . Make something of them, the man had said. Fat chance. Fat, *fat* chance.

Sorley sat over the keys of the piano. He was trembling. His body was full. Just touch him, he thought, and he'd spill over. Because after twenty-two years of being involved with choirs, he'd suddenly found gold. Pure gold from the dusty music and the smell of throat-pastilles. It filled the darkness above him and splashed down the walls . . . The relaxed, the sheer *unforced* quality of the voice.

It finished.

Maunder's clicking footsteps came up the aisle. He stopped by the piano and took off his glasses. He wasn't a man given to emotion.

But then he surprised Sorley. 'Moving,' he said. 'Moving is the only word. And you're right . . . character . . . that rare thing in one so young, the person coming through the voice.'

He went over to Joffrey and shook his hand.

TEN

Haskell was driving the car that had the window winder-handles missing and the child-locks on. Sitting on his left was John Daltrey, and Daltrey was a mess. His shirt was in shreds where Haskell had ripped it. His scalded left hand was wrapped in a towel. And his eyes still had that dull grey colour they'd had in the steamy bathroom.

That had been yesterday. Today they were out driving. They'd come fifteen miles out of Bristol on the motorway and turned off into the country. Fields were on their left, stubble-fields with the scattered red of beech leaves along their headlands. And Daltrey looked out at the autumn colours in disbelief.

'Hask,' he said softly. 'Hask, my son, we're good mates.'

'Sure we are,' Haskell said.

'I mean, we've known each other since school . . . Edmonton . . . And after that it was National Service. We had some good times in Krautland, didn't we? Made a few bob?'

'Yes, we did.'

'And back at home, the building sites. Until we found the sweet life, Hask, the sweet life. And I mean, we always went in on everything together.'

'We did, Johnno. We did.'

'What I'm trying to say is, Hask, we never split up till Dawn and I got married, and moved out Bristol way. And even then we used to meet up, go racing, or go off weekends. You'd get on the phone to me, or I'd get on the phone to you.'

'That's it.' Haskell let the silence hang.

Daltrey looked out of the window uneasily. The fields on his left became steeper, became scrubland and woods.

Haskell turned to him. 'Only this time it was me getting on the phone to you,' he said suddenly.

'What?'

'This last time, when was it, couple of months back?'

'That's right, Hask. July.'

'And I told you I was coming out Bristol way.'

'Yes.'

'But I never said why I was coming.'

'And I never asked, Hask, did I?'

'No, you didn't. But, if you remember, I came out to your place one night. I bought a bottle of Armagnac for you, and chocolates for Dawn. And you cooked in your kitchen, and we had a good evening.'

'Course we did.'

'But then, after Dawn went to bed,' Haskell said, 'I asked you to do something very small and very simple for me. And I asked it because we were good mates, like you said.'

'Yes,' Daltrey said.

'And what I asked, this very small and simple thing,' Haskell went on, 'was for you to contact a man in a pub near here. A man who was a company director in a small firm. I asked you to give him a sealed packet containing money. And pick up a packet of classified files in return.'

'Yes,' Daltrey said, quieter.

'And when you buggered that up, when you *really* buggered that up, and left me out on the road with half the Law in the West Country on my back . . .' Haskell paused. '. . . I had to stick your hand in a bath of near-boiling water to find out what went wrong.'

Daltrey sank down in his seat, turned away.

And Haskell tried to hold on to his anger. Anger didn't do any good.

'For Christ's sake, Johnno,' he said. 'What I've been asking myself, all the time I've been driving . . . What made you take twenty? Twenty out of a hundred? *Grand*?' The anger broke through. 'Was it because you'd been out Bristol way some time? And you thought your back was protected?'

Daltrey didn't answer.

'Or was it because you thought a hundred grand was way above Bristol rates? And you'd forgotten about London rates?

Top London rates? Johnno, didn't it ever occur to you this thing was special?'

Maybe a quarter of an hour later the road was winding between low hills. And Haskell was driving slowly, looking for the lay-by he remembered from before. It came up after a long bend. And he pulled over onto the gravel and parked.

'What's happening here?' Daltrey asked. And then, as Haskell started getting out of the car, 'Where – where are you going?'

'Nowhere,' Haskell said. 'I'll be back in a moment.'

He found the footpath he remembered from before too, and started climbing through autumn trees. At first the light around him was an old gold colour, but higher up the branches were bare where the wind had got to them. And he came out onto open farmland where a tractor was ploughing red furrows under a white sky.

He followed the path upwards until he reached the top of the hill and could look down on the far side. There was a road down there, the same road he'd been driving on, but now going in a wide sweeping curve round the hill. Halfway along it a stone bridge went over a river, and there was a works entrance that was stone as well. Old stone, Victorian, as Haskell knew.

He looked down at the works entrance, at the poplar trees to one side, and the river that widened into a mill-race. Which was all you could see when you passed by on the road. While from up here you could see a lot more.

There were modern factory sheds lying back behind the trees. There was a brick and glass administration block, where even at this moment a certain company director was working.

And to the right, in Dispatch, were two white vans.

Haskell looked until he was shivering in the cold wind. Then he turned away. He went back past the farmland where the tractor was ploughing. He walked down through the bare trees and then the leafy trees with their golden glow. And by the time he came in sight of the road again, he'd decided how to do it. He slipped off his trouser-belt and put it in his pocket.

He got back into the car.

'What are you going to do, Hask? I mean . . . ?'

'Nothing, Johnno. Don't worry.'

'Nothing?'

'All that's going to happen,' Haskell said, 'is you and I are going to take a quiet walk up through the trees.'

'The trees? Away from the road?'

'I can't take you on the road, Johnno, can I? Not the way you look right now?'

'No.' Daltrey glanced around him. 'But . . . why go walking?'

'Little business transaction,' Haskell said. 'I'm shy twenty grand, aren't I? But we can sort that out. Put the books straight. Nice and easy.'

Daltrey wasn't sure.

'Let's get your seat-belt off,' Haskell said.

His hand went to the seat-belt button and pressed it. But then he held on to the webbing, low down, between the seats.

'Looks like it's stuck,' he said. 'It does that sometimes. Just give it a jerk up at the top.'

Both of Daltrey's hands went to the mounting. And Haskell moved. He slipped the trouser-belt from his pocket and got it round Daltrey's neck. He took a loop round each hand and braced fist against forearm.

It took some time for a man to die like that. And while it was happening, Haskell went through what he'd have to do afterwards. Drive on to some lane and get Daltrey into the boot. Bend his knees up so he was small. Cover him with his coat. And get the coat cleaned later, in London.

ELEVEN

It became one of those magical autumn days as Haskell drove back towards the motorway with the body. The kind of day when you went through beeches that were the unbelievable red-brown colour of toffee. And where chestnut leaves fell like flames on the road ahead.

All very different, he thought, from the time when he'd started on this thing, when he'd first met Landon-Higgins. It had been summer then. The trees in Kensington Gardens had that dry folded look of July. And on the walk over to the Round Pond there'd been couples sprawled on the grass, black and stick-like against the sun.

Landon-Higgins had walked beside him with those short steps of his, breathing heavily. And Haskell had wondered what he was doing with a man who talked like a Tory minister, or even a retired Tory minister, his face purple in the heat.

But the man was surprisingly tough, pacing himself, and talking in short bursts. 'You don't know me. I don't know you,' he said. 'But we share a mutual friend. Man called Grately.'

'Harry Grately?'

'Harry, yes.'

Which meant that Haskell knew the racket . . . town hall sales. The prime sites, bus depots, nurses' homes, and schools that were being sold off by councils nowadays. Cheap, if planning wasn't through. And cheaper still if the ratepayers around didn't know they were being moved on to allow for access streets.

'So you're in that business,' Haskell said. 'Wrapping cheques round bricks and lugging them through planning department windows.'

'No, not me. Very boring, that.'

'What then?'

But the man left the question unanswered. They were nearing the Round Pond by now, and the kids of all ages with their model boats. There was a young boy on a bench with a yacht, and Landon-Higgins bent close to him. 'Sod off,' he whispered. The boy went.

Landon-Higgins sat down on the bench. 'That's better,' he said. 'Promised myself I'd only walk another half mile in my life.'

Haskell sat next to him.

And the man began. 'All I know about you is what Harry Gratley told me,' he said. 'You don't work all that often, but when you do, it has to be special.'

And maybe this was special, Haskell thought, if Landon-Higgins was going to risk his blood pressure and walk all the way out to this bench in the heat.

'At risk of blowing my own trumpet, I'm reasonably well known in the City,' the man went on. 'And about a year ago I was asked onto the board of a group of companies. Worldwide they are, water-pumps, water-softeners, little jollies like that. And profitable too on the face of it, except that the numbers had started to go wrong.'

Haskell nodded.

'Anyway, I managed to help sort them out,' Landon-Higgins said. 'And then, with time to sit back, I looked further down the list of companies. And there, right at the bottom, was a factory nobody seemed to know much about. North east of Bristol it was, small, and not much to look at. Just an old Victorian works entrance by a road.'

Again Haskell nodded.

'But, d'you see, there was one rather interesting thing about this factory. I mean, although it was part of the group, it wasn't serviced by the group's computer. Had its own, on site. Classified. And all there was at head office was a terminal for unclassified stuff. Which, you understand, wasn't to be played with by just anyone. Not even by me who'd just helped to pull the whole shebang up by its bootstraps.'

Landon-Higgins stretched his huge bulk out on the bench. 'So what I did was, I danced rather prettily. Managed to get to this terminal for a short period of time. And we had a jolly chat. About Yenefex and Euroslopes and little insanities like that. But then I punched up another heading on the screen . . . Weedings . . . Which turned out to be the screening of the factory personnel. And pretty hefty screening at that. Yes-no at government level.'

'Government level?' Haskell asked. 'You mean it's a government site?'

'Hold on.' The man raised a hand. 'All I'm saying for the moment is that this computer-chat was done in a jolly frame of mind, an idle frame of mind. And it was still jolly and idle and roses-round-the-door as I checked out the personnel. And what d'you think I found?'

'You tell me.'

'All right. A teensy-weensy electronic nudge. Just the slightest computer *moue* about a certain person,' Landon-Higgins said. 'A person very near the top. A company director. A powerful man who had directorships elsewhere. But what the computer had noticed was his run of really *rather* good luck on the market.'

And he smiled. 'We come to the most beautiful words in the English language . . . "Dealing on a recognised stock exchange, knowingly in possession of unpublished and price-sensitive information".'

'Insider dealing,' Haskell said.

'Exactly. And, d'you see, this company director's run of luck only lasted so long. It finished with the Guinness affair.'

'You mean, he was involved in that?' Haskell asked.

'Dropped out just in time. Never got his name in the papers,' Landon-Higgins said. 'But *I* knew. And I began to keep a pretty close eye on him.'

He smiled again. 'And then, d'you see? After a decent interval, when the feller had recovered his testicles . . . I managed to swing a couple of really rather incredible deals his way. Without, of course, him knowing where they came from.'

'And they worked? These deals of yours?'

'Oh, he got quite rich. And he began to rely on the sort of gossip I was feeding him.' Landon-Higgins shrugged. 'Until the day came when my gossip was bad. And I *do* mean bad. And I *do* mean he was in over his head. For example, he could sell his condo in Florida, sell both his planes, sell his concubine and his concubine's Saluki, but he'd *still* have to come up with a quick and definite hundred grand before he could again fart with his missus in bed.'

Haskell grinned. 'Fine,' he said. 'But what I don't see is how I figure in all this.'

'Simple. I want you to get this company director a hundred grand.'

'Hundred?'

'I've made quite a few hundreds recently.'

'But,' Haskell said, 'me, personally?'

'No, through an intermediary. A trusted intermediary.'

'And that's all you want?'

'Good heavens, no,' Landon-Higgins said. 'There are lots of other things too. To do with your . . . profession.'

Haskell turned away.

'Oh, come on. Don't be coy. You know people. People who would indulge in, let's say, photocopying work.'

'Photocopying?'

'And other people. People who would maybe go with you on a rather atha-letical little jaunt.'

Haskell turned back. He leaned close. 'Let's have it straight,' he said. 'This factory you're on about, what do they make there?'

'Ah, yes, the product. I forgot to mention that.' Landon-Higgins wiped his face. 'But I said, didn't I, that overall the group of companies was concerned with water? Water-pumps, water-softeners, and the like?'

'Yes.'

'Well, this little factory outside Bristol is concerned with water too. They have a stream running alongside the worksheds. And they clean it, the water, very thoroughly. They're good at that.'

'Get on with it.'

'And as for the raw materials, there's something called "cotton-comber". Then there's plastic. Then metal of various kinds, according to customers' requirements. Oh, and then . . .'

'Come on.'

Landon-Higgins smiled again. He waved an arm out across the park. 'Let's say that when we leave here, I want to buy a box of matches. Let's say I've only got a fifty pound note. Let's say I go into a bank to change it. And what happens? The cashier holds the fifty up to the light, doesn't he? Looking for forgeries? Looking for the watermark and metallic thread?'

Haskell nodded.

'But, let's say he's looking at a forgery that's *got* this watermark and metallic thread. Let's say he's got a forgery printed on the correct Bank of England paper.'

And Haskell got there.

'Every forgery detected in this country,' Landon-Higgins said, 'has been detected for one reason, and one reason only . . . the paper.'

'Yes,' Haskell said.

'So, let us talk about a factory that produces the real thing. Let's say it ships the paper out to the Bank of England printers when required. By road. In white vans. Let's say that these vans have a payload of four tons. And that a ton of paper equals a million banknotes . . . And that in the case of the higher denomination shipments, the fifties and twenties, you're talking about paper worth one . . . hundred . . . and . . . ten . . . million . . . pounds.'

Haskell looked at the man's face, the jowl, the sweating cheeks, and the hard black eyes.

'*Yes*,' he said.

TWELVE

A fat boy, as Joffrey well knew, skated on thin ice. Or even very thin ice if, for example, he'd just been chosen for a solo over the heads of a dozen other choristers.

Including Morpurgo and Hallam.

So Joffrey kept out of their way. He kept out of everyone's way. Until the following Wednesday afternoon, that was, when it no longer mattered. Because on Wednesday afternoons the choir had something else to occupy their minds. A little game that they played.

It went like this. On Wednesdays there was early evensong over at the cathedral. Which meant that the choir had early football on their own. Which meant in turn that they had to be out on the playing fields by a quarter past two at the latest.

And they never were, not if Sorley was in charge.

On this particular Wednesday Sorley turned up exactly at two o'clock. He counted heads, and found that three boys were missing. And it took him five minutes to find Armstrong and Gavaine hiding in the library. And another ten to find Gillick behind the sheds, cutting up his football vest with scissors.

By a quarter past two Sorley had them all assembled in Middle School. 'Right,' he said, 'just a short game. Twenty minutes each way.'

'Oh, what, Sir?'

'But, how can we play, Sir? Football, I mean? Ralston's always captain of one team, and Ralston's excused games.'

'Anyway, Sir, why's he excused games?'

'You know perfectly well,' Sorley said.

'Do we, Sir?'

'Yes, it's because the choir made that broadcast of choral evensong recently on Radio 3, and Ralston missed crucial work for his exams.'

'Oh, crucial, Sir. Absolutely crucial.'

'But, we all missed crucial work, Sir. We were all in that broadcast.'

'I missed crucial history, Sir.'

'I missed crucial Latin.'

'And I'm only halfway through my crucial *Penthouse*.'

'What was that, Morpurgo?' Sorley asked.

'Oh, Sir. Nothing, Sir.'

But Sorley sighed heavily, a sure sign he was weakening. 'Look,' he said, 'it's twenty-five past two now. Soon it'll be too late to start anything.'

'Oh, yes, Sir.'

'Far too late, Sir.'

'Far too late to get out to the playing fields *and* be back for evensong at four.'

'And, Sir, in case you've forgotten,' Morpurgo said. 'Mr

Maunder the organist is away. Which means you'll have to prepare the service . . . A great responsibility on your shoulders.'

Sorley frowned. He looked responsible. He looked responsibly at his watch, responsibly at the autumn day outside.

And it was this last that did it, the thought of going out into that cold wind in his games shorts. 'Well, look,' he said, 'if you promise me you've got work to do.'

'Oh, we have, Sir.'

'Really we have.'

'Then get on with it,' Sorley said. 'But keep it quiet. Remember I'll be in my study across the hall.'

And they did keep it quiet, for all of ten minutes. But then Ralston tired of working. Felstead and Avery tired of Trivial Pursuit. And Morpurgo tired of his *Penthouse*.

The talk drifted to the subject of Maunder. Maunder the organist, the sharp-suited, the ambitious . . . Why he was away.

'Gone up to London,' Ralston said. 'I heard him talking about it to Sorley.'

'London? Why's he gone up there?'

'Dunno,' Ralston said.

'I do,' Morpurgo said. 'Gone to see his agent.'

'Oh, what?'

'What?'

They all turned towards Morpurgo, the small clever boy with the large head.

'Maunder hasn't got an *agent*.'

'Course he has,' Morpurgo said. 'Whizz-kid like him in the music business. On his way up. Crucial to a man like that.'

'Crucial, absolutely crucial,' Hallam said, echoing him.

'I don't believe it.'

'Oh, yes,' Morpurgo insisted. 'And what's more, he needs an agent, definitely. I mean, look at that evensong we broadcast on Radio 3. Disaster, wasn't it?'

'Total,' Hallam said.

'And then look at the evensong that Winchester broadcast the week before,' Morpurgo went on. 'Which turned out to be one of your all-time greats.'

'And you can bet Maunder was in a sweat about that,' Hallam said. 'You know how he just loves Winchester.'

'Too right.' Morpurgo climbed up on his desk and got their attention. 'So, even as we speak,' he said, 'Maunder's in London with this agent of his. In his office. And what the man's saying to him is this . . . "My boy," he's saying, "you're in trouble. You blew the live broadcast on Radio 3, and you just have to live with that fact. So my advice to you is, forget the live gigs. What your career needs right now is an album. A hit album. A hit evensong, say. Or a hit communion."'

'True,' Hallam said.

'"And how you go about it, my boy,"' Morpurgo went on, '"is look at where the gravy is. Look at Winchester. They got a nice sound there. And they did this Lloyd-Webber Requiem, didn't they? Flaccido Flamingo. Big band. A real sockaroony. Golden disc."'

'Platinum, more like,' Hallam said.

'"Because you can do it, my boy,"' Morpurgo tapped the side of his nose. '"Just get that fine talent of yours to work. Think up some tracks for the A side, tracks for the B side . . . And a great album title."'

'Tricky,' Hallam said. 'Really tricky.' He looked round at the others. 'Anybody got any ideas?'

'For what?'

'An album title.'

'What about carols?' Felstead asked.

Morpurgo shook his head. 'Been done.'

'What about anthems?' Avery asked. '"The Greatest Hits Of C. V. Stanford"?'

'Not commercial,' Morpurgo said.

'All right then, psalms,' Ralston said. 'A photo of the choir in soft focus on the front. And it's called, "These You Have Loved".'

'Could be gay,' Morpurgo said.

He looked on round the room, until his gaze reached Joffrey. 'What about the fat boy?' he asked. 'He got any ideas?'

Joffrey didn't answer.

'He's not saying very much this afternoon,' Hallam said.

'Not saying much any afternoon,' Avery said.

'Come on, fat boy,' Morpurgo stood up. 'You're being a bore, a crashing bore.'

And Joffrey thought about it a moment, then he decided to speak.

'If you want a big-selling record,' he said, 'it's like my father always says, you've got to look at the market-leader.'

'And what might that be?'

'One of the supergroups,' Joffrey said. 'Like Floyd, maybe. You've got to put out the kind of album they do.'

'Which is?'

'Well, a big album. Plain. No group's name on the front. Just this one tiny picture.'

'Picture?'

And suddenly Joffrey saw it. 'Polaroid of God,' he said. 'And the title, well, you'd have to call it "Holy Christ".'

There was a shocked silence.

Morpurgo walked through it to the window. He hopped frog-like up onto the sill. Then he turned and looked at Joffrey. 'Quite like that,' he said. And he laughed.

Everybody laughed.

THIRTEEN

The ice stayed firm under the fat boy's feet that afternoon. In fact it became even firmer. People asked his opinion, included him in their schemes. And he became, wait for it, popular.

It all began in the cathedral, just before evensong, when Joffrey discovered that Morpurgo and he were paired off as duty choristers. Something that normally would have filled him with dread.

But Morpurgo was all smiles.

He led the way along the choirstalls in the fading afternoon sun. And he laid out the service sheets, while Joffrey set out the psalters. Then together they went up the chancel steps to the great brass eagle of the lectern.

One boy alone couldn't turn the pages of the heavy bible, and so they both did it, marking up the first and second lesson. Then Morpurgo looked out past the eagle's wing at the congregation. And he saw the group of smartly-dressed women, sitting together. Mothers of boys who were in the choir.

'Got a few lunatic-mothers in this afternoon,' he said, 'come to hear their little darlings sing.'

'Quite a few, yes,' Joffrey said.

Morpurgo leaned closer. 'Well, it's Wednesday, isn't it?' he asked. 'Early closing? They can't flash their plastic round the shops?'

And Joffrey couldn't believe it. Morpurgo had cracked a joke, for him.

The two boys returned to the chancel rail, bowed to the altar, then started back down the aisle. And as they were passing the lunatic-mothers, Morpurgo whispered again.

'I've got an idea,' he said.

'What's that?'

'Well, you saw the service sheet, didn't you? The psalm that's down for this evening? Psalm 78?'

'Yes.'

'Well, d'you think?' Morpurgo asked. 'D'you think we should play the lunatic-mothers' game?'

Back in the robing-room, Morpurgo gathered the others round. 'How about it?' he asked.

'What?'

'The lunatic-mothers' game?'

'But, we *can't*,' Armstrong said. 'I mean, the last time we played it, Maunder got into a fearful bait.'

'Maunder's away, cretin.'

'So he is.'

'There's only Sorley. And Sorley's a pushover.'

'That's right.'

'And what's more,' Morpurgo said. 'Today's psalm is psalm 78.'

'What's that supposed to mean?'

'It's not only long, it's one of the longest in the book,' Morpurgo said. 'Seventy-three verses, no less.'

'So?'

'So a lot of us could play,' Morpurgo said. 'A lot of us could chip in with our 10p stakes.'

There was a pause. Morpurgo looked round at them. 'All right, let's have a show of hands. Who's in?'

Ten, thirteen, then sixteen of the choristers put up their hands.

'Sixteen times 10p equals £1.60,' Morpurgo said. 'So let's not just talk about a prize, gentlemen. Let's talk about a mega-prize . . . A packet of Rothman's mega-King Size, no less. Winning team takes all.'

And he picked Joffrey for his team.

'The psalm for this evening is taken from the evening of the fifteenth day,' the Precentor intoned into his microphone. 'Psalm 78. "Hear my law O my people: incline your ears unto the words of my mouth."'

Up in the organ-loft, Sorley played the first line of the chant. The choir got to their feet, and began. Everybody sang the first six verses, as marked. Then the decani choristers sang the second six, and cantoris the third six. And then, as was usual with a long psalm in the middle of the week, there were solos. Each boy-treble took two verses in turn. It was a custom Maunder had started, to build up their voices, build up their confidence.

Ralston, as always, had the first solo. And the boy concentrated. He tried hard. He sang with all the purity and simple tone that had made him head chorister.

But Morpurgo, watching the group of lunatic-mothers sitting in their chairs, saw there was no score.

Gavaine came next. And it wasn't just a question of voice with

Gavaine. He had a husky tone which was appealing, and a certain rather nauseating prettiness.

But Morpurgo, still watching the lunatic-mothers closely, saw there was no score.

Next, at verse 22, there came a change to a single chant. And the full choir sang three verses to establish the new vocal line and the change of key.

Then it was Joffrey's turn. Morpurgo had put him in to bat number two for his team . . . And Joffrey, Morpurgo suddenly saw, was going for the big one. For a start he slid past the boy next to him in one swift movement. Which got him directly into the last shaft of sunlight to hit the stalls. And secondly he looked directly up into this light, rounding his mouth and his fat face.

'"He raineth down the manna also upon them for to eat,"' he sang, hitting the first note with a heavy vibrato.

'Dreadful,' Morpurgo whispered.

'"And gave them food from heaven."' Joffrey scooped up towards the high note with a ghastly *portamento*.

'Outrageous,' Morpurgo whispered.

And somebody else thought so too. The lay-clerk beating time across the aisle had a look of horror on his face.

'"And man did eat . . ."' Joffrey was really milking it now, slowing right down, even managing a catch in his voice, '". . . angel's foo-ood."'

'Out*rageous*,' Morpurgo whispered.

But it worked. As he watched, Morpurgo saw one of the lunatic-mothers bend forward suddenly. And, her eyes glistening, snatch her handkerchief from her bag.

'"For he sent them meat enough,"' Joffrey finished.

'Not to mention twenty Rothman's,' Morpurgo whispered.

FOURTEEN

For the second time in ten days Haskell went into the Soho restaurant where there was the green light of ferns. He walked through to the alcove-table and found that Landon-Higgins was already there. He was ordering a bottle of Meursault from the wine-waiter, and wondering about a sherry.

'I should,' Haskell said as he sat down. 'I should make it a big one.'

'Why?'

And when the wine-waiter had gone, Haskell pushed a small news-clipping across the table.

'What's this? Local paper? Bristol?' Landon-Higgins read the headline. 'Prominent Businessman Missing?'

'That's right,' Haskell said.

'Who is it?'

'The man you wanted me to use. The intermediary as you called him.'

'The what?'

'The man who was supposed to give your company director friend a hundred grand.'

'*Supposed* to?' Landon-Higgins came forward at that.

'He didn't pass it all on,' Haskell said. 'Which was why we didn't get all the information we needed.'

'Jesus,' Landon-Higgins said. 'For Jesus' sake, how much went missing?'

'Twenty grand.'

The man swore under his breath. 'And what's happened to him now?'

'He's dead,' Haskell said. 'I killed him.'

'You *what*?'

The wine-waiter returned with the sherry. Landon-Higgins took it and drank. He was looking all round him, his mind racing. Then suddenly he called the waiter back. 'Is the white wine cold?'

'Yes, sir.'

'All right, we'll have it straight away.'

Haskell watched as the sherry disappeared. He watched as Landon-Higgins bit into the Meursault, one glass, then two. And he knew what was coming.

It came quietly.

'Now you can do what you fucking like, out in those fucking impenetrable streets where you operate,' the man said. 'But you don't fucking include me.'

'Maybe I do,' Haskell said, just as quietly.

'What d'you mean?'

'And maybe I want you to know that.'

'What?'

Haskell sat back in his chair. 'You told me this thing was special,' he said. 'It's more than that. It's the most special thing I ever saw in my life.'

Landon-Higgins didn't answer.

'And I'm going on with it,' Haskell said. '*We're* going on with it.'

'No.' Landon-Higgins shook his head. 'My dear feller, if you think for one moment—'

The waiter came to take their order. Haskell said he'd have the carbonnade of beef. Landon-Higgins said he'd start with the coquilles and go on to the Dover sole. He also ordered another bottle of wine.

Which made Haskell think it was going to be easy. Until he saw that the drink didn't seem to harm Landon-Higgins. It stoked him up, fuelled his large body, and coaled those hard black eyes.

The man's voice became very precise. 'I always think,' he said, 'that a truly successful business lunch is one where you sit down to good food with a trusted partner . . . and find out just how bad things really are.'

'Maybe,' Haskell said.

'And in this case what we're talking about is information, what we know . . . And what do we know exactly? That there's a small factory outside Bristol which, despite its rather touching Victorian appearance, has a security system installed by the Ministry of Defence. Star Wars time.'

Haskell nodded.

'Which forces us to turn our attention elsewhere. In particular to shipments dispatched from this factory by road. And what do we find there? Star Wars time too. A white van upgraded from four to six tons fully laden, on account of all the steel plating and hardware on board. And a surveillance system that starts with concealed aerials in wing-mirrors, and finishes with a red light flashing every time the driver scratches his arse.'

'That's right.'

'And we have all that information,' Landon-Higgins went on. 'And yet, when you and your experts get out on the road, the whole thing's a total cock-up.'

'Yes,' Haskell said. 'I accept that.'

'Oh, you do? And yet you still think we should have another crack at it?'

'Yes.'

'Why's that?'

'Because I've been doing a great deal of thinking,' Haskell said. 'About information, as a matter of fact. About that computer, the one at your head office. The one you said you could get to.'

'What about it?'

'I think it can tell us more.'

Landon-Higgins was irritated. 'Correction,' he said. 'It can't tell us any more. I told you before, it's just a terminal, hooked in to the mainframe down at the factory. And of *course* all the security decisions are taken down there. In-house. Classified.'

'All right then, what can you get on this terminal?'

'Just the data necessary for the group board . . . flow scans, currency slopes, auditing, personnel.'

'Fine,' Haskell said. 'And as we both know, that includes personnel screening.'

'The files show up, yes.'

'Fine,' Haskell said again.

'My dear feller, what are you on about? D'you want me to go through the whole damn tomfoolery again? Checking out the workforce? Going right through the production department? Then admin? Then security?'

'Well, let's just think about it,' Haskell said. 'I mean, production, they're out, aren't they? It's a fully automated process. All they do there is press buttons?'

'Yes.'

'And admin's out as well?'

'Definitely,' Landon-Higgins said. 'I mean, if this company director had five-sixths of his money, *and* he's had no comebacks since . . . Then he's going to stay at home at night with his Horlicks, isn't he? And answer absolutely no phone calls?'

'Right,' Haskell said. 'Which only leaves security.'

Landon-Higgins sighed. His voice became quiet again, and patient. 'But we've said it so often, haven't we? This factory is Victorian. It's old. It's had the Bank of England contract an awful long time . . . And why? Because its security system's always been so good. I mean, in the old days there was an estate around it. The workers had free houses. They had free firewood, and free sermons on Sundays. While outside, their mates could only face life on penny gin.'

'What's all that supposed to mean?'

'Simple,' Landon-Higgins said. 'Nowadays free houses equals help with mortgages. Free firewood equals Bupa. Free sermons equal Access cards . . . Security employees do very nicely thank you. They're exactly the last people I'd try.'

Coquilles, brown bread, and a fingerbowl were placed in front of Landon-Higgins. He bent over the dish and sniffed at it. Then he tucked his napkin in his collar.

Haskell helped himself to a slice of bread. 'Maybe we should waste a couple of minutes on security people,' he said.

'Can't see why.' Landon-Higgins chewed delicately on a mouthful.

'Look, bear with me. Just think back to that day when we

were on the road,' Haskell said. 'What happened? We stopped the van. It went into some kind of security-state and locked on its brakes. We started work with the cutting gear . . .'

'And then stood around like lemons.'

'Agreed,' Haskell said. 'But what happened in the end? The van drove off.'

'So you said.'

'And why did it do that?'

'Maybe some radio-controller or someone told it to drive off,' Landon-Higgins said.

Haskell leaned forward over the table. 'No,' he said. 'I told you once before, didn't I? We had the radio jammed.'

Landon-Higgins frowned.

'What I mean is,' Haskell said, 'it was the van-driver who decided to drive off. He over-rode the system.'

'Possible.'

'And to over-ride it, he had to *know* the system.'

'Possible too, yes.'

'And drivers,' Haskell said, 'are on the security payroll.'

Landon-Higgins looked back down to his scallop-shell. He loaded his fork again. 'Don't want to be boring and repeat myself,' he said, 'but drivers earn an awful lot of money. They have pretty houses, pretty wives. They have the most *touching* company loyalty . . .'

'And they have to renew their HGV licences every couple of years,' Haskell said.

'What?'

'And to do that, they have to have a medical.'

Again Landon-Higgins frowned. His fork paused halfway to his mouth.

Haskell watched him. 'All right, I've got a job for you,' he said. 'You go back to that head office of yours. You find your way back to that computer terminal. You punch in drivers. You go back over five-six years, and you see if any have failed their medical. If they've been given the golden handshake, the Official Secrets Act to sign, and been pushed out into the cold, cold world.'

* * *

The empty scallop shell was cleared away. The Dover sole and the carbonnade were brought. And Haskell spun it out, helping himself to vegetables, and ordering a glass of house red. He wanted to give Landon-Higgins time.

Because the man was thinking hard.

'*I* do that?' he asked. 'All that for you?'

'Yes,' Haskell said.

'Even after that little news-item you showed me before lunch?'

'Especially after that.'

The man moved. He put down his knife and fork, and pulled out his napkin from his collar. 'Oh, no,' he said, 'I'm out.'

Haskell said it carefully, 'Quite an interesting situation, really.'

'What is?'

'Well, you. You're a guy who knows his way around. Knows how to cover his tracks. How to get out when he wants to.'

'Oh, yes.'

'In the City,' Haskell said.

Landon-Higgins stared at him. 'What d'you mean?'

'That day we first met, that day in the park,' Haskell said, 'you mentioned something about me having . . . rather atha-letical friends.'

Landon-Higgins didn't answer.

'I have,' Haskell said, 'got rather atha-letical friends.'

Landon-Higgins didn't say much after that. He didn't eat much either. But he drank, and began to lose his battle with the wine.

Because a map of veins started to spread across his face. And it wasn't just the drink, Haskell saw, it was anger too. But maybe anger was necessary, he thought. Maybe it would open up a chink in the man.

Haskell leaned forward again. 'Listen,' he said, 'there's still something I need to know.'

'You do?'

'Yes.'

The man sighed. 'What's that?'

'Simple,' Haskell said. 'I mean, right back in the beginning it was you who came to me, wasn't it? You found me out?'

'Yes.'

'So, what made you do it? What made you fix up that meeting in the park?'

'Wish I bloody knew.'

'No, I'm serious,' Haskell said. 'I mean, you've pulled some strokes in your time, haven't you? But you've never stepped over this kind of line.'

'No.'

'Why then?'

The man reached out and poured himself some more wine.

'Come on,' Haskell said.

'All right. Money has to be the short answer.'

'You're not pushed.'

'There's money and money.'

'Course there is, but . . .'

The map of veins and anger spread. 'How it is, I've got a Rolls Royce, a 1934 Phantom Continental,' the man said. 'I like to drive it into the members' carpark at Goodwood and park among the modern tupperware Rolls Royces. I like to keep my wooden-hulled schooner down at Cannes, and varnished hulls cost a *fortune* to keep in the Med nowadays. Oh, and there are other things . . . Attending performances down at Glyndebourne when the Americans aren't there. Shooting grouse when the Americans aren't there. Buying Impressionist paintings when the Americans aren't there.'

Haskell thought about this for a moment. He wasn't sure.

And Landon-Higgins noticed. 'All right, it's not just money,' he said, 'it's knowing it'll continue.'

'And won't it?'

'Not money like that.'

'Why not?'

'The City,' Landon-Higgins said. 'Even you must have heard about the changes there.'

'Big Bang, you mean?'

'Yes.'

'But has it affected you?'

'Oh, yes.' And the man was serious. 'Look, I'm here to tell

you that not one person knew what was going to happen before it happened. Not one person knew while it was happening. And they're only just beginning to find out now.'

He finished his wine at a gulp. 'Oh, there was lots of talk,' he said. 'First it was going to be a Porsche and a farmhouse for everybody. Then it was going to be a lot of Porsches going cheap . . . Then there was going to be just this exclusive playground for multi-nationals. I mean, the Swiss were losing money to get in. My dear feller, the *Swiss* losing money . . . But then . . . Then the real news broke out.'

'What was that?' Haskell asked.

'All at once,' Landon-Higgins said, 'words like Concert Parties and Chinese Walls and Arbitrageurs started appearing on the front pages of newspapers . . . I mean, have you the faintest fucking idea what an Arbitrageur does?'

'No.'

'What's I'm trying to say is this . . . We all knew we'd been pushed off the Stock Exchange floor by machines. We all knew how many electronic deals per second, and so on. But what we didn't know about was the kind of machine that was coming in later. My dear feller, I've mentioned the Guinness affair to you before, haven't I? People due to go inside? But, d'you know why? There's something called the Serious Fraud Office now. And they're using the kind of computers that check flight-lists and hotel-registers worldwide for terrorists.' His eyes widened in horror. '*Terrorists.*'

FIFTEEN

Melchior went through the school gates in the growing dusk and started out across the court. Rain was coming and there was a blackness in the air. But it comforted him somehow, just as this time of early October always comforted him. The shadows of deanery and chapter house closed in around him as he walked, and there was the smell of woodsmoke from the canons' lodgings.

Coming to the edge of the green he paused and looked up. And, he thought, he'd seen the cathedral in all its moods, but this was his favourite. A last line of sun was clinging to the nave roof. The dark cloud above was thick with rain. And the vast building, new white stone and old brown, bristling with spires and buttresses, was like some huge mottled animal crouching down before the night.

He looked for a long time. Because he knew that tomorrow everything would change. Tomorrow a convoy of scaffolding lorries would arrive. They would be unloaded. A scaffolding tower would rise up below thc tower. The parts of a great crane would be hoisted up onto the nave roof and erected there. And then the real work would begin, of replacing two-hundred-year-old roofing lead, and eight-hundred-year-old timber and stone.

And while Melchior had known for a long time that the repairs were due; while he knew they were the result of a long and difficult appeal; the fact remained. For the next eight months the court would be invaded by strangers.

Which was why Melchior lingered now, listening to the sounds he knew. The cathedral clock striking the half-hour. The creak of the south door opening. And the voices of the choir as they came out from early evensong.

Melchior watched them take the pavement on the far side of the green. And, as ever, he looked for one boy in particular, Joffrey.

But Joffrey's troubles of a fortnight ago seemed to have gone. He was no longer walking alone but in a group, headed of course by the clever boy Morpurgo. And they were talking in that schoolboy language that picked up new words one week and dropped them the next. This week's words, as far as Melchior could hear, seemed to be silent cabbage.

Silent cabbage?

Smiling to himself, he continued his walk around the court. It took him ten minutes, and by the time he reached the school again rain had begun to fall. He went up to his study for his schoolbooks and gown, and then on to the masters' common room, where he knew they would be having tea.

By the large enamel teapot he found the deputy headmaster Gerald Alexander Fraser.

Gaf, as he was known to everyone in the school, turned round. He saw the rain on Melchior's jacket. 'Been out for your constitutional?' he asked.

'That's right.'

'Do you any good?'

'Yes,' Melchior said. 'I saw the choir, as a matter of fact. And young Joffrey seems much better. Really quite happy.'

'Happy?' Gaf balanced tea, biscuits, and schoolbooks with long years of practice. 'Happy's not what I'd call any of the choir at the moment. Peculiar, more like.'

'Peculiar?'

'Yes. There's something up with those little boys. And it's been up for a day or two now.'

'What d'you mean?'

'Think about it,' Gaf said. 'There've been no snide remarks from that lad Morpurgo. No disruptions in the choirstalls. And – though frankly I'm not sure about this – I think some of them have been disappearing from view at a certain time of day.'

'What time of day?' Melchior asked.

'Now. Right now, if you want to know,' Gaf said. 'Masters' tea time, when there's only that idiot Sorley to look after them.'

'Anybody could give Sorley the slip.'

'Quite.'

'Well, look,' Melchior said, 'what I'm asking, old son, is keep an ear tuned, will you?'

'Consider it done,' Gaf said. 'As a matter of fact I've got quite a few of them next period. IVA French.'

'Oh, God,' Melchior said.

'Oh, God is right.'

IVA French. And the classroom with the smell of schoolboy sweat, schoolboy effort, Gaf thought. A smell calculated to sink the heart of man or dog. He sighed to himself and began the lesson, moving through the class and flipping chalky exercise books onto desks. Then he returned to the blackboard.

'Right,' he said. 'Open your books, which I have marked generously and with the warmest of hearts, as ever. And open your text books, please, to page thirty-three.'

There was the flap of book-pages, the flap of old leaves. And then, nothing. Silence from the entire class . . . Too quiet, Gaf thought. Something was up, just as he'd said.

He cleared his throat. 'Page thirty-three,' he repeated. 'The French passage I asked you to translate in prep last night. Which begins: *Au printemps, quand il faisait beau, le fils et la jeune fille du fermier* . . .' He paused, and then singled out a boy. 'Which translates, Morpurgo?'

'*Au printemps, quand il faisait beau* . . . In spring, when it was fine,' Morpurgo said, '*le fils et la jeune fille du fermier* . . . the son and daughter of the farmer . . .'

'Correct, Morpurgo. Quite correct,' Gaf said. 'And how do you know that?'

'Because, Sir,' Morpurgo said, 'I'm given it at the top of the page. I mean, in the list of new words, it gives certain phrases.'

'Such as?'

'Well, Sir. *Au printemps*, in spring. And then, *il fait beau*, it is fine. *Il faisait beau*, it was fine.'

'Correct, Morpurgo. You are given these two expressions. In fact, Morpurgo, you are given the translation of the first six words of the passage. All you have to do is look up to the top of the page, see these six words, and copy them down.'

'Yes, Sir.'

'Now, all of you, it seems, made use of that assistance,' Gaf went on, 'with the single exception of young Armstrong here . . .' He and the entire class turned to face Armstrong, who sank lower in his chair.

'Now, Armstrong, as it turns out,' Gaf continued, 'did not look up to the top of the page. Armstrong, understandably weighed down by the ever-increasing price of Mars bars, kept his eyes low. And Armstrong floundered. Let us examine what he did. He turned to his dictionary and looked up each word individually. He looked up *au*, and found it meant to. He looked up *printemps*, and found it meant spring. *Quand*, he found was when. *Il* was he. *Faisait*, he found came from *faire*, to make. *Beau* was beautiful. And so on . . .'

He paused, and they waited.

'So Armstrong came up with this little gem,' Gaf told them. 'A touching little story which begins thus . . . "To spring when he was making beautiful the son and daughter of the farmer . . ." See what I mean? "To spring when he was making beautiful the son and daughter of the farmer was a trick of the *lowest order*." D'you understand?'

They nodded. They understood. But they didn't laugh. Strange, Gaf thought. So he tried harder.

'What little picture does this conjure up?' he asked. 'A creature crouching in a bush perhaps? Some threatening creature, ready to spring out? A gorilla perhaps? And then again, this nasty Froggy man? This He? This man making up the nasty Froggy son and daughter of the farmer with lipstick and eyebrow pencil? I mean, everybody knows Froggy boys are pooftahs . . . But, wait for it, this gorilla, understandably upset by lipstick and pooftahs, suddenly springs out of the bush shouting Geronimo . . .'

Now, even Gaf had to admit, this was averagely funny. Perhaps more than averagely funny.

But the thing was, the class didn't laugh. They smiled at him politely. IVA French smiled *politely*.

And, as the lesson wore on, Gaf realised something else. They weren't going to laugh at his jokes, because they had their own joke. There was some private running gag that linked them all together, secret, exciting, and bursting to come out.

'I just don't know what it is,' he said to Melchior in the common room later. 'I don't even know who the instigator of the joke is, the focus of the whole thing. All I know is, it's there.'

'Perhaps this instigator, this focus as you call it, could be the boy Gillick,' a voice said.

Both men turned.

Haldane was standing close to them, Haldane the maths master.

'How d'you mean?' Melchior asked.

'Well, I had IVA for maths, second period this evening,' Haldane said. 'And there was something strange to do with Gillick, very strange indeed.'

'As far as Gillick's concerned,' Gaf said, 'strange is hardly the word I'd use. Bizarre, more like. Or grotesque, sub-gothic . . .'

But Melchior interrupted him. 'What was it about Gillick?' he asked Haldane. 'What was this strange thing?'

'Well,' Haldane said, 'I had my back turned to the class, working out an equation on the board. And there was this giggling building up behind me . . . I turned . . . And Gillick, who a moment before had been sitting quite normally at his desk – Gillick now had this . . . steam about him . . . this puff of steam, hanging over his head.'

SIXTEEN

Haldane the maths master was almost right.

And Gaf was almost right too when he'd described Gillick as being bizarre, grotesque, sub-gothic.

To begin at the beginning.

In any group of prep-school boys, small, lonely, and prey to strange obsessions, there has to be the smallest, the loneliest, prey to the strangest obsessions.

Gillick was just such a one. He was tiny for his age. His hair seemed thin, the skin of his face transparent. There were nerve-ends leaping from the corners of his mouth to his eyes. And inside him a certain tiredness of soul.

And Gillick's obsession was destroying his clothes.

There had been the time, for example, when Sorley had been trying to organise early games, when boys had gone missing, and Gillick had been found behind the sheds, cutting up his football vest with scissors.

There had been the time in a chemistry class, when Gillick had tried to destroy his blazer with dilute sulphuric acid. And another time on the playing fields, when he'd spent the whole of the afternoon with a magnifying glass, trying to set fire to his shoes.

Nobody really asked Gillick why. Nobody was close enough to him to bother. As Morpurgo said, 'Nobody's friends with Gillick, and I don't blame them.'

But recently all that had changed. In the past week Gillick had achieved a certain notoriety.

And it had been due, in part, to Joffrey.

Because it had been exactly a week ago, at early evensong, that Joffrey had won the Rothman's mega-King Size for his team. And afterwards, during masters' tea time, they'd gathered to smoke them out of a dormitory window.

Now, smoking out of a dormitory window was usually of the suck and puff variety. But, if people like Morpurgo and Joffrey were running the show, then there were going to be those who inhaled. Inhaled three or four puffs in quick succession, became dizzy, sensuous even, and thought of *Penthouse* magazine and A Life of Sordid Sin.

But Gillick, it turned out, didn't feel any such effect. Gillick, when asked by Joffrey what inhaling was like, said, 'It tastes of cabbage.'

'Cabbage?' Joffrey asked.

And then he found that Gillick wasn't doing what the others did. The boy *thought* he was. But, instead of inhaling, he was swallowing the smoke. Swallowing mouthfuls and mouthfuls. Which firstly made the smoke taste like cabbage. And secondly brought him fame.

* * *

It was the end of the school day. The day-boys had left for home, and the choir were getting ready for supper. Or were meant to be. In fact Morpurgo was arranging a little ceremony.

He had shut the door of Middle School and put a boy outside on watch. He had assembled the choir in a semi-circle, and now stood in its centre.

'Middle School Council, Extraordinary Meeting,' he announced. 'Very extraordinary.'

The others fell silent.

'It concerns news of great importance,' Morpurgo went on. 'News, in fact, which comes to us from our good friend Joffrey.'

Joffrey took a bow.

And Morpurgo, making a grand gesture of it, produced a handwritten document from behind his back.

He unrolled it and showed the writing, beautifully-formed calligraphic writing. It was in the form of a list, giving dates and names, and then achievements. An exact copy, in fact, of the honours-boards that looked down from the walls.

Morpurgo cleared his throat. 'Gentlemen,' he said, 'we live in a highly competitive society where success is greatly esteemed. Around you, for example, you will see names that have achieved greatness in the long jump, the hundred yards, and throwing the cricket-ball. But here and now we are gathered to witness the greatest honour this school can bestow . . . Gillick is about to have a fart named after him.'

They all nodded.

'Now, there have been great farts and immortal farts,' Morpurgo said, referring to the list in his hand. 'There was, for example, Plugs, which was attributed to a boy called Shaughnessy. There was the Yellow Drifter, attributed to Allbright. There was Slams, attributed to Jackson. Which was later surpassed by Philbrick's immortal Slams A Dozen.'

They nodded again, impressed.

'Next on the list of anyone's immortals,' Morpurgo went on, 'has to come Symington's Seventeen Seconder, witnessed by at least three disinterested parties. But now – ' and he waved a hand importantly, ' – we come to a new contender for immortality.

Gentlemen, I give you . . . *anus mirabilis* . . . young Gillick and his supremely original . . . Silent Cabbage.'

Gillick stood on his own, concentrating for a moment. Then, nodding that he was ready, he loosened his belt. There was no sound, but a filmy gauze of tobacco smoke came slowly up past his shirt, past his small shoulders, and hung in a thin cloud above his head.

There was applause.

SEVENTEEN

Haskell came in from the garden of his Chorleywood house, and answered the phone. It was Landon-Higgins.

'I've got names for you,' the man said.

'What?'

'The names of drivers who've left a certain factory. Two of them.'

'That's good,' Haskell said.

'Is that all you can say?'

'No.' Haskell softened his voice. 'Two drivers then. You did well.'

'Damn right. Have you got a pen?'

Haskell found one.

'Okay, the first is Slattery, initials G. H., born 1931.'

'Yes.'

'LOS, which is length of service, twenty-seven years.'

'Yes.'

'RMS negative, 1.4.83.'

'What's RMS negative?'

'I was coming to that,' Landon-Higgins said. 'Required medical standard negative. It means he failed the HGV medical.'

'Right,' Haskell said. 'And the other one?'

'Larcombe, S. A.,' Landon-Higgins said. 'Born 1943; LOS twelve years; RMS negative, 19.6.87.'

'Last year then. Which could be just right for us, couldn't it? He could have all the right info.'

'Yes,' Landon-Higgins said.

'What about addresses?'

The man gave them to him. They were both in Bristol, and Haskell wrote them down. 'Anything else?' he asked.

'Yes, the lump sum they received when they left,' Landon-Higgins said. 'I told you they were well looked after by the firm, didn't I?'

'You did.'

'Well, Slattery got forty-four thousand. And Larcombe nineteen and a half.'

'Terrific,' Haskell said. Then he thought a moment. 'Any idea why they failed their HGVs, these two?'

'No, that would have been in the medical file.'

'And you didn't look at that?'

'Not after going through wages and personnel.'

'Why? Too risky?'

'In a way.'

'What way?' Haskell asked. 'I have to know these things.'

'Well, it's the time somebody like me spends in the computer wing.'

'Not the operating of the machine itself?'

'No.'

'Why not?'

'Because I'm sixty-three years old and I'm a Harrovian,' the man told him.

'What's that supposed to mean?'

'Simple. A Harrovian of my age doesn't even know how to *stand* in front of a computer,' Landon-Higgins said. 'His suit's just not cut that way.'

EIGHTEEN

The next morning, early, Haskell drove down the M4 to Bristol. It took him no more than half an hour to find the address of the first man, Slattery. And Slattery had been well looked after by his firm, just as Landon-Higgins had said.

He had a house out in the Bristol suburbs, a new development with a bit of ranch-style about it, and a smart line in carports and patios. Under each carport a brand new Vauxhall or Ford stood on the concrete. Around each patio was a low ornamental wall. There was the feeling of everything being cemented down, solid and owned.

And Slattery, retired security driver, was outside. It was lunchtime, and he was barbecuing for friends. There were sausages and burgers and litres of Italian wine. There were the running gags of television. But what stood out a mile was the thing that Haskell, for all his watching and waiting, could never fight against . . . contentment.

He gave it up and drove to the Unicorn Hotel. He worked on a street-map for a while, and then in the early evening went out to find the second man, Larcombe.

Who was a different story altogether.

Larcombe didn't live out in some smart new development, but near the centre of the city. South of the river, that was, and one of the old dockland areas that hadn't been tarted up.

It was a long street that seemed to go on forever over Bristol's folds and dips. It was rain and brick. It was small front gardens that seemed to be bursting through their walls, and broken pavements where the weeds showed through. And for a strange moment Haskell had the idea that vegetation could force the street apart and take it over.

He moved closer. Larcombe, he saw, didn't own property in

this city. He rented. And what he rented was a single first-floor room that looked down on a builder's yard.

Haskell got into the yard. He broke the lock of a timber-loft and found a window that looked straight onto Larcombe's. And then he saw the man. He was pale and lardlike. He had sandy hair and a slack and strangely womanlike face. He had a bed, a stack of lager cans and a video. And the rest was just four grubby-fingered walls keeping inside from out.

So why? Haskell asked himself. Why, after a job that had paid three hundred a week, aside from the overtime and company mortgage? Why, after a lump sum of nineteen and a half grand?

He didn't get any answers. He just watched Larcombe sitting fatly on his bed and sipping lager. Then getting up, passing a comb through his hair, and going out.

The pub was called the Lamb and Flag. It was roll-up fags. It was beer-stained surfaces wiped down with a beery cloth. It had posters for long-forgotten drinks, and a dartboard cratered like the moon. And the barman was something else. Short, fair-haired, but black as black inside, he looked up from his paper just long enough to serve Haskell a scotch.

Haskell turned away. He saw that Larcombe was the only other person in the bar, sitting at a corner table, and he went and sat nearby. Then someone else came in, a young man walking strangely on elevated heels.

'Evening, Jarvis,' the barman said. 'Pint?'

'Yes.' Jarvis's hand shook as he took the pint, as he swallowed it in silence.

Two more people came in.

'Evening, Steve. Pint?'

'That's it.'

'Evening, Dorothy. Cider?'

'Yes.'

'How are you then, Dorothy?'

'Knackered,' was all the dark wispy-haired woman said.

They stood there, Jarvis, Steve, and Dorothy, like vessels bruising themselves at the bar. Until they filled. Until they were firmer and their hands no longer shook. While the barman stood apart from them, reading the same paragraph of the paper over and over again.

Silence, until the barman joined the group, drinking shorts to their pints. And then there was his laugh, his wind-up fairground laugh, always exactly the same. Though sometimes it lasted longer if they put money in his slot, if they bought him shorts.

And then later, as the drink built up in him, he talked more. Though always contradicting what they said.

'Yes, but against that . . .'

'Agreed, but that said . . .'

Contradicting and winning every argument. Until, looking away more and more often to the clock, he suddenly smiled. 'Chaps and chapesses, time to go home.'

They finished up their drinks, Jarvis, Steve, and Dorothy, and he ushered them to the door. And to each he said, 'Be good.'

But Larcombe wasn't good, Haskell saw. He saw it through the window of his room. Because once back there, the man pulled the video close to the bed and switched it on. And Haskell could see the screen. He could see how Larcombe watched a certain part of the tape, then rewound and watched it again. How he did this four more times. And the last time, the communication between man and machine was something Haskell could feel from fully twenty yards away.

At lunchtime the next day Haskell followed him to the pub again. He sat at the next table, and, feeling his way, got into conversation. Which wasn't difficult because, after a couple of tries, he found Larcombe was prepared to talk about one thing, big-band jazz.

Then Haskell changed the subject.

'Nice place, this,' he said.

'I like it,' Larcombe said. 'It's a real pub. None of your plastic food.'

'It's like pubs used to be. I mean, somebody's managed to hold onto that,' Haskell agreed. 'And what I particularly like, I don't know, is the decor.'

'Decor?'

'Yes, I mean, like that over there.'

'What over where?'

'The colour of that lino round the bar,' Haskell said. 'That colour, it's hard to get. Years and years of bad cleaning, that is. The mop just being wiped over. And a dirty mop at that.'

'What?' Larcombe looked at him strangely.

'And it's not just that,' Haskell went on. 'I mean, look at the lino, those heelmarks on it . . . No stiletto-marks, see what I mean?'

'No.'

'Well, how long since stilettos've been in fashion? How long since a woman's been in here, standing by the bar?'

Larcombe looked at him even more strangely. 'I only came in for a quiet drink,' he said.

'Course you did,' Haskell told him. 'Only, like I was saying, no women come in here, do they? Not unless you count Dorothy last night, and her buckets of cider.'

'What?'

'No women means death to a pub,' Haskell said. 'And I know because I've run pubs in my time. To attract the punters you've got to have women around.'

'What?'

'That is, unless you've got a woman back at home,' Haskell went on. 'I mean, on a video. Where you see it through and wind it back. And then see it through again.'

'*What?*' Suddenly Larcombe kicked back his chair and moved quickly to the door.

The barman swung round. Haskell smiled at him. Then got up and followed.

Larcombe was still moving quickly, away up the long street with the cracked pavements. But Haskell, keeping to the smoother tarmac of the road, caught him easily.

They both stopped.

'I can understand about the video,' Haskell said. 'But what I don't get is the three hundred a week you were earning. Not to mention the lump sum of nineteen and a half grand . . . What happened to all of that?'

And at first there was Larcombe's huge shock. Shock that had his arms up as if warding off blows.

But then there was the answer.

Because Haskell didn't need to be told. Suddenly he saw the long straight street through Larcombe's eyes. The cracks in the pavement, the cracks in the walls, the vegetation growing through . . . It could vanish, Haskell saw. The whole street could just vanish and fly up in the air.

'When you left that job,' he said then. 'When you had the medical and they retired you at the age of forty-five . . . How long did they say you'd got?'

'Three months,' Larcombe said. 'Six months, top.'

NINETEEN

Back in his room, Larcombe's voice was soft. And his face had that womanlike quality Haskell had seen before. It was the mouth mostly, and the pale sandy eyelashes.

'No, it's not Aids,' he said. 'Nothing dramatic like that.'

'What is it then?' Haskell asked.

The man wet his lips. 'They got a name for it,' he said. 'Asymptomatic cardio-vascular disease.'

'And what's that in English?'

'In English all it is . . . All it . . .'

The mouth trembled and gave up. Haskell got to his feet. He went over to the stack of lager cans, opened two of them, and gave one to Larcombe.

The man drank. He seemed calmer. 'All right. Look, what was happening . . . I mean, I was doing my job, picking up my money, and having these pains every now and then. Sort of stomach pains. Indigestion, I thought it was.'

'And you didn't go to a doctor?'

'Why should I? With indigestion?' The man shrugged. 'But then, I don't know, it got so bad I didn't recover. I mean, the pain went but I felt bad after. Really bad . . . And with the job I was doing . . .'

'There was stress,' Haskell said.

'That's right. So, I thought, maybe an ulcer. And, I thought, I've got this medical coming up anyway, for my HGV . . . So the doctor'll find this ulcer, I thought, and he'll put me on eggs and fish and stuff.'

'Yes,' Haskell said.

'I went in through the surgery door thinking that,' Larcombe went on. 'And I came out as if the door fell on me.'

'Yes.'

'Forty-five years old I was. And I remember what the doctor said to me. "If it's any comfort," he said, "it's happening to people of your age all the time. It's the stress, of course. And it's over-smoking and over-drinking. It's eating junk food. It's under-exercising."'

Larcombe paused. 'Any comfort, Christ,' he said. 'The doctor made these phone-calls. I was down for tests. And I was down for this heart operation. But it seemed my case was tricky. They were rushing the thing through. Rushing it.'

Haskell didn't say anything. There wasn't anything to say.

'So I went back home,' Larcombe told him. 'And I didn't say anything to her at first. But then the bad pain started, and I fainted a couple of times. So I told her, and she cried, and I cried . . . You do, you know.'

Haskell nodded.

'So then I went into hospital for tests. I was there a couple of days, and every day I rang and asked her to visit me. And she said she would, but . . .'

'She *said* she would?' Haskell asked.

'It was as much of a shock to me at the time,' Larcombe said. 'But the thing is, with the tests they don't put you under. What they do is they make a hole in your artery, high up in your arm. They slide this tiny camera inside, and on through until it's looking at your heart . . . And, how it was, you see, the doctor told her that.'

'For Christ's sake, man, what are you talking about?'

Larcombe shrugged. He didn't look at Haskell. 'She's never been able to stand the sight of blood,' he said. 'Never been able to look at so much as a rabbit run over on the road. And I told myself I'd always known that. I didn't blame her or anything.'

He paused again, and then his voice was lower. 'I left hospital after that. And the tests were bad. I mean, the operation was going to be a bit of a gamble, and no gamble at all if I ducked out. What's more, there were going to be tubes and blood-drips and stuff. A lot of stuff . . . Anyway I sat with her at home, and she held my hand, and promised faithfully she'd visit me this time.'

'But you knew she wouldn't?'

'Oh, I knew a lot of things right then,' Larcombe said. 'You do when your mind's rushing like crazy. I mean, I knew I'd been away a lot with my job. I knew we didn't have kids because she'd never wanted them . . . And I knew as I watched her in the kitchen she'd had fitted out in this yellow, and in the lounge she'd fitted out in this green, I knew what she was thinking. I was out of a job, I mean, and there wasn't going to be any more help with this big mortgage . . . All she could see was the whole thing going out of the window.'

Haskell felt cold. 'So what happened then?' he asked. 'After you'd worked all this out?'

Larcombe took a pull from his lager. 'Well, it got a bit weird,' he said. 'She sort of closed in on herself, didn't want to touch me. And, as far as that went, I wanted to. Touch her, you know . . . I mean, I said it was weird. I was meant to be dying, but I was all kind of pumped up. Full of it, you know what I mean? Like you feel with a hangover after a heavy night?'

'Yes,' Haskell said.

'And gradually it got out of hand. It got to the point where things got stupid, really stupid, and so I made arrangements. I was going to give her everything, the savings I had and the lump sum. Enough for her to get a good flat somewhere. And I was going to . . .'

'Get out,' Haskell said. 'The hell out.'

'That's it.' Larcombe nodded. 'I mean, I told her I was due at the hospital again. But I wasn't. And I wasn't going back there either. Not for the operation. Not for anything.'

There was an edge of bravery in his voice. A child's bravery, it seemed.

'Well,' he said then, 'aren't you going to ask me what I did?'

'No, I don't have to.' Haskell looked round at the lager cans, and the video cases on the floor. 'All I'm going to ask you is one thing.'

'What's that?'

'Your wife, you're not going back to her? Whatever happens? You're not going to feel sick, really sick, and crawl back home?'

'No,' Larcombe said, 'definitely not.'

That bravery in his voice again. He took another pull at his lager, and it left a clown-white blob of foam on his lip.

Which helped.

Because now Haskell tried not to think of the man, that fine sandy hair of his, the freckled skin, the pulse under the skin . . . All he thought of was the job in hand.

'Listen,' he said, 'I have to say this to you. You're going to die, and I'm sorry, and there's nothing I can do.'

Larcombe didn't answer.

'And I can't say anything like the doctor said. I mean, "If it's any comfort." Except . . .'

'Except what?'

Haskell sat there with his black hair and his black tailored suit, and he took Larcombe up to the top of the mountain.

'That video over there,' he said, 'where there's the picture of the woman with the boots and stuff . . . I can get that for you for real in London tomorrow night.'

'No,' Larcombe said. But his face had gone liquid, and he hated it.

'Or that other video next to it. Where it's these three women together on the motor cruiser . . . I can set that up the night after, down on Brighton Marina.'

'No.'

'Because if that's what you want . . . Pissing it up, and screwing, and getting your head crooked . . . I've got money. A lot of money.'

But then there was a change to Larcombe. Ideas were sinking into him, inch by inch, past the hate and the soft mouth. 'What is all this about money?' he said.

Haskell shrugged.

'I mean, why've you been on at me all the time? Why pick me up? Follow me? What d'you want?'

Haskell thought for a long moment. Then he told him what he wanted, everything he wanted, from first to last.

Larcombe didn't reply.

Not for six hours.

But then, when it was dark, and Haskell was dozing on a chair, he heard movement and suddenly woke up.

Larcombe was different. He had a clean shirt on, a clean suit, his face was firm. And he was dropping the videos into the waste-paper basket.

Haskell could read the news. 'So we haven't got a deal,' he said.

'Oh, yes, we have.'

'Have?'

Larcombe pointed to the waste-paper basket. 'I don't want any more of that.'

'What do you want then?'

'Simple,' Larcombe said. 'I can't go on on my own. I thought I could, but I can't.'

TWENTY

The days passed slowly in Middle School.

It was the slack time. The time when half term seemed just as far away as ever, when money for cigarettes ran out, and when *Penthouse* magazine could no longer bring to mind A Life of Sordid Sin.

Morpurgo flicked through its pages, scowling at the splayed legs and pointing fingers. 'Gristle,' he said. 'Just gristle. What we want is real live meat.'

Morpurgo, eleven and a half years old.

'Where are you going to find that?' Hallam asked, eleven years and four months. 'We're not allowed near meat here. We're watched over every minute of the day.'

'What about the hols?' Morpurgo asked. 'What about when our lunatic-mothers are freezing ninety-seven quiches, and we're out on our bikes? We all know the world is full of panting harlots.'

'Of course,' Hallam said.

'Of course,' Gillick said, eleven years and one month.

Morpurgo stood up. 'So let us recall the hols. Let us liven up this rancid afternoon with tales of the Labia Minora.'

Not many of them knew what he meant. And those that did shifted uneasily.

'Oh, come on,' Morpurgo said.

It turned out that Gavaine had seen his sister's girlfriend's coonie.

'Everybody in this world has seen his sister's girlfriend's coonie,' Morpurgo said. 'Come on. Anyone else?'

It turned out that Amstrong had walked his dog one evening and seen a couple he'd thought at first were having a fit.

'Not *enough*,' Morpurgo hissed. 'I want Sordid Sin. I want troilism and priapism and AC-DC.'

By now nobody knew what he meant. But nobody had the nerve to ask.

'No score last hols then? From the entire Middle School?'

They turned away. All except Hallam, and his face became cunning. 'What about the fat boy?' he asked. 'I'm sure he—'

'Hal, I've told you before,' Morpurgo cut in. 'Joffrey is no longer the fat boy. A person of some substance, yes. But nevertheless our friend.'

'Friend,' Hallam said sarcastically. 'Well, I'm sure he scored, what with his svelte good looks.'

'Hal,' Morpurgo said again.

But Hallam went on. 'I mean, you can see it, can't you?' he said. 'Friend Joffrey, swording across the dance-floor, lean and mean and looking for *lerv*.'

A flush appeared high up on Joffrey's cheekbones.

'That's not for you to say,' Morpurgo said.

'No, it's for him.' Hallam was angry. 'And why doesn't he? I mean, everyone else has come clean about last hols.'

Morpurgo shrugged. He turned. 'What about it, Joffrey? Anything to report?'

The flush deepened. 'No,' Joffrey said. 'Not really.'

'Oh, unbe*lievable*.' Hallam spread his hands. 'Joffrey didn't score.'

And Joffrey rounded on him, cheeks flaming. 'Not unless you count this girl,' he said.

'What girl?'

'Oh, just some girl I saw.'

'What?' Morpurgo was interested.

'I don't know. Nothing happened really,' Joffrey told him. 'Nothing like your troily-whatnot and the rest of it.'

'Doesn't matter.'

But Joffrey hesitated. 'A chap doesn't like to tell.'

'A chap likes to hear.'

And, looking past Morpurgo, Joffrey saw the entire Middle

School was waiting. 'Well, this girl,' he said, 'I only saw her for a short time.'

'When?' Morpurgo asked.

'Last hols, when my father took us to Spain.'

'Where in Spain?'

'This yachty place,' Joffrey said. 'Rather smart yachty place as a matter of fact. The King of Spain keeps his yacht there.'

'Lies,' Hallam said.

'Shut up, Hal,' Morpurgo said.

'Anyway,' Joffrey went on, 'we had rooms in a hotel there. And in front of it there was this pontoon-thing sticking out in the water. And people used to dive off it and swim. Except in the siesta-time, I mean, when they were inside sleeping.'

'Go on.'

'Well, one siesta-time I couldn't sleep,' Joffrey said. 'And I walked out there. And then . . . then, sort of hidden behind this canvas thing on the pontoon, I saw this girl. She had this towel over her, against the sun. And she was reading.'

'Lies,' Hallam said again.

'Shut *up*, Hal.'

'But it's all lies.'

'Why should it be?' Morpurgo swung round. 'I mean, he said nothing happened. He just saw this girl. Why lie about that?'

Hallam didn't answer.

'Continue, Joffrey,' Morpurgo said.

'All right, well, this girl, she stopped reading then,' Joffrey said. 'She pulled the towel off her and picked up this bottle of sun-oil. And she oiled everything, including her jigglies. Then she looked round and saw me. And she was startled at first. But then she . . .'

'Morpurgo, listen.'

'Hal, will you *shut* it? I've told you before.'

But this time it wasn't Hallam. It was someone sitting outside the group, someone who wasn't in the choir. Robinson the day-boy.

'What d'you want, Robinson?' Morpurgo asked.

The boy came over and whispered in his ear.

Whispered on.

Until Morpurgo looked round at the others. 'Middle School Council,' he said. 'Extraordinary Meeting. Joffrey excluded.'

The meeting, a huddle of boys in the far corner, seemed to go on forever. But finally Morpurgo turned.

'Joffrey, you disappoint me,' he said. Then rage overtook him, and Joffrey couldn't believe his eyes. Because Morpurgo seemed to get smaller, without moving get smaller and further away . . . until he became the hated froglike figure from before.

'No, you do more than disappoint me, fat boy,' he went on. 'God save us, Hallam was right. Every single word you say is a crashing *lie*!'

Hallam was smiling. And Morpurgo looked past him to Robinson. '*Viz*, the evidence,' he said. '*Viz*, the day-boy Robinson.'

He brought him forward. 'Now, as we all know, Robinson has a brother. A rancid accountant of a brother who has spots and no girlfriends. Who has to drink five pints in an evening to work up the nerve to speak to girls, and by the sixth is past it . . . Hence the collection of *Penthouses* under his bed.'

'That's right,' Robinson said.

'An *entire* collection going back two years,' Morpurgo went on. 'And among them, one with pictures of Tanya the Temperature-Raiser in it . . . Also a story about a girl lying on a pontoon-thing in front of a hotel.'

He turned back to Joffrey. 'Spanish hotel,' he said. 'Smart yachty place. King of Spain's yacht there. And the girl on this pontoon. And a towel over her till she takes it off and does the sun-oil bit.'

Joffrey's face was brick-red.

'You read this *Penthouse*, fat boy, didn't you?'

'No.'

'*Didn't* you?' Morpurgo grabbed his lapel.

And suddenly Joffrey nodded. 'I found it,' he said. 'Found it behind a hedge.'

There was a strange silence, a feeling of tension broken. And the others moved away, leaving Joffrey alone.

'Why does he do it?' Armstrong asked.

'Why lie about everything?'

'*Everything*.'

'I mean, the time he said he flew on Concorde,' Ralston said. 'To Manchester . . . And Concorde doesn't even fly there.'

'Or the time he said he got Botham's autograph at Lord's,' Gavaine said.

'Or the time when Jackson's father got one of the new mega-Jags,' Felstead said. 'And Joffrey said his father had one too.'

'And he didn't even know the new mega-Jag had a different shape,' Avery said. 'All squashed up and square.'

'Why *does* he do it?'

'Search me.'

'Simple,' Hallam said. 'It's his act. He wants to be Mr Big.'

But there was one person who hadn't said anything yet. One person who now held up his hand.

Morpurgo.

'No,' he said, 'it's not that.'

'Not?'

'Think about it,' Morpurgo said. 'The fat boy didn't just say he'd been to Spain or on Concorde, or any of the rest of it.'

'Yes, he did.'

'No, what he actually said was his *father* took him to Spain. His *father* took him on Concorde. His *father* got Botham's autograph and bought the new Jag.'

'Same difference.'

'Not really,' Morpurgo said. 'I mean, cast your minds back . . . When did we last see this famous father of his?'

'What?'

'Oh, what?'

'I don't know.'

'All right, I'll tell you,' Morpurgo said. 'It was over a year ago, at the school play. You remember, don't you, Hal?'

'Yes,' Hallam said.

And Morpurgo, his large clever head on one side, made the connection. 'And when did the lies start?' he asked.

'What?'

'Don't remember.'

'Well, I do,' Morpurgo told them. '*Viz*, shortly after that. After Christmas, at the beginning of the spring term.'

'What's that supposed to mean?'

'Only . . .' Morpurgo spun it out. '. . . Only that maybe his famous father isn't around to take him anywhere any more.'

'I don't get it.'

'Nor me.'

But Hallam did. 'Do I read you right?' he asked. 'Are you talking about the Big D?'

'Well, it certainly smells like divorce.' Morpurgo nodded. 'Smells like those three-day-old shirts and take-away Chinky dinners.'

They all turned back to Joffrey and saw the colour of his face, the sweat.

'My father's away,' he said.

'Oh,' Morpurgo said, 'that explains it.'

'His firm's sent him away. On business.'

'Far away?' Morpurgo asked.

Joffrey swallowed. 'The Third World, Africa,' he said. 'He's company secretary for a new scheme out there. Irrigation scheme.'

'Where in Africa?'

'Kenya.'

'Where exactly?'

'Harare.'

'Harare, my stupid little fat boy, is in Zimbabwe.'

'I *know* that.' Joffrey wiped sweat from his face. 'He's based in Kenya, but at the moment he's in Harare.'

The rest of them turned away.

'Don't you believe me?' Joffrey's voice was strange.

Morpurgo came back towards him. 'What you're trying to say,' he said, 'is you tell lies about everything, every single thing . . . except your rancid father.'

And he wasn't expecting the fist that caught him on the side of the face, nor the shoulder that sent him spinning away over a desk.

Joffrey had weight and fury on his side. And it needed three of the others to pull him away.

TWENTY-ONE

He took the big old-fashioned key from its hiding-place and went up to the cathedral tower. Ran as far up the steps as he could, and then stumbled on, cursing the rest. By the time he'd reached the top his head was pounding. And his hand shaking as he got out the letter from his father.

My dearest son, he read. *It makes me very unhappy not to have seen you for so long. I do hope that Mummy and you had a good time in Lyme Regis, and that Ebo-Dog behaved herself.*

As for life here, the only good news is that the work is going well. I mentioned to you earlier that it's a brand new type of irrigation-scheme we're using, and the results so far have been very encouraging. We're reclaiming land that was previously barren. Seeds will be planted. Crops will grow . . . But, far more to the point the blacks are working well, (yes, I'm allowed to call them blacks nowadays), and they're making life a lot easier for me personally.

Please write . . .

The handwriting blurred and swam on the page. Joffrey shook his head angrily. It was just dust, he told himself, dust blown by the wind and getting in his eyes. But then he knew it wasn't, and he let the tears flow unchecked.

After a while he managed to get hold of himself. He knew he had to, knew he had to go back to school shortly and face the others. He glanced at his watch. There was still time to smoke a cigarette over by the parapet.

But as he approached it he got a shock. Because there was the racket of machinery in the air, the clang of hammers on metal, and the chatter of power-tools.

And as he leaned over he saw it, the huge framework of scaffolding that covered the entire length of the nave. And the men swarming over it, bolting sheets of corrugated iron into a shape like a metal tent. And then, strangest of all, the crane. The great T-shape of yellow girders that had now been hoisted up on top of the cathedral, and stood there like some weird crucifix.

It was the work, Joffrey realised, the work they were doing on the nave roof.

But somehow it annoyed him. He'd come up here to be alone and think his own thoughts. He turned away and followed the parapet round to the east side of the tower. And here he found peace.

Because now he was looking out over open country. Looking a long way. It wasn't just that he was on a high building, it was that the building itself was high . . . Whycliffe Cathedral, thirteenth-century Early English, as he'd been told so often, built on a cliff overlooking the River Whyer.

He could see it looping away with poplars on either side. He could see the allotments, and further out the marshland with its reeds and straggly bushes. And finally the river curving back to meet that other line that crossed the valley, the London Road.

It was a warm October day, and there was a haze out there. The kind of crystally brown haze that reminded Joffrey of summer. And just for a moment he allowed himself to think back.

Not to last summer, the holiday in Lyme Regis. But to the summer before when his father had been there too. At home, of course.

His real home.

With Ebo-Dog and the swimming-pool and the Jag parked in the drive. And, *yes*, the new mega-Jag on order.

The trouble was things changed, he told himself. Things changed so *quickly*.

TWENTY-TWO

Out on the London Road, in the haze, a car was parked. And two men were leaning against it, Haskell and Larcombe.

Haskell was idly kicking at the gravel, and Larcombe had one hand held up against the sun. He was looking back down the valley at the river glinting through the trees. And then on to the tall dark cliff where the cathedral stood, the scaffolding on its roof seemingly set on fire.

Haskell moved towards him. 'You like cathedrals then?'

'Yes.'

'Even with all that metal and junk on top?'

'Yes.'

Larcombe looked on. And suddenly he was shivering, even though he was wearing an overcoat in the warm afternoon.

All of which made Haskell uneasy.

Because it had been a week now, a week they'd spent at the Unicorn Hotel in Bristol. And for the first two days Haskell had had a specialist down from London. The man had examined Larcombe and said give him rest, lots of rest. Give him white meat and salads and fruit juice. Get rid of the bloat of lager and scotch.

But the diet hadn't worked. Larcombe's soft round face had collapsed. His skin had become paper thin, and he'd started feeling the cold. Which was what the specialist had said to look out for, coldness, tiredness, and a bluish colour around the lips.

You could say Haskell was more than uneasy. You could say he was worried.

They got back into the car. Haskell started the engine, turned the heater up to full, and drove away. 'I reckon we've done enough, don't you?' he said.

'Yes.'

'I mean, we've achieved something. We've covered most of the route the white van took that day.'

'Yes.'

'Okay then. It's the motorway, and then back to the hotel.'

Larcombe didn't answer.

'You all right?'

'Fine. Just fine.'

The road swung round towards the south. The sun was low on their right now, and a sign came up, motorway 2 miles.

Larcombe was hunched down in his seat, his face in shadow. 'What about the other stuff?' he asked. 'The stuff you wanted me to look over?'

'It'll keep.'

'But you brought it with you, didn't you? In the briefcase?'

'Yes.'

'I'll have a look at it then.'

Haskell shrugged. He felt back between the seats, found the briefcase, and handed it over.

It was a lightweight case, but Larcombe seemed to find it heavy. And he had trouble with the locks.

Haskell helped him. He pointed to the two files inside. 'The top one deals with the van itself,' he said, 'the drawings and the specs.'

Larcombe glanced through them. 'Jaboulet long wheelbase, up-rated to six tons,' he read. 'Half-inch steel plate round the payload and the crew. Floor reinforced with eighth mesh.'

'Yes, and that's where we tried getting in,' Haskell said. 'Through the floor. Pushing the mesh apart.'

'I see.' Larcombe closed the first file and opened the second. 'And what's this?'

'Surveillance,' Haskell said. 'Electronics. The link-up between the van and control.'

Larcombe found a page. 'PMR,' he said. 'Private mobile radio. Two-way interface. VHF.'

'I had it all checked out by experts.'

'I'm sure,' Larcombe said. 'But, what about this here? Where it says voice-mode and FSK?'

'What about it?'

'Well, presumably you were trying to track the van?'

'Yes.'

'So did you actually hear voice-mode? Voices coming over the air?'

'No,' Haskell said, 'that was the funny thing.'

'Very funny,' Larcombe said.

Haskell looked at him sharply. 'Listen, we had the right equipment, this trick VHF receiver. But when we were waiting, we couldn't get the damn thing to work. Things happen like that, on the day.'

'Quite,' Larcombe said. 'But, when you jammed their radio, that was on VHF as well?'

'Of course.'

The man spread his hands. 'You weren't jamming anything,' he said, 'except the weather forecast on BBC bloody Bristol.'

Haskell didn't understand. And he didn't have time to understand, because the motorway was coming up. He swung onto the feeder-road, and as he did so the sun came round to find Larcombe's face. He looked deathly tired.

'Let's get this straight,' the man said then. 'These files . . . You said that when you got hold of them, there was trouble. Not all of the money got paid.'

'Yes,' Haskell said, fighting the glare ahead.

'And you didn't get all the information you needed?'

'That's right.'

Larcombe sighed. 'You didn't get any of the information you needed. You got junk. Ten-, fifteen-year-old junk.'

'What?'

Haskell kept everything under control. He edged out onto the motorway, found the middle lane, pushed the speed up steadily. And he made his voice quite calm. 'So we never stood a chance?'

'Put it this way,' Larcombe said. 'If I'd been crewing on that van, and known these useless bloody files were missing . . . And then been stopped by a bunch of idiots wearing stocking-masks . . . Christ, I'd've wondered if I'd drifted into the lingerie department of Dickens & Jones.'

TWENTY-THREE

Haskell sat in his dark room at the Unicorn Hotel, looking down at the waterfront. There were lights down there on the quay, and the kick of jazz from the corner-pub. It got louder as a group of people came out. And Haskell watched them. He saw how shiny the night was for young people, how shiny their cars, and the cobblestones under their feet. He admired their racket and energy as they drove away. And in the silence that followed it took him some time to cross the room and pick up the phone.

But he did.

'Hello, room service? This is four-three-eight. Have you got a steak pie on the menu? A large one? And a double order of chips and some brown sauce? Oh, and there's a bar-order too . . . bottle of Haig, six-pack of Tennants, and some glasses.'

Room service arrived. Haskell signed the bill and took the tray next door. Where he found Larcombe in bed.

'You sure you want to do this?' Haskell asked.

Larcombe nodded.

'But that specialist said . . .'

'That bloody specialist had me feeling half-dead.'

'What about all-dead?' Haskell asked. 'What about your doctor giving you six months at the most? You want to make it three months? Two?'

'Yes.'

Haskell put the tray on the bed. 'Okay, I'll get water for the scotch.'

'I've got lager for the scotch.'

Larcombe burst open a can. Foam flecked the sheets. And later, steak pie and chip fat and brown sauce flecked the sheets. While the man ate fast, four or five chips on a fork, and topping up his lager with scotch. Then he lay back, pale and sweating, in the middle of the mess.

'All right,' he said. 'All right, I'll tell you.'

'Doesn't have to be now,' Haskell said.

'Let's get it over with, shall we?'

Haskell nodded and sat down.

The man closed his eyes for a moment, frowning. 'The thing I just don't understand,' he said. 'A van-load of fifties and twenties, I mean a van-load . . . What made you think it'd be so easy?'

'I don't know,' Haskell said.

'Listen, this afternoon we were talking about voice-mode, voices coming over the air . . . Up at *this* grade of security?'

'What d'you mean?' Haskell asked.

'At this level there's four types of run,' Larcombe said. 'There's bullion. There's currency paper, either of high denomination or political sensitivity. There's nukes. And there's Royalty.'

Haskell stared at him.

'Give you an example,' Larcombe went on. 'Couple of years back there was this three-vehicle convoy of Royals. And some erk of a driver, he pressed open-channel by mistake. And loud and clear over the air-waves came this voice, "I'm chucking a left after Kew Bridge." There was a hell of a row about that.'

'I see,' Haskell said. 'It's not voices any more. So what is it?'

Larcombe sipped at his drink. 'Are you technical?'

'I can work on a motor.'

'This is going to be a load of laughs,' the man said. 'Okay, let's start with what you had in that file, that out-of-date file . . . private mobile radio. Voice-mode and FSK. High-power VHF.'

'Easy,' Haskell said. 'Easy.'

But Larcombe held up a hand. 'I'll do it slowly,' he said. 'All you've got is a man in a mobile, which means any kind of vehicle with security status. And he's talking to control.'

'Yes.'

'And he does this by speaking, or by using FSK – frequency shift key – a high-speed jumble of sound.'

'Yes.'

'And with a high-power signal he can talk, or be talked to, over a range of a hundred and fifty miles. Which means that anyone within a hundred and fifty miles can pick up that message. And pretty easily too, because it's on a constant band.'

'If you say so.'

'I do,' Larcombe said. 'And that's why the system was scrapped.'

He reached out, and with his fingernail dislodged a piece of steak pie from the sheet. He chewed on it. 'Okay,' he said, 'are you ready?'

'Ready for what?'

'Nowadays.'

'All right.'

'Well, nowadays,' Larcombe said, 'what you've got is a man operating a computer in a mobile. This computer transmits to a central computer. And then this central computer finds another man-operated computer. Which is control.'

'Why all the computers?' Haskell asked.

'Because I'm talking about very sophisticated machines. I mean, just one of their functions is encrypting.'

'En-whatting?'

'Encrypting, putting messages into code. And each message is processed differently. It's the analog version of the one-time code-pad. Impossible to crack.'

'Terrific,' Haskell said.

'And what's more, this message is on UHF, right up above air traffic control. What's more, it's not on a constant frequency, it can be on any of sixty different channels.'

'You're losing me.'

But Larcombe wasn't to be stopped. 'And what's more, it's not high-power but low-power. This signal doesn't travel a hundred and fifty miles through the air, but a maximum of ten. The rest of the way it goes by underground cable . . . See what I mean?'

'No,' Haskell said. 'No, I don't.'

Larcombe smoothed out his bed. He drew imaginary circles on the sheet. 'Look at it this way. You've got almost the whole country divided up into circles of ten miles radius. In the centre of these you've got aerials. And from these aerials you've got land-lines going away to computer-exchanges in London, Birmingham, et cetera . . . And these computers aren't designed to calculate, just communicate. What they do is patch into the Telecom system.'

'All that?' Haskell asked. 'All *that*? For Christ's sake, one company could never afford it. Even a company that makes paper for the Bank of England.'

'No, of course it couldn't.'

'Well, then?'

Larcombe sipped at his drink. It had changed colour, was almost pure scotch. And he was grinning.

'Ever look at the Sunday papers recently?' he asked. 'Ever see these ads where it's some smart-assed guy in a smart-assed car? Making a phone-call?'

'Car-phones?' Haskell asked.

'You call it car-phones. I call it CR, or cellular radio. I call it a bleeding miracle,' Larcombe said. 'And of course I'm only talking about the basic system, the aerials and landlines and such like . . . Because now we come on to the bolt-on goodies.'

'You're going to lose me again,' Haskell said.

'No, I'm not. Just think simple. Think of a white van going along a road. Think of a man inside it pressing a button marked one.'

'Just that? A button marked one?'

Larcombe nodded. 'And in three seconds a map shows up on a screen in front of him,' he said. 'And control comes on line, telling him he's on time, on route, and is cleared for this sector.'

'Jesus,' Haskell said.

'But now think tricky,' Larcombe told him. 'Think of that man pressing button number two, and getting the next map-sector on the screen. Getting police data on a tail-back in the next county. Getting a route round it and a confirm on police co-operation. Think of him pressing button number three. Which gets him Heathrow, if, say, he's delivering there. And Heathrow security have come up with an unmarked Transit somebody's spotted. So they want the shipment delayed, the speed brought back to forty mph maximum while they make enquiries.'

'Jesus Christ.'

'And now think even more tricky,' Larcombe went on. 'Think of *two-way* information. Think of the security-status of that white van, the speed, the revs, the fuel- and oil-levels, temperatures, brake-pressures, checks on circuitry being transmitted *at all times* to anyone listening. Think of it being a four-way, five-way call if necessary.'

He paused, out of breath. 'And think above all of those messages, those encrypted messages, travelling only ten miles through the air . . . I mean, *that's* security.'

Haskell nodded slowly. He reckoned it was time for a drink. He went over to the tray and poured himself a scotch.

Then he turned back to Larcombe. 'What you're saying is, I can't track this van, because I have to be within ten miles to pick up its signal.'

'Yes.'

'And even if I picked it up, I wouldn't understand it.'

'That's right.'

'So what would I hear?'

Larcombe thought a moment. 'You'd hear a *drrrt*, which would be the memory-recall number. And then you'd hear a jingling, like Christmas bells.'

'But I could jam it all right? There's no problem there?'

Larcombe slid over the bed and took the bottle from his hand. 'That's beautiful,' he said.

'What is?'

'Listen, I told you it was Christmas time, didn't I? You jam that signal, and lights start flashing all over the van. A siren starts up. The brakes lock on progressively, and stay locked . . . And the countdown starts, of course.'

'What's that?'

'The unsecure countdown.'

'You mean, five-four-three-two-one, and the Law arrives?'

'No, not the Law.'

'Not?'

'There aren't any shoot-outs, like on TV,' Larcombe said.

'What happens is, at the end of the countdown, the shipment's incinerated.'

'*What*?'

'Burnt.'

Haskell didn't believe it. 'Fifty-pound notes?'

'No, paper.' Larcombe corrected him. 'The paper for fifty-pound notes. The end product of a paper-making line. And, of course, insured.'

It took Haskell a moment to grasp that kind of thinking. Then he looked up. Because he heard a sound, a strange sound. Larcombe was laughing.

'You find all this funny?' Haskell asked him.

'Me? I'm having a great time.'

TWENTY-FOUR

The next morning, just before ten, Haskell went into Larcombe's room. He saw the empty lager-cans, the two-thirds-empty bottle of scotch, and he knew what the man was going to look like.

But he was wrong. Larcombe was sitting up in bed, eating bacon, eggs, sausages, chops, kidneys, the lot.

Bright-eyed, no trace of a hangover.

'You feel all right this morning then?'

'Yes, good. Really quite good.'

But it wasn't all good. Because there were the other changes to the man too. The way he sat forward. The way his eyes moved quickly, following Haskell around the room. For the first time in a week he was no longer sunk inside himself, but looking out.

And starting to think.

Haskell played for time. He took the empty cup from the breakfast tray, rinsed it in the bathroom, and poured himself coffee.

And Larcombe, still eating, started quietly. 'The good life,' he said. 'Nice men in bow-ties bringing me trays.'

'Yes,' Haskell said.

'And a feller could get used to that. A feller could even look forward to the wages coming his way when this thing's over.'

'That's right.'

'I mean, enough for a three-month cruise around the world . . . Three months . . . You see what that means to a man in my position.'

Haskell nodded.

'Only trouble is earning it.'

'That's easy enough.'

'Not really. Not when you think . . .' Larcombe spun it out. 'There's something neither of us have talked about. Something you've never even mentioned.'

'What's that?'

The man put down his knife and fork. He pushed the tray away. 'Listen,' he said, 'you remember how you found me? In that room? Pissed out of my mind? Broke? My marriage shot away?'

'Yes.'

'Well, you weren't the only person worried about me. I mean, before you came there were mates from work. They looked me up, bought me the odd drink, told me the news.'

And Haskell knew what was coming.

'Including the big news,' Larcombe said, 'about a white van being stopped on the road. An explosion.'

'Yes,' Haskell said.

'For Christ's sake, these people are my *mates*.'

Haskell thought for a while. Then he went to the bed and stood over Larcombe. 'But you just told me,' he said. 'You knew that before. Before the night we first met.'

'What?'

'And that night, it wasn't exactly a snap decision of yours. You were awake five, six hours, thinking . . . And then you said yes.'

'What's that supposed to mean?'

'Only this,' Haskell said. 'I reckon that during those six hours you came up with some way. Some way of cracking this thing where nobody gets hurt.'

There was a long silence. Larcombe looked away.

'I'm right, aren't I?' Haskell asked.

'What?'

'You know how to do it. Nice and easy. No violence.'

And Larcombe looked back. 'Yes,' he said then.

'So where's your problem?'

But it was there on the man's face. That bravery again, that child's bravery. 'All right,' he said, 'what happens if I don't go along with you? What happens to me then?'

Haskell moved away. He sat down. He knew there was an answer, and he found it. 'Nothing happens,' he said.

'Nothing?'

'That's it. I pay your bill. I kick you out. And you go back to where I found you . . . *how* I found you.'

There was an even longer silence. Then Larcombe carefully eased his feet out from under the breakfast tray. He stood up and pulled on the thick hotel bathrobe. He curled his toes into the thick hotel carpet. And finally he walked over to the window and looked out of it, warmed by the radiator there, and the sunlight coming in through the lace curtains.

Haskell got up and went to his own room.

About half an hour later there was a knock, and Larcombe appeared. He was dressed, and wearing his overcoat. 'We're going out,' he said.

'Out? Out where?'

'Back to Whycliffe.'

'But,' Haskell said, 'that's where we were last night.'

'Yes.'

They made good time to Whycliffe, but by the time they reached the old part of the city, the traffic was bad. The Cathedral Square was a mass of lorries, and the narrow streets beyond it were worse. As they inched their way past grey stone buildings, and then what seemed to be the windows of a school, Haskell began to swear.

'Don't worry about it,' Larcombe told him. 'It's always like this. The last stop before the motorway.'

'So why didn't we come along the motorway?' Haskell asked. 'And cut back?'

Larcombe didn't answer.

They crawled on, two car-lengths at a time, following the high wall of the Cathedral Court. Until, as the street narrowed even more, they came to the East Gate, and the sudden glare at the top of the cliffs.

It took them five minutes to thread their way through. And another ten minutes, going steeply downhill, to reach the roundabout at the foot of the cliffs, where the town traffic came in from their right.

But finally they were out in the valley, speeding up for the motorway with the lorries.

'No, don't go too fast,' Larcombe said. 'See that turning coming up on the left? And then beyond it, the lay-by? Stop there.'

'The lay-by?' Haskell asked. 'But, for God's sake, that's *exactly* where we were last night.'

He didn't get any reply, and he pulled over and switched off the engine.

A lorry, a big six-axle container, thundered by on the road. Larcombe waited for the sound to die away. 'It's funny,' he said.

'What is?'

'Well, when you tried to take that white van the last time, you almost got one thing right.'

'Did I now?'

'Yes. I mean, you stopped it over on the other side of Whycliffe, didn't you? But if it had been this side . . .'

'What if it had been this side?' Haskell asked.

But Larcombe held up a hand. 'Listen, what's your big problem? Has to be stopping the van talking to control, doesn't it? Without jamming its radio?'

'Of course.'

'And the radio being, as we said before, CR.'

'Yes.'

Another lorry slammed by. Larcombe turned away from it and looked out towards the river. His voice became thoughtful. 'You know, I did my share of runs, big money runs, in that van. But one thing I never liked, none of us did, was coming this way.'

'Why not?' Haskell asked.

But Larcombe didn't seem to have heard him. 'Only we had to,' he said. 'Had to come this way one time in three, one time in four, or it would have been bad security.'

Haskell leaned closer. 'You still haven't told me,' he said, 'why you didn't like Whycliffe.'

The man shrugged. 'We used to call it the shadow run.'

'Shadow run?'

Larcombe nodded. 'CR,' he said, 'cellular radio, it's all very complicated stuff . . . But, I mean, think of car-phones. Even you must've heard. There've been lots of complaints there.'

'Calls not getting through, you mean?'

'In the city, yes,' Larcombe said, 'where there's too many phones and not enough channels . . . But even out in the country there's problems too. I mean, the CR people themselves only claim to cover nine-tenths of the UK.'

'So?'

'So let me tell you about this other tenth . . . For example, there's a section of road between Chesham and Great Missenden where you're never going to get a call through in a million years. And yet it's only ten miles from the M1, where the reception is perfect.'

'Why's that?' Haskell asked.

'Because the road there's in a steep valley, sheer on both sides,' Larcombe said. 'It's what the CR people call an area of shadow-loss. And for them to break it up, they'd have to install two extra aerials at two hundred thousand quid a ti—'

Another lorry passed, cutting him off. And in the blast of sound, Haskell suddenly screwed round in his seat. He looked back up the valley at the cathedral on top of its cliff.

'What you're trying to tell me,' he said, 'is that this is another of those . . . shadow-whatnot areas.'

'Shadow-loss.' Larcombe nodded. 'Just a small one.'

'How small? How far does it stretch?'

Larcombe pointed. 'From just this side of the cathedral choir school down to the roundabout at the foot of the cliffs.'

'Not far,' Haskell said.

'About half a mile.'

'But, what good's that to us? I mean, a van could cover that in, what, a minute, two minutes?'

'Or twenty-one minutes,' Larcombe said. 'At least, that's what it took us today.'

And suddenly Haskell remembered, the traffic in Whycliffe.

'Twenty-one minutes of radio-silence,' Larcombe went on. 'No jamming.'

Haskell hunched forward, pressing his fingertips hard against his forehead. 'It's still not enough,' he said, 'not for what we've got to do.'

'Maybe not,' Larcombe said. 'But there've been bigger traffic snarl-ups. Thirty minutes. Thirty-five.'

'What?'

'I've driven through them.'

'But that's crazy,' Haskell said. 'Thirty-five minutes of radio-silence? On a high security run? Wouldn't control have something to say about that?'

'Why?' Larcombe asked. 'Control can see this snarl-up on their screens. They've got it backed up by police traffic data, the lot. And then again, it's happening in a *town*. I mean, if the van goes unsecure, there are going to be a million people around to see it . . . the flashing lights, the sirens, the whole Christmas show.'

'And see us,' Haskell said, 'if we're crazy enough to be up there.'

'We're not,' Larcombe said.

'Not?'

Larcombe smiled at him. 'The way I see it. I see a traffic-jam *behind* the van, and a clear road in front . . . I mean, you could fix that up, couldn't you? A big outdoor man like you?'

Haskell still had his fingers pressed against his forehead. 'You're saying it would happen out here? Where we are now?'

'Yes.'

Another lorry thundered by, coming from the direction of the motorway. Haskell nodded towards it. 'It's not on,' he said. 'Well, is it?'

'No, not here exactly. Not on the road.'

'Where then?'

'Remember when we were driving just now?' Larcombe asked. 'Remember that turning to the left? Just before the lay-by?'

Haskell looked round. He saw the turning, the small farm-lane, saw where it went down below the road, hidden by trees.

He was still thinking hard. He knew it was all too easy, and then he knew why. 'Wait a minute. That shadow thing . . . You said it only went as far as the edge of the town, the roundabout . . . For Christ's sake, out here the van'd be transmitting again. Well, wouldn't it?'

'Usually,' Larcombe said. 'Usually, yes.'

'What?'

The man shrugged. 'At the moment I reckon the shadow would come halfway out along the valley here. At least that. I mean, we could check it out. Come back with a UHF receiver. See where the line is.'

Haskell shook him. 'What are you *talking* about?'

'Clutter.'

'What?'

'Clutter. A mass of reflecting surfaces, directly in line with the signal, and bouncing it all to hell.'

And Larcombe swung round, pointed once again at the cathedral. 'Where else in the world,' he asked, 'are you going to find a bloody great raft of corrugated iron, five cricket pitches long, and five cricket pitches up in the air? Not to mention a bloody great crane?'

TWENTY-FIVE

Joffrey looked at the games noticeboard, the list of football teams for this afternoon. And it had happened again, he saw. The same thing. He was down to play in goal for choir B, while Morpurgo and his cronies were strikers for choir A . . . Morpurgo who still hadn't forgiven him for that punch-up in Middle School.

But, Joffrey told himself, he wasn't going to pick up any more bruises. Not this afternoon.

He had a plan.

He went up to the dormitory. He passed by his own bed and came to Rayner's. Rayner who had sinus-trouble, and kept a bottle of nose-drops in his locker.

Which, he said, unblocked him.

Joffrey took the bottle downstairs and searched until he found Sorley. And, ducking back into a doorway, he gave himself a full squirt from the nose-dropper up each nostril.

Then he tapped the man's arm.

'Yes, Joffrey. What is it?'

'Well, Sir, about the football this afternoon. I don't know if I'm up to it, really.'

'What?'

'I'm not well, Sir.'

'Oh? Have you seen matron?'

'No, not yet.'

'So you haven't got a note?'

But then the Seventh Cavalry came to Joffrey's rescue. Twin colums of snot came down from his nose.

He blew it quickly. 'I tink I'b tarting a code.'

And immediately Sorley was concerned. 'Good Heavens,' he said. 'And there's your solo you're meant to be practising this evening.'

Joffrey nodded.

'Tell you what I'll do,' Sorley said. 'I'll cross you off the football team. You just stay inside this afternoon, and wrap up well.'

Joffrey wrapped up well. He took off his school blazer and pullover and went out into the autumn afternoon. And he amazed himself. He left the school behind. He left the cathedral court behind. And, hardly knowing what he was doing, he left the town.

He found himself on the cliffs outside the East Gate. Found himself leaning against the railings and looking out at the view. At the river and the London Road, and the bridge where they crossed far away in the distance.

And suddenly he knew.

Because the valley was exactly as it had been two days ago, when he'd looked down from the cathedral tower. The same huge sun-filled afternoon. And the same haze at its edges, the brownish crystally kind of colour that reminded him of summers long ago.

And he knew he was going to walk out there, far out, as far as the bridge. For one afternoon he was going to get away from the school that had been his torture for the past five weeks.

There was a zig-zag track that went down the cliffs, and Joffrey took it, falling deeper and deeper into shadow. Then at the bottom he came to the cinder towpath by the river, the twin rows of poplars, and the smell of woodsmoke coming from the allotments.

Ten minutes later he was in sunshine again, alone in a wide flat area of marshland. Free . . . free of Middle School, of Morpurgo, of the lot of them.

He walked on, his heels sinking into wet cinders. But after a while he realised he wasn't going to make it to the bridge. It was much further than he'd thought, the river looping far out to his left before coming back.

He stopped and looked to his right. There was a smaller path, he saw, going away through tall reeds. About five hundred yards away it seemed to end in a clump of trees. And he remembered there was a farm-lane there that led up onto the London Road. He'd settle for that.

But as he walked, as he got nearer the road, he realised there was a car parked up there. A car with one window wound down, and something poking out of it. A radio kind of thing, with a long fishing-rod aerial.

Joffrey ducked down among the reeds. Because strange things began to happen. The car moved, went forward to the bridge. It stopped, and there were radio kind of noises. Then it reversed back, stopped again, and there were more noises. It happened again and again, the car going forwards and then reversing, only each time a shorter distance, like a ball on elastic.

Until finally it stopped altogether. As if it had found some imaginary line on the road.

TWENTY-SIX

Joffrey didn't go to the car, it came towards him. It drove down the farm-lane from the London Road and stopped quite close to where he was. A blue Audi, E-registered. And its number was the same as Morpurgo's school number, 114.

Two men got out. One was dark-looking, with black-dyed hair and a black suit. The other was shorter, wearing an overcoat. And it was he who had the radio.

It was like a clock-radio, Joffrey saw, with the same sort of flashing digits that a clock-radio had. Only it was larger, with rows of knobs and switches, and a loudspeaker-grille.

The short man worked it. He pressed different buttons. There was a hum, but no other sound.

'Nothing?' the dark man asked.

'Not a whisper.'

'So we're in shadow?'

'Yeh, just like I said, from all that stuff on the cathedral roof.'

Joffrey didn't understand what this meant. Nor did he understand where the two men were going as they moved off. Until he saw that the track ended by an overgrown gateway. There was a yard beyond, and a building almost hidden by trees. An old barn.

'Told you it was down on the ordnance survey, didn't I?' the dark man said.

'You did.'

'And it could be ideal.'

'So long as nobody uses it.'

'Nobody does,' the dark man said. 'No wheeltracks, are there? And look at the state of that tin roof.'

'Yes.'

'What it is, it's part of an old farm, cut off from the rest by the road. And nobody comes this side now. Nobody's bothering to keep the land drained. It's all gone to hell.'

'You know about things like that, do you?'

'I do,' the dark man said. Then he looked round at the gateway. 'What d'you reckon? Can we get it in through here?'

'Maybe.'

'Maybe. You used to drive the damn thing.'

The short man measured the gap with his eyes. 'Yes,' he said then, 'it'll fit.'

'And if it fits here,' the dark man said, 'it'll get into the barn too. Look at the size of that door.'

He went over to the building. There was a graunching noise as he eased a gap in the door and looked inside.

'Perfect,' he said. 'Out of sight. Out of mind.'

'And out of radio contact.'

'Ye-es.' The dark man stood still a moment, hands in pockets, frowning.

'What's the matter?'

'Well, it's what you said. Radio-contact,' the dark man said. 'I mean, on the day, I reckon one of us ought to be listening in, start to finish.'

'Be an idea.'

'More than that. Be essential . . . I mean, you got any ideas?'

The short man looked away towards the road. 'Well,' he said, 'where we found we were picking up transmission again was up on that bridge . . . *Up* . . . It was the height that did it.'

'And?'

'How about that?' The short man pointed up at the barn roof. 'What d'you reckon? Thirty foot up? Could be out of shadow.'

That word shadow again, Joffrey thought. Something to do with radio, obviously. But what?

Then he saw the two men were together. 'Come on,' the dark man said. 'Give us the magic box.'

The short man unlooped the strap of the radio-thing. 'Okay, it's simple,' he said. 'You switch on. You press extended land mobile. Then you press high-speed scan, which hunts fifteen channels a second.'

'Jesus,' the dark man said. 'I mean, what I don't understand is, we can walk straight out of the Unicorn Hotel, go to the nearest electronics shop in Bristol, and buy one of these things. Who uses them, for God's sake?'

'Freaks.'

'Freaks? But can they listen in to car-phones?'

'They can hear them,' the short man said. 'But they haven't got a chance of knowing what the calls are about, or who's making them.'

'Why's that?'

'Work it out for yourself. Just one receiver, picking up over a ten-mile radius . . . Could be any car passing, couldn't it?'

'I s'pose so.'

The dark man looped the radio over his shoulder and went away to the corner of the barn. He reached up and found handholds, and climbed easily on the broken brickwork. But then he slipped. There was the sound of falling rubble.

'Hey?' the short man called out. 'You okay?'

'Yes.'

'Sure?'

'Yes. Take it easy.'

And in a moment the dark man appeared on top of the tin

roof, straddling it. He held out the radio. 'Extended land mobile?' he called down. 'High-speed scan?'

'That's it.'

'And then?'

'Well, if you're out of shadow,' the short man said, 'you'll see lights for the carrier-channels.'

'Lights where?'

'Just above the switch.'

'Got them,' the dark man said.

'Okay, you're receiving.'

'But I want to hear voices.'

'You will, if a car with a phone comes past.'

And one did. Because a man's voice, small and tinny, came down from the barn roof.

'Look, my love,' it said. 'I keep telling you, how can I make it back to you and the kids tonight? I'm ten miles outside Glasgow.'

'*Glasgow*?' the dark man called down. 'Not possible, is it? This thing's only got a range of ten miles?'

'At the most.'

'Dirty bugger.'

And a minute or so later there was the sound of a car coming from the motorway. 'There he is.' The dark man pointed. 'Got a tart with him on the front seat.'

The short man laughed.

The car passed. The dark man watched it go on in the direction of Whycliffe.

Then suddenly he stiffened.

'Jesus,' he shouted. 'Jesus *Christ*!'

'What's up?'

'I don't believe it.'

'What?'

The dark man was still looking up the road towards the town. 'Only what we're after,' he shouted. 'What we're bloody after.'

The short man turned.

And Joffrey, crouching down among the reed-grasses, turned too. But he couldn't see anything. Just hear a vehicle coming up, passing.

Until, seconds later, the radio started again, up on the roof.

With a *drrrt* sound. Then a sound like bells, speeded up.

Joffrey stood clear of the reeds. And, up on the road, saw the back of a van going away.

A white van.

The air stoked up in his lungs. He understood. He started to run.

TWENTY-SEVEN

He didn't care if he was seen, he just ran. Along the path, then the towpath, then, slower, up the zig-zag track that climbed the cliffs. And all the time, to the pounding of his heart, the same question . . . Who to tell? Who to *tell*?

But he needn't have worried.

Because, as he crossed the court, he saw Gaf inside the school gates, waiting for him.

Anger made Gaf's hands stand out from his body, made him sudden. He grabbed Joffrey. 'The headmaster wants to see you,' he said. 'You're to go straight up there.'

And once again Joffrey went to the study door, opened it, and knocked on the green baize inside.

'Come.'

He stood on the edge of the carpet. He was asked to explain himself, but for some time he kept silent. Then he said it, all of it, in a rush . . . the blue E-registered Audi, the man with the black-dyed hair who came from the Unicorn Hotel, the other man with the machine, the radio-shadow that had something to do with the cathedral roof, the white van . . .

Somebody had to be *told*.

When he looked up, he saw Melchior was angry too. Only anger took him in a different way. It gave him the face of a boy, a bewildered boy. He arranged his pens and coloured pencils on his desk.

'I don't understand you,' he said. 'I simply don't understand you.'

Joffrey kept silent.

'You go missing. Search-parties look everywhere. Then you come back from the valley where you've been on your own . . . *strictly* forbidden . . . and to explain yourself, good God, you come out yet again with this story about a white van.'

'Yes, Sir.'

'I mean, why get yourself into *more* trouble?'

'Sir?'

'My dear boy, we had all this once before, didn't we? At the beginning of term? When you admitted the whole thing was a lie?'

'Yes, Sir.'

'And was it a lie? Then?'

Joffrey didn't answer.

'All right, is it a lie now?'

'No, Sir.'

'It's true?'

'Yes.'

Melchior stood up. 'Why do you persist?' he asked. 'Why?'

And at last Joffrey said it: 'Somebody's got to ring the police, Sir. They've got to—'

'*Enough*!' Anger got the better of Melchior suddenly.

Joffrey flinched.

The man turned away. He looked out of the window at the darkening court. And when he turned back again he was calm.

'It's quite simple,' he said. 'When this lying business cropped up before, we agreed on something, didn't we? We agreed that if there was any repetition, it would be a caning offence.'

Joffrey's throat was dry.

'So, what's going to happen is this,' the man went on. 'I want you to leave me now and go back to school. I want you to return at seven o'clock exactly, after supper, and knock on the door. I want you to tell me that you have been lying. Because if not, I'm afraid, the cane will be used.'

TWENTY-EIGHT

It was six o'clock. The shadows were long from the desk-lamp in Melchior's study, and the ashtray was full. He added a further butt to the pile, and opened the window to let in fresh air.

There was a knock on the door.

'Come,' Melchior shouted.

Sorley came in. Sorley who was even more excited than usual, dancing out in the shadows.

'Headmaster,' he began.

'Yes?'

'I've just left the boy Joffrey. He's upset.'

'As well he might be.'

'I mean, extremely upset. I don't think you understand the strain there.'

'What are you trying to tell me, Mr Sorley?'

The man darted forward into the lamplight. 'I gather it's a question of caning.'

Melchior waited.

Twice the man tried to speak. Finally he made it: 'Caning, headmaster, has been outlawed by the European Commission.'

'Is that so?'

'Yes.'

Melchior shifted in his chair. 'To ease your conscience, Mr Sorley, I haven't caned a boy in ten years. And I can promise you quite categorically there will be no caning tonight.'

'There won't?'

'I'm merely using the threat . . . Which is also, for your information, an extremely rare occurrence.'

'But, even the threat,' Sorley said. 'I mean, don't you see

Joffrey is due to report here at seven o'clock exactly, after supper . . . It's the *ritual* of the thing.'

'What?'

'Headmaster, I'm sure you must regard me as a rather fey musician, who can never keep order, but—'

'I regard you as a very talented sub-organist, and a valuable member of staff.' Melchior was tiring.

And Sorley saw it. 'So there's nothing I can say. Joffrey will just report here and—'

'And say he's been telling lies,' Melchior said.

'But, what if he can't do that? What if he's telling the truth?'

'I don't understand you,' Melchior said for the second time that afternoon.

It was seven. Melchior's ashtray was empty. The air in the study was cold and fresh.

There was a knock on the door.

'Come.'

Joffrey came in, fumbling with the door behind him. He stood trembling on the edge of the carpet.

'What have you got to say?' Melchior asked.

And it was as if there was some machine in the boy's throat, some terrible machine, running down. 'The police have got to be told . . . Have got to be . . . Have got . . .'

Melchior was surprised. He was more than surprised. He was shocked.

'So you're sticking to your story?'

Joffrey nodded.

'Even though you know the consequences?'

He nodded again.

It took some time for Melchior to move. He stood up. He'd got it wrong. He felt old and useless.

'Get that chair, will you?' he asked. 'And bring it over onto the carpet, in front of the desk.'

Joffrey's trembling grew worse.

'That chair,' Melchior said, 'please.'

Joffrey turned and fetched it. He brought it over towards the desk.

Melchior turned too. He checked that the outer door of the study was closed. Then the inner door.

As he came back, he saw that Joffrey was bending over the back of the chair, gripping it with his hands. He was shaking violently.

'No,' Melchior said. 'Sit down.'

'Sit?'

'In the chair.'

Tears burst from Joffrey's eyes.

Melchior took the clean handkerchief from his top pocket. He gave it to Joffrey, rested a hand briefly on his shoulder. Then he sat on the edge of his desk, looking down at him.

Fat boy, they called him, he thought. But thin in Melchior's eyes. Small on a big carpet. Railing at a dreadful world.

He didn't want to begin, but he had to. 'I'm sorry,' he said, 'this is not the way I would have chosen. I'm afraid it's going to be far worse than a caning.'

Joffrey's face was hidden by the handkerchief.

'When you ran away this afternoon, when search-parties went out, I . . . I looked through your desk in case there was a note,' Melchior said. 'I apologise about that.'

And Joffrey looked up, startled.

'There wasn't a note, of course,' the man went on. 'But there was a letter from your father. And a letter from you back to him . . . unposted. But it was addressed to Mr R. H. Joffrey, Experimental Irrigation Centre, Harare, Zimbabwe, Africa.'

Joffrey moved suddenly, came forward. 'It's where he works,' he said, louder. 'In Africa, with the blacks.'

'No, not in Africa,' Melchior said. 'Though he does work with blacks, and it is an irrigation-scheme . . . Only it's down on the Sussex coast. In Ford Prison.'

'No,' Joffrey shouted suddenly.

'Yes.' Melchior was glad he'd checked both doors were closed. 'And you know that as well as I do.'

Joffrey was on his feet, beating at the man.

Melchior held on to him gently. 'He was involved in a big financial scandal in the City,' he said.

'*No*!'

'It was something that was unearthed just after the Guinness affair.' Melchior nodded. 'There were well-known figures involved, and they were brought to trial. Your father escaped with a light sentence. It was said his role was . . . well . . . peripheral.'

Joffrey was limp now, leaning on Melchior.

'I'm not here to judge. That happened in court,' the man went on. 'Nor am I here to remind you of personal unhappiness, except where it has to do with your conduct at school.'

He held on to Joffrey. 'Because of course there is the other matter,' he said. 'The lies you tell. Which, as we all know, began at the same time as your father's . . . predicament.'

Slowly he levered Joffrey back onto his chair. He saw that he was prepared to stay there. That he needed space around him now. And time. To accept.

Melchior needed time too. He walked around his desk to the window. Because it wasn't just this particular scandal, he thought. There had been many others, which had affected many other schools. In fact it had been brought up at the Headmasters' Conference. That, and the other modern parental habit . . . dope.

The useless feeling came over Melchior again. That uselessness when confronted by the present-day world. He could see Joffrey's father standing in front of him. The suit, the bow tie, the closely shaven chins. And the well-informed City humour. An amusing man.

He could see the mother too, far from amusing after the court case. He could hear her saying she was selling her house, had to, to pay the massive fine. And hear her saying she was moving out of the area. She had to do that too.

Melchior didn't understand that, why she'd cut herself off from all her friends. And, worse, why she never came to the school nowadays. Why she sent Joffrey by train and taxi at the beginning of each term. And never turned up for half term, or the school play or prize day.

Because there was a boy facing him, an only child, who had been removed from everything he knew. Whose mother didn't visit during term-time. And who had made up a strange imaginary world.

Melchior turned back. 'This isn't how I'd planned to conduct this little talk of ours,' he said. 'And I'm sorry.'

Joffrey still had his face in his handkerchief.

'But, let me suggest a couple of things,' the man went on. 'Other parents have been very discreet. You and I are the only people in the school who know about your father. You and I are the only people who know why you tell these lies . . . But we need to progress from there, don't we?'

There was no answer.

'Admitting to the big lie, about your father, will remove the need for the others,' Melchior said.

There was a sigh, a jagged sigh, from behind the handkerchief.

'I'm asking you to own up to it, yes or no.'

A long silence. And then a trapped, faraway, 'Yes.'

Melchior left it at that. 'As to what happens now,' he said. 'I am going to leave the study and join my wife for supper. I suggest you stay here for a few moments to compose yourself. Then you must go and rejoin your schoolfellows. And you will have to dream up some punishment that I've given you. Because they will ask. Am I being fair?'

Joffrey nodded.

And Melchior left.

TWENTY-NINE

Joffrey himself left the study some five minutes later. And maybe it was because he was angry, really angry, he didn't exactly know why . . . But he told the big lie, the biggest of his life.

It happened when the others asked if he had been beaten.

And he nodded.

The choir gathered around him. They sang words from the Messiah. They sang, 'And with His Stripes He Hath Healèd', as they pulled down his trousers to see the marks.

And then Joffrey knew he'd gone too far. From their faces he knew nobody was going to believe anything he said again.

And from what they said, nobody was going to *talk* to him.

PART TWO

THIRTY

For the first two days, being sent to Coventry was almost a relief to Joffrey. Nobody looked at him, asked him to pass the salt, or mentioned him by name. But, by the same token, it led to a certain peace and quiet.

By the third day, however, he began to feel uneasy. Because it could go on, he saw. The way things happened at a small prep school would allow it to go on. By and large, Middle School boys spoke only to boys in their year. It wasn't done to look outside. And Morpurgo had the whole of Middle School under his thumb.

But on the third evening Joffrey's life changed. A time began for him that was better than any other he'd known at Whycliffe. He found a corner, a resting-place. And he found someone who made him laugh and told him magical things.

It happened during what was known as the Quiet Time, the twenty-minute period, late at night, between second prep and going up to the dormitory. Because it was then that Joffrey went to the library to change a book. And in the far corner found a boy he'd forgotten about. Gillick.

Gillick the tiny boy with the cropped hair and the nerve-ends that quivered in his face.

And amazingly Gillick, defying Morpurgo's ban, looked up and spoke.

'Hello,' he said, 'aren't you the boy who told those lies about the white van? About people having their arms blown off in an explosion?'

'Yes,' Joffrey said. Because by now he'd stopped trying to sort out what was a lie and what wasn't.

'That's good,' Gillick said. 'Good.'

Thinking about it, Joffrey could understand why it was that Gillick spoke to him. Because the boy was alone too, nearly all the time. There'd been his brief moment of glory over the Silent Cabbage affair. But that had come and gone. If anybody talked about him now, they said he was funny. Or strange.

And Gillick was both of these things.

There'd been the time, of course, when he'd cut up his rugger vests and tried to set fire to his shoes.

There'd been the time when he'd been obsessed by measuring things. When he'd walked round the school with notebook and ruler, jotting down the measurements of windows, railings, and bushes . . . even Ackroyd's foot when Ackroyd was standing still.

And there'd been the time when he'd seen some John Wayne movie on TV.

When he'd got his slippers from the dorm, pushed them into his trouser-pockets so they stuck out like pistols, and walked around like a gunfighter. 'I'm awful fast, Johnny,' he'd say. And then, 'Draw!'

And he'd draw. Once he'd even drawn on Sorley, advancing on him like some grim little midget down a corridor. Frightened, Sorley had backed away. Gillick had said he'd count to three. And he'd counted to three. Then sent the slippers hurtling into the man's stomach.

Sorley hadn't reported him. He didn't know what it was he had to report. Nobody really knew what it was about Gillick.

And nor, for that matter, did Joffrey as he sat next to him now in the library. Because he saw the boy had a razor in his hand, and was cutting every tenth page out of *In the Steps of the Master*.

'Why're you doing that?' Joffrey asked.

Gillick shrugged.

Joffrey watched him count ten pages and make another cut.

'What it is really, I'm decimating,' the boy said. 'Everybody gets that word wrong nowadays, don't they?'

'Yes,' Joffrey said.

They sat in silence for a while.

'But, why do the other things as well?' Joffrey asked then.

'What other things?'

'Well, destroying your clothes, for example?'

'That,' Gillick said. 'That was because my father got into a terrible bait about my clothes-bill. He said he wouldn't buy me any more.'

'I see,' Joffrey said. But he didn't. 'All right, why go round measuring up things? Or being a gunfighter?'

'All part of the same thing, really,' Gillick said.

'What?'

Gillick put down the book and the razor. 'Can you keep a secret?' he asked.

'Yes.'

'Yes, I suppose you can. I suppose you have to, being fat and everything.'

'Well-built,' Joffrey said.

'All right, well-built.' And Gillick looked at him with eyes that were small and sharp and grey. 'What it is, I want to be sent away.'

'Away?'

'Away from school. Leave.'

'But . . . but, d'you think you'll be able to manage it?'

'I've managed it before,' Gillick said. 'This is my seventh school.'

'What?'

'And I've only got to carry on like this till I'm thirteen years and nine months.'

'Why thirteen years and nine months?' Joffrey asked.

'Because that's when I'm due to go to Harrow,' Gillick said. 'And I'm not going to Harrow. I'm not taking any more of this crap.'

THIRTY-ONE

They met the next evening too, during the Quiet Time. And once again Gillick was magical. He did most of the talking, Joffrey most of the listening. And sometimes, looking into his sharp grey eyes, Joffrey saw the light of pure reason.

'How it is,' the boy said, 'if I go to lots of different schools before I'm thirteen, then I'm bound to fail the Harrow exam.'

'Yes,' Joffrey said.

'And then I'll have to go to a state school. Have to.'

'A *state* school?'

Gillick saw his shock. 'Don't believe all that propaganda they give you,' he said. 'A state school is heaven. You don't just get home for half term, you get home *every* weekend and *every* evening.'

Joffrey nodded. It was unthinkable.

'And you don't have to work. All you do is stick your head in a Walkman till you're eighteen.'

'Yes.'

'And then you leave.'

'But,' Joffrey said, 'what happens then?'

'That's easy as far as I'm concerned,' Gillick said. 'When I'm eighteen I get twenty-five thousand pounds.'

'What?'

'From my grandmother.'

Unthinkable.

'And then I'm going to start out on my own.'

'But, what d'you mean? What'll you do?' Joffrey was trying to keep up.

'Something. Something *they've* never thought of.'

'They?'

'The parents.'

'Oh,' Joffrey said. 'But won't they worry about you?'

'They don't worry at the moment,' Gillick said. 'Don't see me all that often.'

'They don't?'

'No, they're abroad a lot. And when they're at home, they're usually at one of their other houses.'

'Other houses? How many have they got?'

'Three,' Gillick said. 'One in London, one in Norfolk, and one at Arbinger Royal near Bristol. Which is where I spend most of the time.'

Joffrey whistled. 'What do they do? Your parents?'

'They don't grow up,' Gillick said. 'That's what they do.'

'Oh,' Joffrey said.

And, he thought, sometimes the light of reason in Gillick's eyes was too pure. Sometimes it was difficult to understand.

But one thing he understood about was not seeing your father. And he wondered if Gillick felt the same as he did. 'Tell me,' he said quietly. 'Tell me about your dad.'

'What about him?'

'Well, is he ever around?'

'Sometimes at weekends,' Gillick said. 'But even then, I mean, he never gets up till around four.'

'Four in the afternoon?'

'Yes. No one can wake him.'

Joffrey frowned. He thought of the very few times his own father had got up late. And that dark green colour of gin bottles. 'What is it?' he asked. 'Drink?'

'No, not drink. Not really.'

'What then?'

'They're out of their skulls most of the time. Sometimes I think they're trying to *kill* themselves.'

'Oh,' Joffrey said again, not understanding.

But he went on. 'What about your mother?' he asked. 'Does she stay in bed a lot too?'

'Yes.'

'Why? Is she unhappy?'

'Unhappy? No,' Gillick said. 'She has a certain quality of life, as she calls it . . . The whoop and wharft, that's what she calls it when she's really up there. Flying.'

Joffrey was lost. Completely lost.

But Gillick didn't seem to notice. 'And your parents?' he asked. 'Is your father much trouble?'

'No,' Joffrey said. 'As a matter of fact, he's away a lot too.'

'I see.'

And Joffrey was about to talk about Africa, about irrigation schemes and blacks, when suddenly he knew it wasn't necessary.

He moistened his lips. 'Can you keep a secret?' he asked.

'Yes,' Gillick said.

'I mean, really, *really* keep a secret?'

THIRTY-TWO

And it was such a relief to talk about his father. Tell the things he'd never told before. To a living soul.

But it didn't matter. All Gillick said was, 'You mean, he was one of the ones who got arrested. And wound up in Ford Prison.'

'Yes,' Joffrey said.

And that was that. The two of them still sat close together in the library, in the corner under the window. There was just the night sky outside, the yellow of the table-lamp between them. And for the rest, shelves of fat books going away into the darkness.

And Joffrey told more about his father. Told about the good times before the police had taken him away. About the big house they'd lived in then with the tennis court. About Ebo-Dog getting hold of the balls and taking them away to the river. Biting through them and not bringing them back.

About Ebo-Dog catching the moorhen . . .

Then something made him look up.

And he couldn't work it out, the expression on Gillick's face. Anger, was it? Or what?

Until he understood.

Gillick was bored.

It was a shock, but Joffrey got over it, *made* himself get over it. He saw how different things were for Gillick, how they were somehow bigger and more important. His three houses. His father who didn't get up till four in the afternoon. And his mother who flew.

While Joffrey's mother didn't even like driving a car for long distances. And his father got up at seven even on Sundays. And though he was funny and laughing with grown-ups, with Joffrey he was strict. Really very strict. Made him wear a sports-jacket and tie when people came, just as he did. Made him eat at table just as he did. Said no one in this world was hurt by a good example.

And wound up in Ford Prison.

Joffrey gasped. He'd never put those two parts of his father together before. Ever.

'What's the matter?' Gillick asked.

'Nothing. Just thinking about . . . you know . . . what happened.'

'Your father?'

'Yes.'

'Don't waste your time on parents,' Gillick said. 'They get what's coming to them.'

And Joffrey gasped again. He felt pain, physical pain. Because suddenly he knew it was true. And just as suddenly he wished he could be more like Gillick, see things the way Gillick saw them . . . Strike out on his own.

He looked away at the library shelves, the big dusty books of the divinity section, the bibles and the lives of saints.

And he thought about a recent letter from his father . . . *Remember you are at a fine school, and privileged to sing in a fine cathedral. Whatever else may fail in life, never turn your back on God.*

'I don't believe in God,' Joffrey said suddenly.

'Who does?' Gillick asked.

'I mean, there can't be a God, can there? He wouldn't let things happen as they do.'

'No.'

'And what's more,' Joffrey grew braver, 'I reckon there are people who know. Quite important people. Scientists maybe.'

'Yes,' Gillick said.

'I mean, maybe scientists have actually . . . proved there isn't a God.'

'Oh, but they have,' Gillick said.

'What?'

'Oh, yes. Didn't you know?'

And Gillick was watching him carefully.

'I don't believe it,' Joffrey said.

'It's up to you.'

'All right, then. Tell me.'

But Gillick was still watching him, taking his time.

'Go on.' Joffrey grabbed his arm.

'Okay,' Gillick said finally. 'Take science. Take physics, for example . . . Take what we're taught here . . .' He seemed to be searching for words.

'Like what?' Joffrey asked. 'Like electricity?'

'Electricity, yes.'

'And what else? Light? Sound-waves?'

'That's it,' Gillick said suddenly. 'Sound-waves.'

'What about them?'

'Well, the thing is about sound-waves,' Gillick said, 'they don't disappear, do they? Just go on forever? Getting fainter and fainter all the time?'

'Yes,' Joffrey said, unsure.

'And the thing is too . . . scientists have got machines that can measure sound-waves. Even from way back, *ages* back. And they've taken them to places like the pyramids. And, of course, the Holy Land.'

'To do what?'

'Find Jesus' voice.'

'And did . . . did they?'

Gillick shook his head. 'Nothing,' he said. 'Absolute zilch.'

Joffrey was appalled.

'Listen,' Gillick leaned even closer, 'you know about priests?

You know that when priests become priests, they take lots of exams? Have lots of interviews?'

'Yes,' Joffrey said.

'All right, then. The last interview they have is with the bishop,' Gillick said. 'And what he tells them is that there is no God, and they'd better keep quiet about it.'

Joffrey whistled. He drew back. 'You sure?'

'Yes.'

'How?'

'Books,' Gillick said.

'What books?' Joffrey looked round at the library shelves.

'Well, they're not going to have them here, are they?' Gillick said. 'Not in a place like this?'

'No.'

'But there are books with all that kind of stuff in them . . . We've got them at home.'

'Oh.'

'Didn't you know?' Gillick looked pleased. 'Didn't you really know?'

There was only a minute or so left before the Quiet Time ended and the dormitory bell rang. And Joffrey's mind was in a whirl. He thought how *old* Gillick seemed. He thought of the boy's three houses with all their books, as against his own house with none. He thought of all the things Gillick had at his fingertips, as against the absolute zilch he knew. And he thought of . . . thought of the one thing he *had* to know.

Except that he couldn't ask it. Couldn't ask anyone in the *world*.

But, looking once again at his watch, he saw it was dormitory time.

He took a deep breath and began.

It wasn't about his father really, he said, but to do with, well, after he'd gone off to prison . . . Because then, for God's sake, then his mother had got so worried about what people would think that she'd moved away. Moved up to this rancid little town in the Midlands, where she knew nobody, nobody at all. And . . . and she'd started to crack up, started talking in lists. Get your Supper from the Oven, Be Sure to Use a Cloth, Turn the Gas Out.

'Everybody's lunatic-mother talks in lists,' Gillick said.

'But she's not just a lunatic-mother, she's mad,' Joffrey insisted. 'She cries all the time, watches me all the time, never lets me go out on my own. And it's been going on now for *eighteen months*.'

'What?' Gillick asked.

'It's true,' Joffrey said. 'And, I don't know, during that time it's as if everything . . . everything . . .'

'Everything what?'

'Well, everything out in the real world has sort of changed, gone on without me. And I . . . I just don't know anything any more.'

'I don't get it.'

Joffrey tried again. 'Look,' he said, 'eighteen months ago it was all right. Here at school, I mean. It was all Mars Bars and cinemas and football. And it was okay. I got by.'

Gillick was watching him in that strange way again, frowning.

'But, how it is now.' Joffrey felt the blush coming. 'Now it's all different. It's all . . . harlots and meat and coonies and *Penthouse* magazine.'

'Yes,' Gillick said.

'*Penthouse* more than anything.' The blush grew. 'Because in there it's all people . . . well, people sucking . . . sucking coonies and sucking dongs. And sucking, you know, well, everything when it happens. And licking sweat. And even once, I mean I *read* it, people . . . peeing . . . over each other.'

'Yes.'

Joffrey was burning, ashamed. 'But . . . but, that's not how it is, is it? Not for everyone? Not for people like . . . our parents . . . and us? I mean, that's just for people who buy *Penthouse* all the time, and those awful vids in the video shop?'

Gillick nodded.

'I mean, for people like . . . us,' Joffrey could hardly get the words out, 'there has to be another way? . . . Different? . . . Different altogether?'

And Gillick was frowning hard.
'Yes,' he said. 'Didn't you *know*?'

THIRTY-THREE

The fine autumn weather had gone. Rain had come. It battered against the windows of the Unicorn Hotel. And in Larcombe's room, Haskell leaned against the window-sill and looked down at the man. He lay there on the bed puffed-up, inflated, like some washed up seal. And there was wreckage that had been washed up with him too. Spread out on the sheets was a litter of Yorkie bars, Crunchie bars, Poppets and Treets.

The situation wasn't what you might call good, Haskell thought.

And then he knew it.

'Listen, I've had it up to here,' Larcombe said. 'Questions, questions, questions the whole time. That's the end of it, okay?'

A gust rattled the window-blinds. The lighting in the room was low. There was just the man's face, taut and angry.

'Anyway, what's the use?' he went on. 'I can't help you with the real one, the big piece of information.'

'What's that?' Haskell asked.

'Well, this factory we keep on about, has it ever occurred to you they don't just make the paper for pounds sterling?'

'Yes,' Haskell said.

'All right, has it ever occurred to you they make paper for a hell of a lot of countries around the world? One hundred and twenty, to be exact?'

'Yes.'

'So what are you? A genius or something? I mean, how're you going to know, out of one hundred and twenty different shipments, which is the one you're after?'

'As it happens,' Haskell said, 'it's not a problem.'

'*Not*?' the man was startled. 'For Christ's sake, nobody in the entire place, apart from the managing director, knows when the next fifties-shipment is due.'

But Larcombe was wrong. At least four people knew, to Haskell's certain knowledge.

First there was the man at the Bank of England, who looked at the bin of fifties and found it was getting low.

Then there was the man he contacted at the printers, to set up a new print-run.

And then the trigger-code that appeared on a certain computer at a certain group headquarters.

Where Landon-Higgins worked.

And where Landon-Higgins danced, rather prettily as he'd said, into the computer-area.

Because the man had phoned Haskell last night. 'M'dear chap,' he'd said, 'seems the Christmas rush is starting. Seems paper has been ordered to whop up the nation's overdraft.'

'Paper?' Haskell had asked. 'When?'

And the answer, he thought now, as he stared at Larcombe's sweating face, was what you might call worrying.

Thursday November 24th.

And today was Thursday 10th.

Fourteen days' time.

THIRTY-FOUR

Then it was Friday 11th. It was thirteen days' time, and it was getting insane.

Because Larcombe looked up from his bed and surprised even Haskell.

'I want a woman,' he said.

'A what?'

'Woman. W-O-M-A-N.'

'No,' Haskell said, 'out of the question.'

'Why?'

'Because I don't know how fit you are.'

'All I've been doing is lying around here eating. I'm fit. Fitter than I've been for months.'

'But I don't know that,' Haskell insisted. 'I mean, when that specialist called, he said—'

'That specialist knew nothing.'

It went on for ten minutes or so, and then Haskell left. He went back to his own room and looked out at the squalls coming over the quays. He wondered if he should get heavy. But then he knew that wasn't the way, not with Larcombe. He had to keep him sweet.

But with a woman? And the way the man was looking right now? The problem was, as he'd said, Haskell just didn't *know*.

Then he thought of a way of keeping the thing sensible. Or ninety per cent sensible. He picked up the phone and dialled a Bristol number.

'Hello, is that Lena?' he asked.

'Speaking.'

'Lena, it's Haskell here.'

'Who?'

He had the feeling he'd been all through this before. 'Haskell,' he said, 'the guy who took you to that Chinky restaurant and showed you Sumo wrestling.'

'Oh, yes. Yes, I remember.'

'Fine,' he said. 'But, look, Lena, I've got a rather unusual request.'

'Oh, dear.' Her voice was guarded.

'No, nothing like that,' he said quickly. 'What it is, I'm ringing on behalf of a friend of mine, business friend.'

'Why doesn't he ring himself?'

'He's shy, Lena, very shy.'

'Is that right?'

'And the thing is too, he's not really on top form. Been told to rest.'

'Well,' Lena said, 'it doesn't really sound as if—'

'Lena,' Haskell cut in. 'Look, why I'm ringing, I remember

last time you introduced me to a certain ladyfriend. Very elegant, she was, very charming, and very sort of careful.'

'Who was that?'

'Julie.'

'The genteel one,' Lena said.

'That's right. Genteel's exactly the word.'

'And you think she could handle it?'

'She'd be perfect,' Haskell said. 'She could take it slow, read the signals, call the whole thing off if necessary.'

There was silence at the other end. 'It isn't part of our normal service,' Lena said then. 'The financial involvement would be higher.'

'I understand that.'

'And then . . .'

'Then what?'

'Well, if it weren't you ringing up . . .'

'It is me, Lena,' Haskell said. 'And if you remember, it was a man called Maxie who put me on to you.'

'Maxie, yes.'

'And what Maxie told me was, you were very reliable, very reliable indeed. You see what I'm on about?'

THIRTY-FIVE

Shortly after lunch there was a knock on the door, and the woman Julie came in. And Haskell remembered things about her. The wide mouth that went with her slight heaviness. The face she kept hidden behind dark hair. And the way she kept picking fussily at her clothes. Genteel, he thought, Lena's word for her, as she sat down awkwardly and faced away.

'I don't know if I'm very good at this,' she began. 'Being passed on from one to the other.'

'No,' he said. 'And I'm sorry.'

'So why do I have to call on you first?'

'To talk,' Haskell said. 'Talk about my friend next door.'

'You make him sound like a patient.'

'No. Nothing like that.'

'What is it like then?'

'Well,' Haskell stood up, 'it's his nerves really.'

'What?'

'He's got nervous. Overdone it.'

'It happens,' she said.

'Yes. Only the doctor's been. Put him on a diet. Said not too much – well, not too much in the way of exertion.'

She looked down. 'For Christ's sake, Lena told me,' she said. 'And she told me too about the money, which is terrific. But what I *don't* need from you is a map.'

Two hours later she came back. And she seemed different, lighter, as if a smile had been on her face in the other room.

'All right?' Haskell asked.

Any trace of the smile went. 'I'm only here for the envelope,' she said.

He got it from his pocket and gave it to her. Then he paused. 'Listen, have you had lunch?'

'No,' she said. 'I mean, yes.'

'You're not hungry?'

'No.'

'A drink then?' He saw the tiredness under her eyes. 'You look as if you could do with one.'

She sighed in exasperation. 'You really want to know, don't you?'

'Know what?'

'How he is next door.'

'I'm worried about his health,' Haskell said. 'I'm here on business with him. Sort of feel responsible.'

'That's nice.'

'Listen,' Haskell said, 'we girls must stick together.'

She was close to him now, looking at his hands, and maybe

remembering the last time in the apartment, when he'd massaged her tiredness away.

'All right,' she said, 'I'll have that drink.'

He poured her a scotch. She sipped. 'As a matter of fact,' she said, 'he's a talker.'

'A whatter?'

'All he wants to do is talk.'

Haskell felt relieved.

'There's quite a lot of that around nowadays,' she said, 'in a place like Bristol.'

'Why Bristol?'

'Big city, Aids,' she said, 'scared businessmen.'

She sipped again. 'Certain amount of costume drama in the business today,' she said. 'People want a show. No contact.'

'I thought you ladies weren't supposed to like that sort of thing.'

'I don't know,' she said. 'Safer.'

'There's that.'

'And it can be quite funny,' she went on. 'I mean, Lena's got this song for them.'

She started humming a tune, an old jazz standard, Haskell remembered. He even got the title – 'Pick Yourself Up'.

And then she sang words. 'Will you remember the famous men?' she sang, 'Who have to fall to rise again? They take a deep breath, Pick themselves up, Jerk themselves off, And start all over again.'

Haskell grinned. 'But, our friend next door?' he asked. 'He doesn't want a show, does he?'

'No, just talk,' she said. 'He's unusual.'

'How's that?'

'A romantic.'

THIRTY-SIX

Throughout the week Joffrey had lived for the Quiet Times when he was alone with Gillick. But now all that was over. Because the weekend had come. And it was *the* weekend, he realised suddenly.

Half term.

When Gillick would be going out with his family.

And Joffrey would be on his own.

He'd had this letter from his mother. She couldn't come, she told him, because her sister had fallen ill. But he knew the real reason. She couldn't face the other parents at school.

By Saturday morning Joffrey was desperate. He knew he shouldn't say anything. It wasn't done to say anything. But in the break he went up to Gillick and touched his arm.

'Listen,' he said, 'is there a chance, I mean, just a chance I could come out with you this afternoon?'

'What?' The boy was surprised.

'Not that I really like to ask.'

Gillick nodded. And then frowned in that strange way of his, as though weighing a great many things up. 'All right,' he said. 'Yes, if you like.'

'You mean it?'

'Course I do. But, what you'll have to do is clear it with Matron, and bring a pair of pyjamas or something.'

'Pyjamas? Why? Will we be staying away?'

'Yes, at Royal, our house at Arbinger Royal.'

'But,' Joffrey said, 'if it's for the night, are you sure your parents won't mind?'

'It's not my parents. They're away. It's my sister.'

'You mean, she's staying at the house alone?'

'Only for the weekend,' Gillick said. 'The thing is, she used to live there. But now she's passed her driving test, she's gone up to live in London.'

'How old is she then?'

'Seventeen,' Gillick told him. 'But don't worry, she's all right. She can be quite funny in a way. And we'll have the place to ourselves, see a few vids, stay up late, go out in her car.'

'Car? What sort has she got?'

'Citroen,' Gillick said. 'A 2CV.'

But after lunch it wasn't a 2CV waiting for them out on the drive, it was a large purring Merc. And there were two men sitting on the front seats.

'Oh, *God*,' Gillick said.

'What's the matter?'

'She bloody promised.'

'Promised what?'

'Not to bring any of her London friends.'

'Oh,' Joffrey said.

'Bunch of Aussies,' Gillick said. 'Aussies and queeros.'

One of the men got out. He was tanned, he wore the crumpled kind of suit that was meant to look crumpled, and he opened the rear door. Joffrey stepped in. And immediately he forgot all about Aussies, because the car surrounded him with its wide luxurious space. There was the smell of leather, of Bond Street, and the gleam of small wrapped parcels.

And beyond the parcels was Gillick's sister.

Zee.

She lay back in one corner, and she was as different from Gillick as she could be. Where he was small and sunk-in, she was smooth. Where his hands were stubby, hers were long. She also looked a lot older than seventeen, and normally Joffrey would have been afraid of her.

But he wasn't. She was like nothing he'd ever seen. She wore colours, dazzling colours, layered and spiky, that were difficult to sort into clothes. She had her hair in layers too, silver and bronze. But it was her eyes. As she looked up, they seemed to widen. Until he felt he could dive into them. In.

He sat a little away from her, next to the parcels. Gillick sat on his left. While far away in front were the two men. One of them turned and asked for directions. And his voice was Australian, just as Gillick had said.

While Zee's voice was soft and dark, with an edge to it like icing.

'You go left out of here,' she said. 'Then go through the arch and left again.'

'Left?' Gillick asked. 'You mean, we're going out of town?'

'Yes.'

'Out to Royal?'

'Don't we usually?'

But Gillick was furious. 'You're not . . . not taking these queeros out to *Royal*?'

The sign for Arbinger Royal came up some half an hour later. It was a long straggling village with yellowstone houses, and hedges that were spattered with mud. Then the road went uphill, and at the top was a set of double gates.

One of the Australians got out. He opened the gates and then drove on. And Joffrey didn't know what he was expecting, but he'd never dreamt that the land would fall away, would widen out into smooth silver grass. And that at the bottom there'd be a huge expanse of water. The Severn Estuary, with, far out on it, the Severn Bridge.

It shone like cobwebs in the haze, the bridge. And the water was gold, with gold wading birds. As they went downhill, Joffrey breathed it all in. The shine of it. And the fact that someone could own this and look out at it every day.

He didn't notice the house, Royal, until they drew up in its shadow. And somehow he'd expected an old house, like the one his parents had once owned. But this was modern, white, and on different levels. And while he knew Gillick had money, like some other boys at school – Hallam, Morpurgo – this was what his father would have called quiet money.

Zee led the way in. She kept turning on switches. And lights kept coming on over paintings, exactly over paintings, fitting their frames. Chandeliers too lit up in the wide hallway. And then there were carpeted steps, cinema-wide, that went down and round.

They were in a long room, filled with the gold of the river and the setting sun. There were books on every wall, Joffrey saw, and he wanted to ask Gillick about the ones that said there was no God. But they moved on, past low tables and zig-zag settees, until they came to a glassed-in walk where the sunset was huge. At the far end was the warm chloriney smell of an indoor pool. But Joffrey didn't see it because he was led away to the right.

It was the kitchen, he saw, but not the sort of scrubbed-table kitchen his parents had once had. This was all shiny enamel and steel. And in the middle of it Zee put down her wrapped parcels. 'Tea,' she said.

She untied the ribbons and showed them sardine-and-tomato sandwiches, éclairs, and Lapsang tea.

'But no milk,' Gillick said.

'There'll be milk here.'

'No, there won't,' he said. 'They've been away. Away *ages*.'

'Fine,' she said. 'Then we'll drink our tea black.'

'I don't like it black.'

'Don't be annoying,' Zee said. 'We've got visitors.'

They sat round the table and started on the sandwiches. Or rather Joffrey and the Australians did. Zee and Gillick hardly touched theirs. They just started bickering, in a brotherly-sisterly way.

It went on and on.

Until Joffrey, reaching out for an éclair, suddenly realised it was serious.

'No,' Gillick was saying. 'No.'

'Why not? It's only a small thing.'

'It isn't. And you know it isn't.'

'But you've done it for me before.'

'Just once,' he said. 'When you went on and on.'

'Even so, you did it.'

'For *you*, yes.'

'What d'you mean by that?' she asked.

He pointed round at the Australians.

'They're my friends.'

'But you've got more friends coming later on,' he said louder. 'You told me that yourself.'

'Just a few.'

'How do I know what you mean by a few?' he shouted. 'It could be *hundreds*.'

'Calm down,' she said. 'Just calm down.'

He sat there, trapped and angry in the white kitchen.

'It's not as advertised,' he said then.

'What?'

'It's not what I told him.' He pointed at Joffrey. 'I said there would just be the three of us. I said we'd stay up late, see a vid . . . . just as we used to do before.'

'Things change,' she said. 'They don't stay the same.'

'They *don't change*!' he shouted at her. 'They *don't*!'

And Joffrey was amazed. Gillick he hardly recognised. He was no longer the boy in the school library, whispering how he was going to get away to a state school, how he knew for a fact there was no God. That reason of his, that pure reason, had gone.

In the silence that followed, Zee nodded at the Australians. They got up and left. Then she turned back to Gillick. 'You know you'll do it for me in the end.'

'I won't.'

'Oh, yes.'

'But how can I?' he asked. 'I don't know where they keep it.'

'You found it last time.'

'I don't know where they keep it *now*,' he said. 'They've moved it.'

'They can't have,' she told him. 'They've been away.'

He glared at her. 'You're as mad as they are. I mean, why can't you use your own stuff? Why's it have to be *theirs*?'

'Because,' Zee said, 'I don't have their kind of money. I can't fly out to Goa and pick up Nepalese Temple Ball.'

* * *

Joffrey left the kitchen too. He knew there was something going on he didn't understand. He found a door along the passage, and opened it. The room inside was empty. And there was a huge TV over in one corner.

But it was complicated. It had one of those remote-control units, and he couldn't see how to switch it on. He gave up and waited. After a while he heard footsteps going upstairs. Then, after another while, coming back down again. And then, silence.

He opened the door and looked back down the passage. Zee and the two Australians were standing in the kitchen with their backs to him. And, he saw, one of them must have found some milk. Because there was a tall glass of it on the table. Only the more he looked at it, the less it seemed like milk. It was too white, and sort of on the move. Swirly.

Zee bent over the glass. She tipped it slightly, and started sucking in as her mouth went down to the rim.

Down to the rim.

The glass was upside-down.

THIRTY-SEVEN

They were sitting, all five of them, on the zig-zag settees. Zee, and then Joffrey and Gillick, on one and the Australians on another. The room was silent. Silence seemed to go through the whole house.

Then Zee giggled. 'Last year it was coroners,' she said.

To Joffrey's left, Gillick sighed. 'Was it?'

'Yes.'

There was an even longer silence, and then she giggled again. 'Dwarfs are confused.'

'Very,' Gillick said.

'Dwarfs are very, very confused.' She turned towards him, but Joffrey was in the way. She was surprised a moment, but then she smiled.

And Joffrey couldn't believe it. She yawned, and her arm stretched out along the settee. Then she sort of slid, and snuggled against him. Her clothes sank in like tissue. There was the softness of her body.

'For God's sake,' Gillick said.

Zee looked round. 'What's the matter?' she asked. 'He's good-looking.'

A rush went through Joffrey. A rush, spreading him upwards and out.

'He's like a tennis-player,' she said.

'Oh, very athletic,' Gillick said.

'What's wrong with that?' she asked. 'Nothing. Absolutely nothing. I'm athletic too.'

'If you say so.'

'I *am*,' she said. 'I play lacs.'

'Yes,' Gillick said.

But Joffrey hardly heard him. He felt Zee move closer. Her cheek on his shoulder. Her scent.

'Lacs,' she said, wriggling slightly.

He started trembling. 'Lax?'

'Yes.'

'What is it?'

'Oh, something,' she said. 'Something girls like me play.'

Then she looked up at him. 'I'll have to teach you sometime.'

Later, Joffrey was with Gillick. And Gillick was in the long glassed-in covered way. He was kicking at the skirting-board, just one part of it, savagely.

And Joffrey knew now wasn't the time to ask. Knew Gillick was furious with everyone. Even him.

But he did.

'Listen,' he said, 'what your sister . . . what Zee . . . told me.'

'What?'

'I mean . . . I mean, about . . . lax.'

Gillick kicked the skirting again.

'Well, was she . . . joking?' Joffrey asked. 'I mean, does she . . . play lax?'

'Course.'

Joffrey held his breath. 'And is it . . . what I think it is? . . . Is it . . . ?'

'What?'

'Well, that *other* thing we talked about? I mean, of . . . doing it with a woman? Not . . . not the way that's in *Penthouse* magazine?'

'Yes, *yes*,' Gillick shouted in fury.

THIRTY-EIGHT

In the Unicorn Hotel it all started quietly enough.

It was early on the Saturday evening, and the woman Julie had come to see Larcombe for the second time. Because Haskell had reckoned a second time was necessary. He'd spent a couple of hours with the man during the day. And even though he was calmer, much calmer, he still wasn't coming up with any answers.

Anyway, round about seven, Julie came along to Haskell's room for her envelope. He gave it to her, poured her a glass of the Chablis he was drinking. And everything went as smooth as silk.

At least in the beginning.

'So how is he next door?' he asked. 'Still the romantic?'

'Oh, yes,' she said.

'What is it then? Chocolates? Flowers?'

'No, as a matter of fact it's little notes.'

'Notes?'

'He hides them around the room for me to find,' she said. 'They've got these little drawings on them.'

'That's nice.'

'Well, it's different,' she said. 'Not to mention welcome after some of my other clients. I mean, this one, he talks about such interesting things.'

'Does he now?'

'Yes, like paintings,' she said. 'I never knew there were so many paintings in Bristol. He's been round all the galleries.'

'Kind of a quiet one,' Haskell said.

'But educated too,' she told him. 'I mean, he's been talking about the cruise he's booking up for next month. And most people, if they've got the money to go cruising, well, it's all cheap booze, isn't it? And five course meals?'

'Mostly, yes.'

'But, with him it's archaeology,' she said. 'He's going on one of those archaeological cruises. Says he's always wanted to do that. Go to Athens and then on through the islands. See all the classical Greek sites, and the Minoans.'

'You know all about that, do you?' Haskell asked.

'No.' She shook her head. 'Not until this afternoon.'

'How's that?'

'Well, he got me to look at these brochures with him. And we talked a lot, and I helped him pick one out. It leaves – when is it now? – the twelfth of next month.'

Haskell stiffened. He heard warning bells.

'The actual cruise starts at Venice,' she went on. 'And he flies out there from Heathrow. And, I don't know, you'll think me stupid, but I even wondered if I'd go and wave him off.'

More warning bells.

Haskell kept his voice offhand. 'You say you helped him choose?'

'Yes.'

'From these brochures?'

'Yes, I went round and picked them up for him.'

'When? Today?'

'That's right. He phoned me. Phoned me this afternoon. I got there just before the travel agents closed.'

Phone-bells, Haskell heard. He'd *phoned* her.

He walked casually into the middle of the room and caught his reflection in the mirror. The black suit and the black-dyed hair. It was time to go to work.

But not with his hands. Not like the last time in that apartment, when he'd smoothed her tiredness away. This time it was going to be room service. It was going to be another bottle of Chablis and a plate of smoked salmon.

And a lot of care.

He filled her glass and he talked softly. And all the time he was steering towards that little chink there was going to be in her, the Bad Time.

Because there always was a Bad Time with women like her, part-timers, who worked for people like Lena.

He took it slowly, and first of all he got to her father. An accountant with a smart house and a Rover up in Solihull . . . which explained the genteel bit.

Then he got to the man her accountant-father hated. A man called Derek. She'd married him. There'd been a kid.

And finally to the break-up of the marriage six years later. The Bad Time.

'It was just one evening, a Wednesday evening,' she said. 'No, not a Wednesday. A Wednesday would have been early closing.'

'Yes,' he said.

'Because I was down in the centre, doing some shopping. And I looked at my watch and saw he'd be finishing work. So I called round there to get a lift back.'

'Yes.'

'The place was just about empty,' she went on. 'There was just one light on, in his office. And he was on the phone. And . . . and it was his voice.'

Pain on that genteel face.

'I'd never heard that voice before, not in all the time we were married,' she said. 'It was quiet and wheedling, just like a kid. And so . . . *phoney*.'

Haskell refilled her glass.

'And then,' she said. 'Then he rang this *other* tart and talked her into going out later in the week. And, for Christ's sake, he was meeting her with friends. Friends *I* knew.'

'Yes,' Haskell said.

'And maybe I shouldn't've had it out with him. But it was that voice, that wheedling voice. The fucking *deviousness*.'

Haskell nodded.

'So of course I left him, took the kid. And of course I was broke.'

'Broke?' Haskell asked. 'Didn't your father help out?'

'No,' she said. 'Not the accountant. Not six years in arrears.'

She finished her glass.

'And then,' she said, 'it was as if word got around. Because people kept having a try at me. Men, I mean. Who knew I had the kid and was broke.'

He filled her glass, and she drank again. She didn't care how much she drank.

'And it was so strange then,' she said. 'It was as if I was going towards this strange country. Where people were smaller. And where they only had two hundred words in their vocabulary. And they played cards with only half the pack. I got bad then. You know, quite bad. Booze and the rest of it . . . and, I don't know, it was in that sort of crowd I met Lena.'

'She's nice,' Haskell said. 'A nice person.'

'Yes, she is.' She nodded. 'And she helped me with the kid. Babysitters, and then a school. It was magic. This posh little school called St Christopher's, up in Clifton . . . And my Rachel going there. Rachel Lambert. I went back to my real name. Couldn't go on with his.'

'Yes,' Haskell said.

'Have you got kids?' she asked then.

'Two. Both boys,' Haskell said. 'Well, they're men now.'

'What do they do?'

'They're both accountants.'

And suddenly she stared at him. 'You . . . you've been toying with me. Just bloody *toying* with me.'

He didn't answer.

'But *why*?'

And then she answered her own question. She saw. 'Finding out . . . finding out about me. And, my God, my little—'

Haskell sat back. He took his time, adjusted the fall of his jacket. 'You're a nice girl, Julie,' he said. 'Maybe too nice for this racket.'

'What?'

'Because there are rules.'

She seemed dazed.

'People like me come to people like you,' he said, 'because they don't want to get close. Don't want to get involved.'

She turned then and looked towards the next door room. 'It's him,' she said.

Haskell shrugged.

'*Course* it's him.' She turned back. 'I mean, there's something wrong. You said it was nerves, but it's his heart. He keeps holding himself there. He's bad. He should be in *hospital*.'

Haskell waited till she'd finished.

'Julie,' he said then, 'you've got no problem with me, none at all. That's if you don't ever see him again, and you put him off when he phones.'

'What?'

'Just ask Lena,' he said. 'Ask her about a man called Maxie. Ask her why Maxie's going to get a phone-call from me, telling him about a girl's name, Rachel Lambert. And a school up in Clif—'

She flew at him suddenly. He held her nails away.

'Talk it over with Lena,' he said. 'She'll tell you it's only insurance. Nothing'll happen . . . You're a nice girl.'

THIRTY-NINE

At Royal, it was a little after ten o'clock. Joffrey and Gillick were in the TV room, watching the end of a video. It finished, and there was a snowstorm on the screen.

But a bigger storm raging through the house.

There was huge rock music. Huge. There were voices, loud, sandpaper Australian voices, and women laughing.

'It's getting out of control,' Gillick said. 'There must be busloads of them. *Busloads.*'

'Yes,' Joffrey said.

'I told her,' Gillick said.

'Told her what?'

'That they'd notice.'

'Who would?' Joffrey asked. 'Who'd notice?'

'The parents. Notice the stuff that's missing from their room.' Then he turned, saw Joffrey's face. 'Don't you understand *anything*?'

No, Joffrey thought. But he didn't say it.

He just listened to the music pounding through the floor. 'Why's it so loud?' he asked.

'What?'

'The music.'

'Because they've got speakers everywhere,' Gillick said.

'Oh.'

'In the walls, behind the pictures, everywhere. They like music.' The boy got up and switched the video off.

And then it happened.

The music stopped. And there was an airplane, a huge jetplane, shrieking as it landed through the house.

Joffrey ducked.

'The sound-effects tapes,' Gillick said in disgust.

'The what?'

'Sound-effects. The parents use them when *they* have parties.'

The jetplane got louder, louder. There was the smack of tyres on tarmac. The scream of engines in reverse.

'I'm going,' Gillick said. 'Not taking any more of this.'

'Going where?'

'Up to bed. Locking the door . . . You coming?'

'Yes,' Joffrey said. But he stayed where he was.

Gillick reached the door. 'Come *on*,' he said.

'Well . . .'

'Well, what?'

'Maybe, in a moment. Not yet.'

'Sod you,' Gillick said. And ran.

The door closed behind him. There came the sudden *blaa-aap* of a ship's siren, filling the house. Then another, rattling the windows.

Joffrey waited, gathering his strength, his amazement. Then he went out too.

He was in the long glass-covered way. There were men there, and women with bright dresses and mysteriously smiling faces. They were round a table, drinking the upside-down milk. No, not drinking, Joffrey saw, but sucking it in. Then straightening up and breathing out smoke.

He didn't go towards them, but walked in the other direction. Because the covered way went on at right-angles. Went along past the columns of the indoor swimming pool, to an area of ferns and spidery plants. They were set in coloured pebbles. And other women were there, a row of them, dancing and holding hands.

There came the sound of a train, an express, rushing up the covered way. Joffrey ducked back against the wall. The dancing women smiled at him, and the train passed. It was only sound, he told himself. Sound coming from the hidden speakers.

Then the woman at the end of the row held out her hand. He took it. He danced next to her, swayed with her, as racing cars rushed all over him and through him, and a football goal was scored. He was very happy. He'd never known such happiness. He felt it coming through the woman's hand. Coming all the way along the row of women as they swayed.

After a while he went on to the end of the covered way. And here he found that a window had been broken. A storm maybe, or maybe the high winds of last winter. Anyway a section of the glass had been mended with plastic sheeting. It flapped and crinkled in the wind. And a group of people was playing a game.

What they were doing was picking up coloured pebbles from around the ferns. Three pebbles each. And then, one by one, they threw them at the shiny plastic. As if there were a target there. Only there wasn't.

And it was very confusing, because there were scores.

For example, as a woman threw and hit the sheet, the others all held up their hands, like skating-judges holding cards. 'Five-point-six,' one of them said.

'Five-point-four,' another.

'Five-dead.'

Joffrey joined the game. He picked up three pebbles, blue, red, and green. He waited his turn, and they let him wait his turn. And then he threw.

There were gasps.

'Five-point-*nine*.'

'Five-point-*nine*.'

'Five-*nine*.'

He threw again, carefully, and hit the self-same spot.

Hisses.

'Three-point-two.'

'Three-point-two.'

'Three-dead.'

The last pebble, the green, he didn't throw. Instead he moved to the end wall of the covered way. Walking through a fire-engine, and a horse-and-cart.

There was a door. He went outside. The grass sloped down, as before, to the wide flat water of the Severn. But a moon shone now. And, to his amazement, the sounds continued.

In that calm night, his footsteps silent on the grass, there was a giant noise. A bolt being slid back. Opening the sky. Then, all around him, the lock of heaven being unlocked.

A part of his mind told him they were still sound-effects. And then the rest of his mind caught up. Because he walked past low plastic mushrooms on the grass, each about two feet wide . . . Loudspeakers . . . loudspeakers outside.

He was cold. And a baby, its chuckles as big as the night, went with him as he walked back to the house. He felt it was the beginning of something. That something important was going to happen.

And it did.

Because now he didn't return along the covered way, but ducked in through the pillars to the pool. And Zee was there, alone by the diving-board, in a pure white bathing costume.

He stared at her.

Ripples of light from the water were playing over her costume, her arms and legs. And he walked towards her. Because he knew he should. Knew now was the time.

Beyond the pillars the game was still going on.

'Five-point-three.'

'Five-seven.'

And church-bells rang.

He went close to her, looking up at her smooth face, and the light that moved across it.

'Can I ask you?' he said. 'Can I ask you something?'

'Yes.'

'It's about . . . lax.'

'You're very sweet,' she said, taking a long time with the words.

'How d'you play it?' he asked.

'What? . . . Lacs?'

'Lax,' he said.

'Well,' she said, 'you have nets.'

'Nets?'

There were starbursts on her face. 'Silken nets,' she said.

'Five-point-eight.'

'Five-eight.'

The church-bells swelled, were huge.

'What else?' he asked.

'A ball,' she told him. And then, frowning, as if it were difficult. 'A great, great ball.'

'Hard?' he asked.

'Olee . . . ,' she said. 'Olee-aginous.'

'Yes,' he said.

'It breathes light,' she said. 'Light cascades from it.' And, as her face came close, it poured out light.

'Five-point-nine.'

'Five-nine.'

'*Six!*'

A choir sang carols.

She kissed him. There was the disturbing, the very disturbing muscle of her tongue. And then she drew away.

'I'll have to phone you sometime,' she told him.

'Yes.'

'And you'll have to prove your affection for me. Prove it to the world.'

'Yes.'

He walked slowly away, then turned back. And he needed the distance. Because he didn't know if he was meant to touch her, or speak to her, or kneel down and kiss her wet footprints on the tiles.

Which, he knew, was love.

FORTY

On the Sunday morning, just before eleven, Haskell went in to see Larcombe. His window was open, the room smelled fresh. And more than that, it was clean. All the litter of the past week or so, the chocolate wrappers, the food trays and bottles, had gone.

'Welcome back to the real world,' Haskell said.

'Yes,' Larcombe said.

'You're looking a lot better.'

'Maybe,' Larcombe said. 'But if I am, there's only one reason for it . . . that woman Julie.'

'You could be right.'

'Kind of funny though,' the man went on. 'I tried ringing her late last night. I tried this morning, again and again. But I don't seem to be able to get through to her.'

'Well, it's Sunday,' Haskell said. 'She's probably taking her kid out.'

He was close to the window, listening to the churches striking eleven across the city.

'The real world,' he repeated. 'As a matter of fact I wanted to talk to you about that.'

'Did you now?'

'Yes. I mean, time's going by, and there are still one or two things we've got to clear up.'

'Such as?'

'Such as the route . . . the route we want a certain white van to follow.'

Larcombe sat up. He looked at Haskell for a moment. 'Okay,' he said, 'get a map. A road atlas'll do. Three miles to the inch.'

'I've got one in my car.'

Haskell went out. And as he did so he thought how he'd wasted two precious days on Larcombe, but maybe he'd got it right. It was that look the man had given him just now. There was a chance the information was going to come out with no ifs or buts, no funnies. Clean.

The road atlas was open on the bed. And Larcombe was bending over it, his hand rasping on his chin.

'Okay,' he said, 'on the surface of it, it all seems tricky.'

Haskell nodded.

'It seems this van, with all its cellular radio and police traffic data, has got it made. It can pick its way round trouble. Got an unlimited choice of routes.'

'Yes.'

'But the thing is, it's all done by computer . . . and what's a computer? Just a cupboard that stores lots of little bits of paper, and sorts them out fast.'

'If you say so.'

'I do. And what's more I say the important thing is the paper . . . the information. Who puts it there, in what order, and why.'

Haskell frowned.

'Which only means,' Larcombe said, 'that you've got to think exactly like they think . . . And then get one jump ahead.'

'All right.' Haskell left it at that.

Larcombe picked up the atlas. He looked at three different pages in turn, the Severn Estuary, the Home Counties and Outer London. 'Fine,' he said. 'Now the van goes from the factory to the Bank of England printers – a distance of eighty-two miles.'

'Yes.'

'And most of that way, say fifty odd miles, is motorway, the M4.'

'Yes.'

'And the motorway's out as far as you're concerned.'

'Why's that?' Haskell asked.

'Because the daytime volume of traffic on the M4 has been worked out,' Larcombe explained. 'I mean, on the eastbound lanes it averages thirty-five vehicles a minute. Which, in your case, is going to be thirty-five witnesses a minute.'

'Yes,' Haskell said. 'But that's daytime. What about night?'

'They won't come at night,' Larcombe said. 'They need the cover of those thirty-five vehicles. I told you, it's all been worked out.'

He put the atlas down, and turned back two pages to the Severn Estuary. 'Okay, so where it's got to be is between the factory and the motorway. Agreed?'

'Agreed.'

'Which means junctions 17 or 16.'

Haskell found them on the map. 'Brinsmead or Whycliffe,' he said.

'Right.' Larcombe straightened. 'And you need them to come Whycliffe way, where you're all set up. But that's exactly the way they're not going to come.'

'Why?' Haskell had his hands out. 'Why aren't they going to come Whycliffe way?'

'Number one,' Larcombe said, 'they came that way last time. We saw them, remember?'

'Yes.'

'Number two, using the same route twice in a row is bad security.'

'Yes.'

'And number three, the Whycliffe run is the shadow run, remember?'

'All right,' Haskell said. 'All right, I'll buy that.'

'Terrific,' Larcombe said. 'So the van heads in the Brinsmead direction, doesn't it?' He pointed at the map. 'And between that and the factory it all looks marvellous. All those roads? A roads and B roads? Looks like they can take any route they like?'

Haskell nodded.

'Until,' Larcombe told him. 'Until you know about things like cut-offs.'

'What-offs?'

And Larcombe frowned. 'Think of it this way,' he said. 'You're in a high security mobile, right? And you're coming up to a fork in the road. Police traffic data tells you both ways are possible, both are free. But you've still got to choose one of them . . . And when you do, you cut off all the possibilities of the other route. All the other roads and forks that could lead on to the motorway.'

'Sounds a bit obvious,' Haskell said.

'So obvious,' Larcombe smiled, 'that in the twenty-eight miles between the factory and the motorway, there are only two cut-offs to Brinsmead.'

Haskell didn't believe it. He bent over the map again. 'But for Christ's sake, there must be five. More than five . . . six . . . seven.'

'Show me,' Larcombe said.

'All right, what about this one? This turning here at Gurlay?'

'Pipe-laying,' Larcombe said.

'What?'

'Pipe-laying out on the Brinsmead road. They've been at it for months. And they've got three sets of traffic lights, stuck way out in the countryside. Bad security.'

Haskell grunted. His finger moved across the map, stabbed at it again. 'This one here then? What's it called? Langston?'

'Level-crossing there.'

'What's wrong with that?'

'Main line from Bristol. A train every twenty minutes,' Larcombe said. 'And *sometimes* they're on time.'

'But,' Haskell said, 'but, even if the crossing-gates are down, you can still chuck a left here.'

'And then another left, and then come back down the road you went up,' Larcombe told him. '*Very* bad security.'

'Yes.'

Haskell stared down at the map. And gradually, as Larcombe talked, he began to see it through his eyes. Just the two different routes to Brinsmead, among the maze of other roads.

'Got it then, have you?' Larcombe asked finally. 'Two cut-offs . . . And once you've blocked those, you've got the van coming on towards you at Whycliffe.'

'Unreal.' Haskell shook his head. 'Just unreal.'

'Not really,' Larcombe said. 'Not when you think you're talking to the man on the job. I mean, the experts can come along and give him lots of pretty buttons to press, lots of radio signals that'll get him switching routes . . . But *he* knows the road.'

FORTY-ONE

Haskell got out on the road. He spent half of the afternoon driving to the first of the cut-offs Larcombe had talked about. And the other half looking for an answer.

He found none.

For the first mile or so the Brinsmead turning was a narrow country road. Then there was a village, a messy mud-streaked kind of village, with high pavements rising up from the street. There was a bus-stop, a butcher's, and a Wavy Line. And on the other side, a house with a police noticeboard.

It was raining again, and the street was deserted. For a long time Haskell stared at it, but couldn't come up with anything. And gradually the ticking of the car-clock began to get to him. It was already Sunday 13th.

And the date he was looking at was Thursday 24th.

Eleven days away.

But suddenly it came to him. *Thursday* 24th. He began to see the street as it would be on a weekday. The people waiting at the bus-stop maybe, the people going into the pub. The freezer-truck parked outside the butcher's. And the cars, Volvos maybe, and Audis like his own, parked outside the Wavy Line.

He got out. He went to the rear of his car and paced out its width. Then he paced on, to the far side of the street and the high pavement there.

Perfect, he thought.

And then, looking up at the house with the police noticeboard . . .

Just *perfect*.

On the Monday it took him even longer to find the answer to the second cut-off. In fact he drove past the spot three times before he parked and went back.

It was a narrow valley between hills, no more than a gap. There was a farmhouse to the left behind a muddy yard. And, to the right, pasture that sloped steeply up to a cattle-trough.

And at first Haskell didn't know why he'd stopped. Or why, now, he went to the gate of the field and stared up at the trough. At the tap rising up from one end of it.

Until he understood. A tap meant a pipe, a pipe coming under the road to the farm. And a pipe could be found by a metal-detector.

And he understood something else too. A sound he'd heard. The hissing of the car-tyres as he'd passed those other three times.

Water.

The road was the lowest point in the valley.

By three in the afternoon he was back in Larcombe's room at the Unicorn Hotel.

'How about water?' he asked. 'Standing water?'

'Could be the answer,' Larcombe said. 'Depends how much.'

'Well, a pool maybe twenty, maybe thirty yards long.'

'And how deep?'

'Two or three feet.'

'That'd do it.' Larcombe nodded. 'You just find the driver who'd go through that . . . all those electrics around. And all that steel.'

'That's what I thought.'

Haskell sat down. He realised he was hungry, and that he'd missed lunch. But now wasn't the time to stop. Not with Larcombe in this kind of mood.

'All right,' he said. 'How about the big one?'

'What's that?'

'Getting in. Into the van.'

'Yes,' Larcombe said. But he didn't say any more, just stared at his hands.

'What's the matter?'

'I don't know.'

'Yes, you do.'

'Okay, it's what we discussed,' Larcombe said. 'What we discussed before.'

'When was that?'

'You remember. When we talked about violence.' The man looked up.

'There won't be any violence.'

'So you said.'

'No, I didn't just say it,' Haskell told him. 'I made you a deal. You show me the way, and I follow it. To the letter.'

Larcombe watched him a moment. Then he made up his mind. 'Okay,' he said. 'How you've got to think of it, you've got to think of a game of chess . . .'

FORTY-TWO

It was the Tuesday, and at long last Haskell had managed to shake himself free of Bristol. He'd left the Unicorn Hotel early, he'd kept to the fast lane all the way up on the M4, and reached London by about twenty past eight.

For a meeting that was way, way overdue.

With Liney.

Liney had been ringing him on and off for the past month. And recently it had been every day. 'It's getting late, Hask, *late*,' he'd said. 'Any more of this and we'll have to cancel.'

'No,' Haskell had told him, 'there's still time.'

And there still was – just – he told himself now, as he drove Liney along the North Circular. The man was sitting on his left, bulky in a new white sheepskin coat. The smell of it filled the car, and the smell of Liney's three-day-old shirt. Animal, Haskell thought, something he trusted.

There was the sound of Elton John on the radio,and the *flak-flak* of the wipers. Outside, the North Circular was blurred by rain. But then the lights of a forecourt showed up, and Haskell slowed. Forecourts were Liney's speciality. And vehicles. He'd been nicking cars since his second year at comprehensive. And by the time he was doing O levels, nicking trucks. He'd always thought big.

Turning onto the forecourt, Haskell drove round to the workshops at the back. Liney got out, hunching himself up against the rain. And Haskell followed him, watching his young man's walk, and the slick of his dark hair showing above the sheepskin.

Elton came at them again as they went into the workshops. Haskell looked round and saw nothing but young men. He felt old. Things were changing, he thought. Nowadays car workshops were like operating theatres. Mechanics were like surgeons, and pulling a surgeon's wage. He walked on past them, following Liney over to the work-bay in the corner.

There were no mechanics there, just a van, a Belgian-made Jaboulet. It was the stretched version, long wheelbase, with high metal sides. And about the only thing it wasn't, Haskell thought, was white.

Liney sat on the workbench. Oil got onto his new white coat, but he didn't care. He was twenty-four, and folding money just slid off his face, leaving no mark there. He thought only of the job in hand.

'So you've got the answer,' he said.

Haskell nodded.

'And no more of that jazz we had last time? No more lobbing explosives down through the ventilator?'

'No,' Haskell said. 'Anyway, that's out as it happens. Right out.'

'Why?'

Haskell slid open the van door. He climbed up until he was standing on the driver's seat and looking back over the roof. 'What they've done,' he said, 'is they've fitted a heavy steel plate, crosswise, just inside the ventilator.'

'Makes sense,' Liney said. 'But how d'you know?'

'That guy Larcombe. He heard it from his mates at work.'

'You sure?'

'Course I'm sure. I did a lot of talking to him.'

Liney thought a moment. 'And this Larcombe?' he asked. 'Where is he now?'

'Back at the Unicorn in Bristol,' Haskell told him. 'I've got Hibbert down there, babysitting, keeping him out of trouble.'

'Hibbert's okay.' Liney nodded. Then he moved round on the bench and pointed at the van. 'All right,' he said, 'tell me how it's done.'

'Well, what you do,' Haskell said, 'is you play chess.'

'You what?'

'You take one of their pieces. Take one of their men.'

Liney's head came up sharply. 'Have I got it right?' he asked.

'You're saying we bust into an armoured van, and get a man out?'

'Not out,' Haskell said. 'We just place him under threat.'

'That's nice.'

'Listen.' Haskell came down from the van. 'If this man's under threat, *real* threat . . . then the rest of them cave in.'

'Why's that?'

'Because, and I quote,' Haskell said, 'it's not company policy to place crew-lives in danger.'

'But how in danger?' Liney asked. 'How the hell d'you get in through all that steel?'

'Well, first,' Haskell said, 'you pick the driver.'

'Oh, you do?'

'Yes, because he's got over-ride. He can over-ride the system, unlock the wheels, and drive away. I mean, he did all that last time, didn't he?'

'Yes,' Liney said. 'Yes, he did.' And suddenly he was thoughtful.

'And what's more,' Haskell went on, 'you've got doors that get you into the cab.'

'Two doors, yes,' Liney said. 'But they slide. And they're steel, in steel runners. You can't crack those.'

'You're right,' Haskell agreed. But then he reached into the cab, pulled a catch there, and walked round to the front of the vehicle.

'The bonnet?' Liney asked.

'That's it,' Haskell told him. 'The only door on the van that hinges . . . And it's steel too, of course, with two dirty great locks . . . here and here.'

Liney got up from the bench. He walked over and saw where Haskell was pointing, in through the top louvre of the radiator.

'And,' Haskell went on, 'you could get one of your cutters in through there, couldn't you? I mean, one of your big jumbo Euro-size cutters?'

Liney measured the gap with his fingers. 'Yes,' he said.

Haskell opened the bonnet. 'And after that, you could get your cutters to work on the air-cleaner, and all the injector-gear, and the battery-mount? *And*, which is the big one, the steering-column?'

'All *that*?'

'Oh, yes,' Haskell said. 'Because, once you've had that lot away, all that's left between you and the man is . . . cardboard.'

FORTY-THREE

Just after half term, a new expression crept into the language of Middle School. A three-word expression, a catchphrase, that was heard again and again.

Not that it started as three words, it started as two. Started, in fact, when Jackson went to see Matron, because his toes were itching more than usual.

Matron told him he had *tinear pedis*.

Which, of course, became *tinear penis*.

And then, more mysteriously, tin your penis.

An expression replacing others such as canker bollocks, (noun, masculine, plural), and slime off, (verb, imperative).

Thus . . .

'Tin your penis.'

'Oh, tin *yours*.'

But this wasn't all. In addition to enriching its language, Middle School began to pick up a rumour. A serious rumour. That the ban on speaking to Joffrey had been broken. And that the strange kid Gillick had broken it. Apparently he'd taken Joffrey out with him for half term.

By Wednesday the rumour reached the ears of Morpurgo, Hallam, and Ralston. They decided to do something about it. And in the morning break, they chased Gillick into the end loo.

But he didn't cower away from them as they'd expected. He just stood there, small and calm.

'You took Joffrey out last Saturday,' Morpurgo said.

'No.'

'Yes, you did. You were seen.'

'No.'

'And seen coming back.'

'Absolutely not.'

'In a big Mercedes.'

'Oh, tin your penis,' Gillick said.

'Tin *yours*.'

They ran at him then. Hallam and Ralston each held on to one arm. Morpurgo grabbed his hair.

He bent close. 'You're friends with Joffrey.'

'No.'

Morpurgo nodded. Hallam and Ralston began twisting the boy's arms.

Gillick showed nothing.

'Yes, you are. Rancid friends.'

'No.'

Morpurgo nodded again. Hallam and Ralston twisted more.

Still Gillick showed nothing.

'Come on,' Morpurgo said.

And suddenly Gillick's eyes filled. The pain caught up. 'All right,' he said.

'All right, what?'

'I was friends with him, but I'm not now.'

'Why?'

'Because he's boring,' Gillick said. 'Fat and boring.'

'Agreed,' Morpurgo said. 'But why were you friends before?'

'Well . . .'

'Come on,' Morpurgo said again.

'Well, at first he was interesting.'

'Interesting?' Hallam asked. 'The fat boy?'

'Yes.'

'Why?'

'It was when he said . . . when he said his father was in Ford Prison.'

'*What*?'

'Oh, what?'

They let go of him and stood back.

'He went there after some big City scandal,' Gillick said. 'He was involved in it.'

'You're joking,' Ralston said.

'Unbe*lievable*,' Hallam said.

But Morpurgo shook his head. 'No, it's not, Hal,' he said. 'In fact it explains a lot.'

'Such as?'

'Well,' Morpurgo said, 'just think about the lies. The lies he told about his father.'

'Yes,' Hallam said, 'I see. I see what you mean.'

And the three of them faced each other, thinking back over the term.

But then Gillick spoke.

'No, you don't see,' he said. 'You don't see at all.'

'What?'

'Oh, what?'

They turned. Gillick was leaning against the tiled wall now. And he was no longer calm, he was strange. Strange and angry.

'That fat boy,' he said viciously. 'Ever since his father went to prison, he's gone all sort of soft inside, like a jelly. He's . . . he's only just holding on.'

'What d'you mean?'

'He doesn't understand anything. He gets everything wrong.'

'Like what?'

'Well,' Gillick said, 'he says he's in love.'

'What?'

'In love with my sister.'

'But your sister's *old*.'

'She's *seventeen*.'

'I know,' Gillick said. 'But he's in love with her.'

'Why on earth?'

'Because she kissed him.'

'Him? The *fat* boy?'

'Yes, at a party.'

'Oh, I get it,' Ralston said. 'At a party.'

'But there's more to it than that,' Gillick said. 'She told him she was going to teach him about lacs.'

'What?'

'Lacs?'

'Lacrosse, you mean?'

'The girls' game? The one they play with those nets?'

'Yes,' Gillick said. 'But Joffrey, the fat boy, the jelly, he got it all wrong. He thought it was something sexy, to do with sex.'

'*What*?'

'Exactly,' Gillick said. 'Only the point is, she *let* him think it too. She played him along.'

'What was she? Drunk or something?'

'No, not drunk.' And Gillick's voice rose. Suddenly he worked himself into a fury. 'You'll see,' he said. 'You'll see when your sister gets to be seventeen. Because then she'll become like everyone else. She'll become sick. She'll eat sicky things like cocktail eats and raw steak. She'll drink sicky things like brandy. And she'll *do* sicky things . . . Just sick.'

The three of them stood there, lost.

But finally it was Hallam who spoke. 'Listen, Gillick,' he said. 'When we started, you said something about all this being interesting. But it isn't interesting, it's *weird*, just like every other thing about you.'

'That's right,' Ralston said.

But Gillick looked straight back at them. 'Maybe,' he said. 'But then again, maybe not.'

'What are you talking about?'

The boy shrugged. 'There's one thing I left out,' he said. 'At the party . . . the party I was talking about . . . my sister promised to ring Joffrey.'

'Ring him?'

'Why?'

'Well, she did it . . . did it for a joke.'

'What?'

'But what *he* thinks,' Gillick said, '*he* thinks it's all to do with love and lacs and all that jelly fat-boy stuff.'

'I still don't get.'

'Don't you?' Gillick asked. 'Well, have you seen Joffrey

recently? Have you seen how he's mooning around everywhere? Just mooning, waiting for her to ring?'

'Well, he is mooning, yes.'

Gillick drew himself up. He came closer. 'And as it happens,' he said, 'I can do my sister's voice on the phone, sound just like her.'

FORTY-FOUR

Just before lunch the three older boys were together in Middle School.

'Weird,' Hallam said.

'Just weird,' Ralston agreed.

'But kind of funny too,' Morpurgo said. 'The fat boy thinking that lacs is something sexy.'

They giggled.

'And quite funny too,' he went on, 'about Gillick's sister saying – what was it? – he had to prove his love for her. Prove it to the world.'

They giggled again, their heads close together.

Until Hallam drew back from the group. 'But, what I don't see is how it fits together,' he said. 'I mean, all that . . . and Gillick ringing up, pretending to be his sister.'

'Simple,' Morpurgo said. 'What we do is, we think of something for the fat boy to do, something really wild. And then Gillick gets him to do it.'

'Like what?'

'Proving his love.'

'But how?'

Morpurgo stood up importantly. 'The fat boy,' he said, 'will speak fat-boy love to the world. He will be filled with beauty.'

'Beauty?'

'Beauty is all around us.' Morpurgo spread his arms. 'We meet it every day at choir practice, in the anthems, in the psalms . . .

And in the words of the psalms, the fat boy will tell it out among the heathen.'

'What?'

'He will sing of his handmaiden. He will praise her name unto the uttermost parts of the earth.'

'Don't get it,' Ralston said.

'Oh, come on, Morpurgo,' Hallam said. 'In plain English, tell us what you're on about.'

In plain English Morpurgo did.

And they started giggling again, uncontrollably, as they understood.

It was only later, when they were sitting down to lunch in the dining-hall, that Hallam mentioned it.

'Why?' he asked.

'Why what?'

'Why d'you think Gillick told us all that? I mean, all that sicky stuff about his sister? He didn't have to, did he? Not his own sister?'

'Point,' Ralston said.

The two of them looked at Morpurgo.

He thought for a moment but then shook his head. 'Absolutely no idea.'

And he still had no idea, after lunch, when he came across Gillick in the library. The boy looked as weird as ever. He was hunched over a table, scowling, and working on a large sheet of white paper.

'What you doing?' Morpurgo asked.

'Nothing.' Gillick covered it up with his arms.

'Come on. Show.'

'No, really, it's not important.'

But Morpurgo leaned forward and snatched the paper away. He saw it had a minutely-detailed drawing on it. Some sort of floor-plan, with different rooms, and different things in them that looked like machines.

'What is it?' he asked.

'Ohhh,' Gillick said, 'I don't know.'

'Course you do.'

'Well, all right then, it's a sort of a factory.'

'Factory?'

'Yes.'

'What kind?'

And Gillick smiled strangely. 'A penis-tinning factory,' he said.

'A what?'

'For tinning penises.'

Morpurgo drew back. He was chilled.

'Look,' Gillick said, 'it works like this . . .' His finger pointed to the top of the plan. 'The donors come in here.'

'Donors?' Morpurgo asked. '*Donors*?'

'Yes,' Gillick said. 'Aussies and queeros. By order.'

Morpurgo felt the chill spread through him.

While Gillick's finger moved on. 'And these donors,' he said, 'they go over to these holes in the wall here and put their penises in. And, behind the wall, this machinery starts up, this automatic milking-machinery . . . and then . . .' He pointed. 'Then, at the moment of climax, these knives come down. They chop the penises off, which go along this conveyor-belt here . . . And at the same time these containers here come along by another route . . . They all meet up in the canning-room . . . the tins are sealed . . . and you've got the finished product. Tinned penis in sperm sauce.'

FORTY-FIVE

It was late on the Wednesday evening, and Haskell was reading from a list. 'Jack Shannon driving the recovery-vehicle,' he said.

'Yes,' Liney said.

'Bazzer driving the first van, the one that's waiting on the road.'

'Yes.'

'And he doubles on the second van, the getaway.'

'Right.'

'Then there has to be your boy, Mike Whitrow, on the cutting-gear.'

'Whitty's the best. He's safe.'

'And I reckoned George Gartside as his mate.'

'Yes.'

'Then Trevor up on the roof with the radio-phone.'

'Fine.'

'And then you and me,' Haskell said. 'Which wraps it up on-site.'

Liney nodded.

'So . . . moving away,' Haskell went on, 'I'm putting McIver, Jock McIver's son, down the road by the roundabout.'

'McIver, yes.'

'And Gummer driving the big six-axle, up in Whycliffe.'

'Yes.'

'Dave Rowan as his mate.'

'Yes.'

'And as for the rest, there's going to be four back down the road with radio-phones. And four more taking care of the cut-offs. Anyway, this is what I thought.' Haskell handed over a second list with eight names.

'Hamish, Jack Freely, Pawson . . . yes, yes, yes.' Liney read them. 'Most of them have worked with us before.'

'All bar two.'

'But, Christ, it's a lot.' Liney frowned. 'I mean, eight here, plus . . . how many did you do before?'

'Ten, with you and me.'

'Eighteen, my Christ.'

'Plus four vehicles, four on-site alone,' Haskell said. 'We've got a lot of work to do with them tomorrow.'

FORTY-SIX

The line of buildings stood alone under a huge Essex sky. And they had a strange smell about them, sweet, sickly, like uncooked sausage-meat. It hung everywhere. Over the tall asbestos sheds, over the grain-hoppers and the diesel tanks, and the wartime concrete road that linked them.

But it was strongest, the smell, where one of the shed-doors was open. And inside was a vast area of shadow. It was just possible to see the thick grey covering on the floor. And the grey dust that hung in the air.

There was a squawking. A white turkey came out. Except that it was difficult to see it as a turkey. Its neck and back were bald where they had been pecked. It shambled, belly-down, on buckled legs. And it moved in circles, blinded by the daylight.

A man came out after it. He was white too, slab-white, and powdered with the grey dust. He went after the turkey. Easily he scooped it up and threw it back into the shed. Then he leaned against the door and lit a cigarette.

A second man, taller, joined him. They looked out at the flat Essex land. At where the old wartime concrete became old wartime runway, stretching away. And at the dots far off in the distance.

Nine or ten men.

And four vehicles.

'Still there then?' the tall man said.

'Yeh. Same as this morning.'

'What's it all at?'

'Search me. They put down this load of traffic-cones, and then they drive round them.'

'That right?'

'Yeh, and they got stop-watches an' all.'

'How d'you know that?'

'Guv'nor told me.'

'He let them in then?'

'Yeh.'

'And put the money in his back pocket?'

'No, not this one. This one's Ministry.'

'Fuckin' Ag and Fish?'

'No, fuckin' Transport. Ministry of fuckin' tow-bars and turnin'-circles.'

FORTY-SEVEN

The pub was next to the petrol forecourt on the North Circular Road. It was raining hard outside. And inside, men were lingering, lining up the drinks. Making a session of it, they said, a real Sunday lunchtime session.

But over in the corner two men were drinking slowly. Their heads were close together, and they were worried.

'For Christ's sake,' Haskell said, 'we were doing all right. We were doing fine . . . And then, bang, three days lost in a row.'

'Yes,' Liney said.

'Three days, three deliveries of Jaboulet spares, and *six* steering-columns.'

'I know,' Liney said. 'But it'll come right in the end. That boy Whitrow – Whitty – he's ace.'

'Ace?' Haskell asked. 'He's never got below twelve minutes cutting out those columns. And never below eighteen for the whole job.'

'You've got to understand,' Liney said, 'that Belgian gear, it's good nowadays.'

'Maybe,' Haskell said. 'But listen . . . forget eighteen minutes. I was counting on half that. Always was.'

'Half?'

Haskell leaned closer. 'You know me,' he said. 'I always leave time at the end. None of that James Hunt stuff. None of that ninety miles an hour. The only way to do it is drive away easy, with time in hand. That way we all get home.'

'Agreed,' Liney said. 'Agreed. But, Hask, we've worked on those steering-columns a hell of a time now. Maybe it *is* eighteen minutes. Maybe you'll have to settle for that.'

'Not possible,' Haskell said.

'You mean it?'

'I do.'

'All right then. So what do we do? You got any other ideas?'

'No.'

Liney looked at him hard. 'You sure?' he asked. 'Not like you not to have any ideas.'

Haskell turned away. 'I'll get some more drinks.'

And Liney watched him go, frowning.

In five minutes Haskell was back. He put the two glasses down. 'All right,' he said, 'since you ask, the only idea I've had is to make a change.'

'What change?'

'To the team.'

Liney sipped slowly. 'Who's out then?' he asked.

'Gartside,' Haskell said. 'George Gartside.'

'Him? The one who's working as Whitty's mate? But he's okay, isn't he? Reliable?'

'But not fast,' Haskell said. 'What I reckon is, if Whitty gets a new mate, then maybe we'll get the time down.'

'Maybe.' Liney was surprised. 'Can't say I see it like that though.'

The two men drank.

'Okay,' Liney said then. 'Who're you going to put in his place?'

'I've got one or two names.'

'Such as?'

'You know the sort of people.' Haskell shrugged.

'Well, so long as it isn't Redman. That's all.'

'Redman?'

'The guy who was with us last time. The guy who played Jack the Lad with the explosives.'

'Not him,' Haskell said. 'Jesus. Never again.'

FORTY-EIGHT

That evening Haskell drove south of the river, following a street-map. He came to a street of small terraced houses, and parked. And on the bell-push of a ground-floor flat found the name, G. Gartside.

He rang.

A five-year-old girl dragged the door open, panting.

'Your dad in?' Haskell asked.

She nodded. 'In the front.'

Haskell went through to the front room. It had sheets over the furniture, newspaper over the floor. And half of the room was white, the other half blue.

Gartside turned, paint-roller in hand. He had loose hair falling into his eyes, and he was eager. 'Hi, Hask.'

'How you doing?'

'Okay, getting through it.' He dipped the roller. 'She wants blue. Blue this time.'

'Going to be a boy then?'

'That's what she reckons, yes,' Gartside said.

'When's it due?'

''Nother couple of months.'

A second young girl came in then, smaller, around four. She had a mug of tea in her hands, and holding it carefully, she took it over to her father.

'Thanks, Moo,' he said.

The girl turned towards Haskell. 'You want some cuppa tea?'

Haskell bent down. He picked her up. 'No,' he said, 'I just had some.'

He held her. She was rigid in his hands. And her smile was rigid too. He let her go.

When they were alone again, Haskell went over to Gartside.

He had a wedge of fifties in his hand, and he stuffed them in the man's top pocket.

'What's that for?'

'Severance,' Haskell said.

'What?' The man was startled. 'You mean, I'm out? You're not taking me?'

'No, I'm not,' Haskell said. 'I'm sorry. Nothing personal.'

Gartside put his tea down. 'What is it then? My work's all right, isn't it?'

'Your work's fine.'

'What then?'

Haskell looked round at the door the girl had gone through. 'You've got two kids. Got another on the way.'

'What?'

'And I don't believe in mixing that with . . . what I've got in mind.'

'What?' Gartside looked at him sharply. 'You mean violence, don't you?'

Haskell nodded.

'But you said there wasn't going to be no violence. You always said that.'

'There's the *chance*,' Haskell said. 'Has to be, with a job like this.'

Gartside took a step away. He leaned against the wall, the blue, forgetting he'd just painted it. 'Bit sudden, isn't it?' he asked. 'I mean, it's not like you to change your mind.'

'No,' Haskell said.

FORTY-NINE

In the south-eastern corner of the cathedral court, quite close to the school, there was a phone-box. And on the Monday morning, not long after breakfast-time, three boys were crammed into it. Morpurgo, Hallam, and Gillick.

Gillick had the phone. 'Hello,' he said, 'is that Joffrey?'

'Yes,' Joffrey's voice said.

'*Zee* here,' Gillick said, curving the word, making it low.

'Who?'

'Zee. You re*mem*ber me? From the party?'

'Yes. Oh, yes, of course.'

'Because I re*mem*ber you, Joffrey. The ath*let*ic one, like a *ten*nis-player.'

Hallam snorted into his handkerchief.

'I said I'd ring, didn't I?' Gillick went on.

'Yes . . . Yes, you did.'

'To talk about *lacs*,' Gillick said. 'You seemed to be so *in*terested in it at the time.'

Hallam doubled up.

But the humour of the situation took Morpurgo in a different way. Just as he'd done once before, he spread his hands, opened his mouth – and began to sing verses from the psalms.

'O, how sweet are thy words unto my throat,' he sang. 'Yea, sweeter than honey unto my mouth.'

Gillick shot him a warning glance as he spoke again. 'Because I do want to talk to you, Joffrey darling, I *do*,' he said. 'But first I want you to *convince* me of your love.'

'O God, my heart is ready,' Morpurgo sang, 'my heart is ready: I will sing and give praise with the best member that I have.'

It was night, late at night. And in the dormitory one person was awake, waiting. And three people were awake, watching.

The cathedral clock chimed midnight.

Joffrey got out of bed, fully dressed. He took his shoes with him, and padded away down the dormitory to the stairs.

Morpurgo, Hallam, and Gillick sat up. They grinned at each other in the darkness. Then Morpurgo began chanting.

'Thou hast proved and visited my heart in the night-season,' he chanted.

'Yes,' Hallam said.

'My loins are filled with a sore disease,' Morpurgo went on, 'and there is no whole part in my body. I am feeble and sore smitten: I have roared for the very disquietness of my heart. Lord, thou knowest all my desire.'

'Yes, yes,' Hallam said.

The two of them got out of bed. They went to the window. And in a moment saw Joffrey coming out into the kitchen garden below. They watched him go away to the potting-shed.

And, a moment later, come out with a spade.

'Thou hast shewed thy people heavy things: thou hast given us a drink of deadly wine,' Morpurgo chanted. 'Thou hast given a token for such as fear thee: that they may triumph because of the truth.'

They watched Joffrey carry the spade to the far garden-wall, on the town side.

'I will rejoice and divide Sichem: and mete out the valley of Succoth,' Morpurgo chanted louder. 'Gilead is mine and Manasses is mine: Ephraim also is the strength of my head. Judah is my lawgiver.'

'Shh,' Gillick said.

But Morpurgo wasn't to be shushed. 'Moab is my washpot. Over Edom I will cast out my shoe: Philistia be thou glad of me . . . *Who* will lead me into the strong city?'

They watched Joffrey go over the wall and into the town.

He was frightened as he walked through the streets with the spade over his shoulder. He kept away from the lights, and quickened his pace until he came to the Cathedral Square. There were only a couple of people about, and nobody saw him as he edged his way left towards the line of bus-stops. And the railings of the Priory Gardens just beyond.

He climbed the railings in the shadow of an overhanging bush. He shouldered the spade again and tramped through more bushes and undergrowth until he came out onto a path. And he saw where he was making for. A grass bank ahead of him that rose maybe twenty feet up from the path, with flowerbeds on either side.

He reached the grass and paced it out. He found the spot where he should start digging, and wondered a moment about being seen. But, as he looked back, he realised the lights of the Cathedral Square were some hundred and fifty yards away.

He dug the spade in, dug it in three times more, and lifted a turf. It was much more difficult than he'd imagined. He knew there was meant to be a steady rhythm to digging, his father had told him that, but he couldn't find it. His foot kept slipping off the spade. He couldn't get his weight over it properly. And he kept striking flints.

And then it started to rain.

He dug on and on, gasping. His clothes stuck to him, and he thought about other clothes melting around a soft body. He thought about a girl in a white costume by a swimming pool, and her face leaning over him, sparkling with light.

And he kept that face in his mind all the time he dug.

Three and a half hours.

He didn't finish until the cathedral clock struck four.

At seven-thirty in the morning the bus-queues began to form outside the Priory Gardens. Long queues, men and women hunched in the rain, looking hopelessly back towards the bus station.

Then one of them turned.

And through the railings saw it, some hundred and fifty yards away. The lover's heart cut out of the turf. With the initial J at one end of the arrow, and Z at the other.

FIFTY

'It's not enough,' Morpurgo shouted. 'Just a small heart on a piece of grass.'

'Small?' Gillick asked.

'It's twenty feet by twenty,' Hallam said.

'Not big enough!' Morpurgo shouted louder. 'Not high enough! Not enough people to see!'

'What d'you want?' Gillick asked him. 'A plane sign-writing in the sky?'

'No,' Morpurgo said.

And began ranting again: 'My heart is smitten down and withered like grass: so that I forget to eat my bread.'

'What?'

'I am become like a pelican in the wilderness: and like an owl that is in the desert.'

'Oh, what?'

'My soul thirsteth for thee,' Morpurgo ranted on. 'As long as I live will I magnify thee in this manner: and *lift up* my hands . . .'

'Up? Is that it?' Hallam asked.

'You mean, on top of a house?' Gillick asked.

'On top of a hill?'

Morpurgo raised his hands in despair. 'Many oxen are about me: fat bulls of Basan close me in on every side,' he groaned. 'O, deliver my soul from the calamities which they bring on me, and my *darling* from the lions.'

'*Your* darling?'

'You mean, Joffrey's darling.'

And Morpurgo nodded. 'I will declare her name unto my brethren: in the midst of the *congregation* will I praise her.'

'Congregation?' Gillick asked.

'Oh, I get it,' Hallam said. 'Congregation – church – ' He looked at Morpurgo. 'Cathedral?'

'Of *course*.' Morpurgo sank wearily into a chair.

'But, you said up.' Gillick frowned. 'D'you mean high up on the cathedral? The tower?'

'Where the fat boy goes when he wants to be alone?'

'No,' Morpurgo said, 'higher.'

'What's higher than the tower?'

'Think,' Morpurgo said.

'But there isn't anything.'

'*Think*,' Morpurgo said again. 'What's that dirty great yellow thing stuck up on the nave roof? Miles high?'

'The crane?'

'Yes,' Morpurgo said. 'Right up on the top of it.'

'Yesss,' Hallam said.

But Gillick was alarmed suddenly.

'You can't mean up *there*?' he asked.

'Why not?' Morpurgo looked at him in surprise.

'Well,' Gillick said. 'I mean—'

'You mean what?'

'Well,' Gillick said again, 'I know I started this business, this phoning Joffrey business. But . . .' He shivered. 'Climbing up that crane, it's too dangerous.'

'Not at all,' Morpurgo said. 'There's a ladder going all the way up, with curving bar-things all round it.'

'Quite,' Hallam said.

'But, the *height* of it,' Gillick insisted. 'You yourself said it was miles high. The top must be, what, a hundred and fifty feet from the ground?'

'The fat boy's good at heights. Very,' Morpurgo said. 'Remember when he stood on top of the tower that time, waving down at us? Right up on the parapet? Smoking a fag?'

'Smoking and not holding on,' Hallam said.

But Gillick tried one last time. 'Joffrey didn't get any sleep last night,' he said. 'He's exhausted. I mean, he could slip. He could—'

'All right, we'll leave it for a couple of days. Make it Thursday or Friday, the end of the week,' Morpurgo said. 'I grant you, the fat boy's never been exactly noted for his strength.'

Gillick nodded unhappily.

And Morpurgo was off again. 'He hath no pleasure in the strength of an horse,' he chanted. 'Neither delighteth he in any man's legs.'

FIFTY-ONE

It was the Tuesday afternoon, Tuesday 22nd November. Two days before the off.

Liney was driving Haskell's car. He was crouching tiredly over the wheel, and his new white sheepskin was no longer white. It was mud-streaked and oil-streaked and slept-in.

And the car windscreen was mud-streaked too. This morning they'd covered a lot of ground, following the route the white van would take on Thursday. They'd started at the paper-making factory, stopped at the two cut-offs along the route, and then again in Whycliffe. In each place Haskell had shown Liney how it was going to go, and how the news was going to come in by radio-phone.

Now, at just after two o'clock, they were leaving Whycliffe and driving out along the river-valley.

'Next on the left,' Haskell said. 'That farm-track there.'

Liney nodded. He signalled, made the turn, and there was a different sound from the tyres as they went down through the trees.

Rain was still falling. It made deep puddles of the potholes along the track, and inside the yard-gate it was slippery. Haskell got out. He went over to the barn and opened the door. And showed Liney the space there was inside.

'Vehicle one, vehicle two, vehicle three, vehicle four,' he said.

'Plenty of room, yes.' Liney nodded.

'And over here, by this wall, the cutting-gear and the generator.'

'Yes.' Liney thought about that for a moment. 'And does it

still bother you? The time Whitty's taking with that cutting-gear?'

'It does,' Haskell said.

'He's got it down to fifteen minutes, start to finish.'

'Still nowhere near.'

'So what do we do?'

'Go along with it. Have to.'

Both men stood looking out at the yard and the rain. Then Haskell thought of something. He went back to the car and got out Larcombe's scanner, the device that looked like a clock-radio.

'What's up?' Liney asked.

'Nothing. Just going to show you the phone-exchange.'

'The what?'

'Where the calls come in to from out on the road.'

Haskell walked away to the corner of the barn. He started climbing carefully, avoiding the loose bricks he'd slipped on last time, and a moment or so later was straddling the tin roof. He pulled the scanner round onto his lap. He read the instructions that Larcombe had taped on to the machine. Then he switched on, pressed extended land mobile, and high-speed scan.

And heard it.

'. . . That's twenty, two-zero, items stock-list niner-five-two . . . colour rose, spell R-Roger, O-Oscar, S-Sugar, E-Ena . . .'

Haskell bent towards Liney. 'You listening?'

'Yes,' Liney said.

'. . . And ten, one-zero, items stock-list six . . .'

'Want any more?'

'No,' Liney said.

Haskell switched off. 'I'll come back down then.'

And he did, moving carefully over the wet bricks of the barn.

Liney looked from him to the machine in his hands. 'And it's radio silence down here?' he asked. 'That shadow thing you were on about?'

Haskell nodded. He switched on again.

'. . . Magenta, spell M-Mother, A-Apple, G-George, E-Ena . . .'

'Jesus,' Haskell said. 'Jesus *Christ*!'

But he was still in control, still kept to the speed limit as he took the motorway back to Bristol. It took him twenty-five minutes there, and twenty-five minutes back.

With Larcombe.

The man seemed bewildered. After three weeks in a hotel-room he was slow-moving and puffy, hating the rain.

But then the rain lifted. Under an edge of cloud the sun came out, just to the right of the cathedral on the cliff.

Larcombe stared at it, on and on, the metalwork on its roof, and the flare from the sun as the crane moved.

Then he worked the scanner, listening as the signal came and went.

'That's it,' he said finally.

'What's it?' Haskell asked.

'The crane. The crane up on that roof.'

'What are you talking about?'

Larcombe pointed. 'When it's east-west, right across us, it's bouncing signals up into the stratosphere . . . But when it comes round, more than halfway round, it lets the signals through.'

'Jesus,' Haskell said. 'But why now? Why the Jesus didn't we find this out before?'

Larcombe turned to him. 'All I can think of,' he said, 'when we were here before, I mean all the time we were working out the shadow, maybe they had that crane in its east-west position. Don't ask me why.'

FIFTY-TWO

Things happened quickly. Haskell took Larcombe back to his room in the Unicorn. And then in his own room he talked to Liney.

'I want a crane-man down here,' he said.

'Better than that,' Liney said. 'I'll get on to Maurice. He's got a wedge of dockland he's turning into millions.'

'No,' Haskell said. 'No Maurice. No dockland king who's going to spread the word around. I want a crane-man, a man who drives a crane, and who needs a quick and easy grand.'

Liney nodded. He got the point.

The crane-man came down on the Intercity. He was in his twenties, all faded denim and blond hair. And nervous, needing to be behind a pint during opening hours.

By now it was eight-thirty and they were back in Whycliffe, parked on the Cathedral Square. The three of them got out and looked up at the great west front of the building. And the crane high above, its red lights swaying gently in the darkness.

'Moored east to west along the roof,' the crane-man said. 'It's how I'd leave it anyway.'

'And leave it like that at night?'

'Oh, yes.'

'But,' Haskell asked, 'can it be locked in that position?'

'It is locked now.'

'I mean, locked permanently. Immobilised.'

The crane-man looked at him.

'It's what you're down here for,' Haskell said. 'Why we're flashing around this kind of money.'

The man turned away. He thought for a long moment. 'Okay,' he said then.

'You mean, okay, it can be done?'

'Yes.'

'Climb up there, get into that cab, and . . . ?'

'The cab's not locked,' the man said. 'You can't go looking for keys at that height. The only key is for the motor.'

'And you don't need that?'

'No.'

'Right,' Haskell said. 'So talk me through it.'

The crane-man shrugged. 'Well, for a start, it's a Detlev.'

'What is?'

'The crane. You can see the name up there on the jib.'

Haskell saw. He nodded.

'And it's not more than three-four years old. So it fits into current EEC regs.'

'Terrific.'

'Well, it is as far as you're concerned, because it means it's got manual on the trim.'

'What?'

'Look.' The man pointed. 'The counterweight, see that? That big weight hanging down from the after-jib? Behind the cab?'

'Yes.'

'Well, that slides. It goes further out for hi-load. And it does it automatically. An automated system.'

'So?' Haskell asked.

'So, EEC regs insist on manual over-ride. Which is this wheel on the driver's left. It's painted red. And it's got this red safety-bar over it.'

'You mean, you can lift up this bar and turn the wheel?'

'A child could,' the crane-man said. 'It's geared right down.'

'And what happens then?'

'One hell of a lot.'

'Tell me.'

'Look up there.' The man pointed again. 'All the upper part of the crane, the cab and the jib, moves round, doesn't it? On a bloody great crown-wheel and pinion.'

'If you say so.'

'And once you trim that counterweight back, I mean with no

load on the hook . . . Then the whole sodding thing'll tip back, strip the splines off the pinion, seize up . . . Take days to free it.'

Haskell breathed out a long slow sigh of relief.

They left the square and walked on the town side of the cathedral. And, rounding a corner, came to the hoardings of the big work-site. A battery of floodlights shone down on it, and a tower of scaffolding rose up.

'There we are. Easy,' Haskell said. 'Just get you over the fence and up the ladder.'

The crane-man turned. 'You reckon?'

'I do.'

'Take a closer look,' the man said.

Liney went off into the shadows. He was away some time, and when he came back he was frowning. 'Security firm,' he said. 'Some outfit called Site Secure.'

'You mean, one ex-copper,' Haskell said, 'scared of the dark.'

'No, three men inside the gate,' Liney told him. 'And closed-circuit TV.'

'What?'

'Oh, yes,' the crane-man said.

Haskell swung round. 'You know these people?'

'Come across them in dockland, yes.' The man nodded. 'They work three-handed minimum. They've got a system of ID cards with photos. And they know everyone who comes into that site. Everyone.'

'But why?' Haskell was amazed. 'Why all that?'

'Try thousands and thousands of quidsworth of roofing lead,' the crane-man said. 'I mean, work it out, this is a building of some size.'

And it was, Haskell realised, as he moved in closer. Because the rain had lifted, there were just a few high clouds, and he could see tall flying buttresses, spires, and huge cliffs of stone going up into the moonlight.

They walked right round the cathedral, and by the time they'd finished, Haskell was worried.

'What d'you reckon?' he asked Liney. 'D'you reckon Arnold could handle this?'

'Don't know,' Liney said. 'We could ask him.'

The crane-man walked between them. 'Who's Arnold?' he asked.

'A man,' Haskell said, 'who does a bit of night-climbing.'

'Well, he'd have to be the human fly. He'd have to have done the north face of the Eiger.'

He moved away and touched one of the flying buttresses. 'Your Arnold,' he said, 'would be all right for the first six foot of this, where there's moulding. But after that, I mean look at it, it's straight up for fifty foot, dead smooth. And smooth and curving at the top.'

He moved further away, reaching the wall. 'And this,' he said, 'has to be, what, forty foot up, smooth, to that window? And after the window, what? Another forty foot?'

He came back towards them. 'You still don't get it, do you?' he said. 'They didn't just build big in those days. They built *massive*.'

FIFTY-THREE

Massive.

The next morning Haskell stood inside the nave. The great pillars and arches stretched away from him. They rose high above his head. And it was strange. For a moment he was a kid again, on a school trip to Westminster, and it all came back. The darkness, the smell of cold stone, the piled-up tombs. And the *space* . . . A chunk of decaying air, he told himself, the size of a hill.

Then Liney touched his arm, and he remembered why he was here. It was 9.30 am. And by this time tomorrow a certain white van would already be on its way.

He walked out across the flagstones and came to a postcard stall. 'Excuse me,' he said to the woman there, 'I was wondering about a conducted tour.'

She smiled at him brightly. 'The next one starts in about half an hour,' she said. 'It leaves from the west door.'

'And does it include the tower? Or the roof?'

'Good Heavens, no,' she said. 'The public aren't allowed up there. Far too dangerous.'

'Dangerous?'

'Yes. You see, both tower and roof can only be reached by the bellchamber steps.' She pointed to the far end of the nave, and the door there set into a pillar. 'And, I mean, you'd think, wouldn't you, it would be quite a simple climb? Straight up?'

'You would,' Haskell said.

'Not a bit of it.' She smiled again. 'You have to walk halfway round the galleries of the cathedral, the triforium and the clerestory. Very high up. Quite a drop.'

'Yes,' Haskell said. 'But the thing is, I've got a friend who's very interested in photography. I mean, he sells to magazines and things. And he thought, you know, the view from up there . . .'

The woman shook her head. 'For photographers' passes you have to apply to the Dean. In writing. Stating *bona fide* affiliations.'

'And how long's that going to take?'

'About a week.'

Haskell thanked her and moved away to where Liney was waiting. 'Get a locksmith down here,' he said.

It was just before one. There were now only twenty hours before the off. And Haskell was pacing back and forwards on the cathedral steps.

A car drew up, a red Italian Lamborghini, and the locksmith

got out. He looked about nineteen. He ran an antiques shop in the Fulham Road. And he sold, Haskell knew, to customers who had to enjoy what they bought in private.

Moving easily, he climbed the steps and looked up at the cathedral. 'Worth the trip out here,' he said. 'Wonderful example of Norman architecture. Waters the garden of the soul.'

'All that,' Haskell said.

He led the way in through the west door. They walked among the whispers and footsteps of the nave, and stopped by the bellchamber door.

It was old black oak, with rows of black iron studs. And it was about a foot smaller than the young man as he stood by it.

He bent to the keyhole. He looked at it, and then he turned. 'No,' he said.

'No? Just like that?'

'Not by tonight.'

Haskell stared at him. 'You mean it?'

The young man smoothed back his hair. 'The key to this lock is about a foot long. It weighs about four pounds. And the flat, the part that goes into the lock, will have an intricately chased design. Perhaps foliated. Perhaps, given the period of the building, *fleur-de-lys*.'

'*Fleur-de*-what?'

'Like those designs you see on carpets.'

'So you can't make one up then? A key?'

'I could. But it would take about a fortnight.'

Haskell turned away. He leaned against the pillar. 'Jesus.'

'You are,' the young man said, 'talking about the son of the house.'

Haskell turned back. 'Okay then. Can you cut us through the door?'

'Yes, I could do that too,' the young man said. 'But it might rather take the *edge* off evensong.'

'I meant tonight,' Haskell said tiredly. 'Getting yourself shut in here with your tools.'

The young man nodded. He ran his hand over the woodwork.

'Problems,' he said. 'You've got a door the size of a broom-cupboard, and a lock the size of a chair. You've got oak that's twice as old as a Tudor beam – ever try to cut through one of those? – and a great deal of massive iron.'

'You're the expert.'

'Too right. And the only answer here is safe-blower's gear. A thermic lance.'

'If we could get one in here.'

'And if,' the young man pointed to the roof of the nave, 'we wanted to leave a cloud of white smoke hanging up there . . . for the police to find.'

Haskell hadn't thought of that. 'No,' he said. 'That's out. No traces.'

'Difficult.' The young man frowned. 'All right, the only other way is to go for the tongues of the lock itself. Cut stone. And mortar it back in place afterwards.'

'Cut *stone*?'

In answer, the young man took a metal rule from his pocket. He slid it along the surface of the door and on into the surrounding arch.

'That's the overlap,' he said. 'Eight inches behind the jamb-stones.'

'What?'

'Which is eight inches by, say, three-foot-six. And two-foot-six deep . . . Just short of six cubic feet.'

'How long will that take?' Haskell asked.

'Well, I'd have to use a mason's cutter, to fit the stones back in later.'

'How long?'

The young man thought. 'The whole job, plus making good . . . Ten hours. Ten hours minimum.'

'No,' Haskell said.

'What d'you mean, no?'

'Listen,' Haskell said. 'I've done some research into this house of God. And the Lady Chapel, whatever that is, is open for private prayer until ten tonight. And tomorrow morning the guy comes in to do the boilers at six.'

'Eight hours,' the young man said.

'Right.'

'Sorry. Can't be done.'

Haskell smashed the flat of his hand against the pillar. 'It's only a *door*.'

The young man straightened. 'D'you want my celebrated lecture on Norman cathedrals?' he asked. 'D'you want to hear about belltower doors? The doors that guarded the bells, the message, the *power*? My dear man, you're talking about the fortress of God.'

Alone, Haskell went out into the court. He saw the chain-link railings with their old-fashioned spikes. He saw the leaded windows of the lodging-houses. And he saw the servant carrying the lunch plate with the metal warming-cover.

There was the silence of a castle keep. All around Haskell was the high court wall. While behind him was the cathedral.

The fortress of God.

And for the first time he understood. He'd come too far. He knew nothing here.

Then he turned and looked at the tower.

And saw the boy up there in the school blazer.

FIFTY-FOUR

There were other boys in blazers. They were coming out of the school that was in the corner of the court, and disappearing through an archway.

Haskell followed. He turned into a street on his left. And at first it was narrow, between old bow-fronted houses. But then it widened out to a gravel walk, and rows of chestnut trees.

The boys ahead of him went through another gate. There was grass beyond, a playing field, and a football game going on.

Haskell went in. He saw boys and parents standing on the touchline. And maybe it was a school match, he thought, because there were shouts for Whycliffe, and shouts for St John's.

The shouts were high and thin. And the football was on the thin side too. Nobody went in on a tackle, nobody meant to hit the ball with their head. These kids were all brain, Haskell thought, brain and nerve-ends. They were like ghosts out on the grass, ghosts who would come back in thirty years as cabinet ministers.

He moved closer. People turned to look at him, and for the second time this afternoon he knew he was out of his depth. Because the field, and its high flint wall, was all of a piece with the cathedral. It was parents in Barbour jackets. It was a master pedalling by on a wheezing bike. It was talk of James and name-tapes and Tunisia.

He gave up. And he was about to turn away when he heard it.

Like a blast from the street.

'You know what I'm talking about . . . Temple Ball.'

It was a girl, Haskell saw, a girl in bright flashy colours. And she was speaking very softly to the schoolkid next to her, who was maybe her brother.

'Just five grammes,' she said.

'No,' he said.

'Five. They'll never miss it.'

'No.'

The match was still going on, but the girl and the kid left early. They went out to a Citroen 2CV parked on the gravel. She opened the door. 'You won't change your mind?' she asked.

'No,' he said, 'I won't.'

Sun was coming low through the trees. The rain, which had eased off last night, seemed to have gone altogether. And as the girl drove off, she raised a cloud of golden dust.

Haskell watched. It was a fine scene, he thought. Almost like one of those TV adverts where they tried to sell you Citroens or mortgages or insurance.

Only this time it was dope.

He waited for the kid to come back to the gate, and then he stopped him. 'Excuse me.'

'What?' The kid looked up.

'I thought choirboys were meant to be good little boys,' Haskell said. 'I didn't think they sold their sisters Nepalese Temple Ball.'

The kid changed. He was scared. 'I—'

Haskell grabbed him and took him on to where the trees curved round, out of sight. He sat him on a bench.

'You're in trouble, kid. You're pulling in funny-fag money.'

'What? . . . No . . . *No*.'

'Oh, yes, you are.'

'I'm *not*,' the boy said. 'I mean, she's had stuff from me before, but never for—' He stopped suddenly.

'Oh, before, was it?' Haskell asked.

'No.'

'But that's what you just said.'

'No.'

'We'll see.'

But suddenly the kid showed defiance. 'I don't care what you do,' he said. 'I just don't care.'

Haskell was surprised. 'Is that right?'

'Yes. I don't mind being slung out of school. I *want* to be slung out of school. I've been trying for three terms now.'

And Haskell could only admire. 'Listen,' he said, 'I'm not talking about that school of yours, all those future prime ministers. I'm talking about you not making it up to the rank of *postman*.'

'What?'

'You're dealing, kid. You're bloody dealing. Don't you understand?'

'But you can't believe that?'

'Course I can,' Haskell said. 'I've known kids your age, *and* younger. The court-records are full of them. What was it? Your old man's stash?'

'No.'

'Hidden away in his bedroom?'

'No.'

But the boy's head drooped, and Haskell could see the name-tape inside his collar. He grabbed a handful of shirt and read it.

'Well, E. J. Gillick, school number 102,' he said, 'we're getting somewhere. I mean, finding your old man's house should be easy enough.'

There was a long silence. Then Gillick spoke. 'Who . . . who are you?'

'Never mind who I am,' Haskell said. 'It's what I want.'

'What's that?'

And Haskell looked at his watch. Ten past three. There wasn't *time*. He had to go straight in.

'Information,' he said.

'What are you talking about?'

'It goes like this,' Haskell said. 'I was having a look round the cathedral, and round the court. Only a moment ago, I mean. And I looked up and saw this schoolkid on the tower.'

Gillick was amazed. He couldn't keep up.

'You know him?' Haskell asked.

'What?'

'Do you?'

'Yes,' Gillick said strangely. 'Yes.'

'All right. What's he doing up there?'

No answer.

'I need to know.'

'What's this got to do with the other thing? The thing you were on about before?'

'It just has,' Haskell said. 'So, about that kid, why's he up on the tower?'

'Ohhh,' Gillick said. 'He just . . . goes there sometimes.'

'Why?'

'I don't know. To have a smoke. Moon about.'

Haskell frowned. He didn't understand. So he asked the big question, 'How's he get up there?'

'Ohhh,' Gillick said again. 'He's got a key.'

'Key?'

'Yes, to the bellchamber door.'

Haskell sat quite still. He felt air moving across his face, felt every plank of the bench he was sitting on.

And he knew he had to be careful. Very careful. Knew he had to come up with something a young kid would go for.

Then he got it. It was when he was thinking back to lunchtime, and the locksmith arriving in his red Lamborghini.

'Listen, kid,' he said, 'I don't come from here. I come from London. And I run a business selling very old things to people. Antiques, all right? But special. There's no bill of sale. Nobody ever lets on they buy from me. And I don't let on where I get my stuff . . . you understand?'

Gillick frowned. 'I'm not sure.'

'What I mean is, a business like mine depends on whispers. And right now the whisper is from here, this place . . .' Haskell pointed back through the trees. 'The workmen up on the cathedral roof.'

'You mean?' Gillick asked. 'You mean, they've found something?'

'Could be.'

'What is it?'

Haskell shrugged. 'All I'm saying is, I need that key to get up there. Need it tonight. Definitely.'

'But,' Gillick was startled, 'what's it got to do with me? I don't know where it is.'

'You know someone who does.'

'Yes, but—'

Haskell leaned closer. 'And you'd better get it for me . . . E. J. Gillick, school number 102, see what I mean? Better get it by choir practice this evening. Which I happen to know is at quarter to five.'

FIFTY-FIVE

It was ten past five, and practice was nearly over. The chancel was a great cave of shadow above the yellow lights of the stalls.

Out in the centre of the aisle, Sorley leaned against the piano. He glanced at his watch. 'We've just got time for one more,' he said. 'So, shall we take another look at number seven?'

A rustle of paper went through the choir. And Gillick, like the boys around him, found the Corpus Christi Carol.

'Now, as I'm sure you'll remember,' Sorley went on, 'the first verse is men, the second tenors, the third basses, and the last verse full . . . While the chorus, printed in italics as you can see, is full throughout.'

He played a chord on the piano, raised his baton.

'Down in yon forest there stands a hall,' the men sang.

'The bells of Paradise I heard them ring,' Gillick sang, with the others.

'It's covered all over with purple and pall.' The men again.

'And I love my Lord Jesus above anything.'

Sorley turned towards the tenors.

And Gillick turned too, looking for Joffrey.

And suddenly he was afraid.

'The bells of Paradise I heard them ring.'

The stupid rancid jelly of a fat boy.

Joffrey wasn't saying anything.

Wouldn't even look in his direction.

'And I love my Lord Jesus above anything.'

The basses began their verse, and Gillick looked further, past the Dean's stall and the rood-screen, to the much larger shadow of the nave.

And he was even more afraid.

'The bells of Paradise I heard them ring.'

The man was standing there, some way away. The tall man in the dark suit.

'And I love my Lord Jesus above anything.'

That story of his, Gillick thought, about workmen finding something on the cathedral roof.

I mean, who in the world would believe that?'

After choir practice Gillick hid himself in the robing-room. And he thought he'd got away with it.

Until, that was, Sorley found him.

'Gillick? What are you doing boy? You're meant to be duty chorister?'

'Am I, Sir?'

'Of course you are. You know that as well as I do.'

'No, Sir, I thought it was tomorrow.'

'You thought nothing of the kind. For Heaven's sake, boy, Jackson's already done half your work. He's nearly done *all* of it.'

'Oh, Sir, I'm sorry.'

'But there's still something you can do.' Sorley came towards him. 'Go and change the hymn-numbers down in the nave.'

'The nave, Sir?'

'Yes. Here's the list for tomorrow. Get a move on.'

Sorley was watching from the rood-screen, and Gillick knew he had to go down the steps to the nave. But there was a patch of bright light there. He had to force himself to run through it, before reaching the pillar where the hymn-board hung.

The bottom of it was in shadow. He crouched down, looking all round him. He couldn't see the man in the dark suit, but he knew he was there.

The only thing, Gillick thought, was to move fast. He reached for the box where the hymn-numbers were kept, and began to find the ones on Sorley's list.

Then he heard footsteps, getting closer.

They stopped.

'All right, kid, have you got it?'

'What?' Gillick asked.

'You know what. The key.'

'Well,' Gillick said.

'You haven't got it?'

'No, not exactly.'

'Why not?'

'It's the other boy, the boy who goes up on the tower,' Gillick said. 'I mean, normally he tells me everything, *everything* . . . But the key, for some reason he . . .'

The man came closer. And he was unlike any other man Gillick had known. His suit wasn't dark, it was black. And there was his hair too. Dyed. Fitting his head strangely, like a black cap.

He got hold of Gillick and took him round the pillar into shadow. There were flower vases there, and metal vase-stands. And beyond them a tomb. A statue of the Christ with an angel.

Gillick looked back. For a moment he hoped Sorley was still watching. But he had gone. And, with the distant sound of the choir-door closing, gone altogether.

All right, Gillick thought, a verger. *One* of them had to be on duty.

But then he heard the rattle of the boiler being stoked, miles away under the north transept.

The man bent over him. 'I told you I wanted it by tonight.'

'Yes,' Gillick said, 'but I can't get it. He's got it hidden somewhere.'

'Where?'

'I don't know.'

'No idea?'

'No,' Gillick said. 'Only that it's too big for him to put in his pocket. So he can't take it over to school. It has to be here somewhere, in the cathedral.'

The man looked round at the tomb. And then at the next archway with its tomb. All the niches and cornices going away down the long nave.

He turned back.

'You never see him hanging round a particular place?' he asked. 'Before he goes up to the tower?'

'No.'

'Never? I mean, when does he usually go up there?'

'During the day. The afternoon.'

'And not in the evening? Like now?'

'No,' Gillick said. But all at once he thought of what Morpurgo had in mind for the fat boy, later in the week.

And the man saw, saw it in his face. There was some sort of instinct that he had.

And suddenly he moved. He reached down into the shadows. He got hold of one of the metal vase-stands. Raised it up. And then smashed it down onto the statue of the Christ, breaking off a foot.

There was a huge sound. A sound like the rushing of wind. Like a storm of meteorites crashing around the nave walls.

Gillick was terrified.

'You're not telling me it all,' the man said.

'No,' Gillick said. 'What I mean is there's . . . there's . . .'

'There's what?'

'A sort of . . . bet,' Gillick said. 'This boy . . . this boy I was telling you about . . . He's going up on the roof. One evening, I mean.'

'When?'

'Day or two's time. Thursday or Friday.'

'And today's Wednesday.'

'Yes.'

Slowly the man bent towards him again. 'It couldn't be today?'

'What?'

'This evening?'

'I . . . I don't know.'

'You mean, there's no reason why not?'

'No.'

The pores of the man's face, the roots of his dyed hair, were close. 'Who's in on this bet?' he asked.

'A group of us.'

'You as well?'

'Yes.'

'And who's the one who's fixing the time?'

'Well, me,' Gillick said. 'I s'pose I do that.'

'All right, make it tonight. This evening.'

'Yes,' Gillick said.

'I'll be waiting here. I'll know.'

'Yes.'

There was a pause. 'So what time will he come?' the man asked then.

'Well,' Gillick said, 'what we thought . . . we thought second prep. We thought he could say he was feeling ill, and—'

'What time's that?'

'Half past seven.'

'Do it,' the man said.

Gillick looked down. He saw the broken foot of the Christ. He was trembling.

And the man noticed. His voice was softer. 'So what's this kid going up on the roof for?' he asked. 'What is this bet?'

Gillick told him.

And it was strange. He heard the man hiss in his breath. Saw how his eyes began racing. Saw how he looked away at the pillar, just a section of the bare stone, as if trying to slow his thoughts down.

It went on and on. Then the man turned back. He spoke again.

FIFTY-SIX

Haskell went back to his own world. He walked in the new part of town, the shopping precinct, among the bright neon signs and the neon-coloured clothes. He saw mothers who couldn't handle young kids, teenagers who couldn't handle pavements, and old men who couldn't handle the whole blasted world.

And he needed that, all of that. Needed to be away from the cathedral to see if he was making any kind of sense.

And he was, he told himself. Nothing had changed. It had always been a straight line, he'd gone after the key and he'd got it. He was going to watch this kid coming into the cathedral tonight, see where he took the key from, and where he put it back. Which meant two separate chances. Nothing could go wrong.

But in addition there was a third chance. An extra to the programme that had nothing to do with keys.

Because Liney and the crane-man were going to be out in the cathedral court. They were going to be looking up and watching the lights of the crane.

It was something Haskell had suddenly thought of when that Gillick kid had talked about the bet. That unbelievable bet.

And it was icing, Haskell thought. If it worked, it worked. If it didn't, it didn't.

But the thing was, it was so simple.

FIFTY-SEVEN

It was twenty to eight as Joffrey crossed the south transept. The cathedral was dark. There were lights in the Lady Chapel away to his right, and a single light far off in the other direction, by the west door.

He could see no sign of the verger on duty, but he could hear Sorley up in the organ-loft, practising. Bach it was, Joffrey knew, and the lines of the music built up as he stopped in the shadow of a war memorial.

It was a roll of honour for the dead. There were helmets and crossed rifles, and then a huge book carved out of stone. Joffrey climbed up onto its plinth, reached to the top of the book, the dust there, and brought down the key.

Taking it with him, he went to the belltower door. He unlocked it, then locked it once again behind him. There was the smell of cold stone. The steps of the spiral staircase ahead of him were dim. Eighty of them in all, he remembered, up to the level of the roof. And he would have to count them carefully, very carefully. He couldn't afford to switch on a light.

He reached the top, panting, and came out onto the clerestory. Not that there was anything clear about the storey at night. The darkness stretched below him like a huge chasm. And the organ, the great fugue, piled up in waves that dashed against the vaulting, making him dizzy.

He walked out along the gallery, feeling the unevenness of the rubble under his feet, and trying to remember where the bigger stones were. His left hand gripped the iron rail. But every now and then he had to let go where there were pillars.

Suddenly his foot caught a large stone. And he fell out – *outwards*. There was a huge rush of space. Then his right hand behind him found iron, the rail. Grabbed onto it. His head was pumping. And the tiny chessboard of the chancel floor, far far below, was like travelling chess, lurching up and down.

He hung on a moment. Then hauled himself back. And in the roar and pounding surf of the organ, had to admit it.

He was scared rotten.

He was even more scared out on the nave roof. The wind was strong, buffeting against the corrugated iron to his right, and setting up a drumming sound. He reached the foot of the crane and looked up. At the red lights of the crosspiece high above him, swaying up and down against the stars.

He took a deep breath and started climbing.

It was scary all right. His hands were sweaty, and slipped on the rungs of the ladder. And the metal hoops behind him were man-size, too far back for him to lean against.

He climbed on, up into the shrieking wind and the night. There was a swaying movement he hadn't expected. The whole world seemed to be on the move. He shut his eyes.

Then, all at once, the next rung of the ladder seemed different. It had grease on it, and he realised he was in the middle of the cog-and-wheel part that turned the crane around. He climbed with extra care, hooking the heels of his shoes onto the rungs, and gripping harder with his hands.

Until finally . . .

Safety. Or safety for the moment at least. He was out of the wind and inside the cab.

He sat on the driver's seat and waited till his breathing calmed. Then he thought about what Gillick had told him. Or rather, with a real burst of panic, about what would have happened if Gillick *hadn't* told him.

Gillick, it seemed, was as scared about the climb as he was. And this evening he'd talked to a man down in the court. A man who knew about cranes. And *he'd* told him there was a safety-device you had to operate if you wanted to climb up above the cab. A wheel, painted red, on the driver's left. With a red-painted bar over it.

Joffrey lifted the bar. He wound the wheel back, as he'd been told. And suddenly had to bite down his fear. Because, with a huge graunching noise, the whole of the cab lurched back.

And it wasn't just the cab. The great crosspiece of the crane kicked up and swung against the stars. Until gradually it slowed, and Joffrey's heart slowed with it. Because he knew the crane was locked now, safe.

He was out on the long metal crosspiece, the wind and stars shrieking round him. He held on with one hand. And with the other eased something out from inside his sweater.

It was a rolled-up bedsheet. One he'd taken from the dormitory earlier. One he'd tied strings to, all the way round. And painted with a message.

Now, unrolling only the first part in the wind, he tied strings to girders. Tied more as he unrolled more, inching his way along.

Further and further in the shrieking wind, until it was done.

ZEE QUEEN OF ALL was stretched out in huge letters against the crane. And tomorrow Zee herself would see it. Just as she'd seen the lover's heart in the Priory Gardens. She'd told him that. Told him how proud she was.

And, he realised suddenly, she wouldn't even have to come into Whycliffe to see this. She could see it from miles away.

Tomorrow, he thought, when the sun came up, the shadow of the crane – the shadow of his love – would go out across the countryside.

FIFTY-EIGHT

The car came closer in the dawn. Haskell watched Liney park at the end of the farm-track and open the driver's door. And as the interior light came on, he saw Larcombe sitting in the back with his cases from the Unicorn Hotel.

The man got out. He walked slowly through the yard-gate and picked his way through the puddles. His face was blue in the half-light, and he was shivering.

Haskell gave him the radio-scanner. He waited for him to extend the aerial and switch on. Then check the top-end UHF bands for carrier-channels.

'Well?' he asked.

'Just a moment.'

Haskell waited on.

Until: 'No doubt about it,' Larcombe said. 'We're in shadow.'

PART THREE

FIFTY-NINE

Maynard went up into the white van. It was steel inside, bright steel, and there was the flicker of striplights.

Maynard put his lunch-bag into his locker, and then turned as Renwick came in. Renwick who was riding shotgun on this trip. Maynard watched him slide the steel outer door shut, spin the heavy safe-wheel in its centre, and switch on the magno-locks.

He watched him do the same with the inner door of the payload compartment, and then turn his attention to the racks.

There were sixteen of them, bright steel again, on each side of the gangway. And each of them held a flat steel case, three foot by four.

Thirty-two cases in all.

Renwick pressed buttons. Steel bars slid across, and a white disc lit up above each column of racks. Then a red disc as the heat-shields locked. And finally a yellow disc as the incinerator pilots lit.

Start to finish it took Renwick four minutes. And then he too put his lunch-bag in his locker.

'What you got?' Maynard asked him.

'Pâté.'

'Do what?'

'French country pâté,' Renwick said. 'My missus gets it from Waitrose.'

'That's all I need,' Maynard said. 'Duck-farts all day.'

He turned to his console, switched on the three main grids and the supplementaries. And immediately Nanton's voice came through on the intercom.

'What are you? Asleep in there?'

George Nanton the driver.

'No,' Maynard said.

'Well, have you done the checks?'

'Yes,' Maynard lied.

'Checked the helmets and the bullet-proofers?'

'Yes.'

'And the operation of the toilet?'

'Yes.'

'Give us a route then, will you?'

'One minute.'

Renwick leaned over Maynard. 'What's up with Nanny?' he asked.

'Oh,' Maynard said, 'it was that PTD we had earlier.'

'What was that then?'

'Some farm, twenty-two miles away.'

'Twenty-two miles?'

'That's it. Seems there's a leak from a cattle-trough. Seems the road's flooded.'

Renwick blew out his cheeks. 'Doesn't seem a lot to worry about,' he said.

'No,' Maynard shrugged. 'But it happens to be on the second cut-off to Brinsmead. And you know how Nanny feels about cut-offs.'

'I do, darling,' Renwick said. 'I do.'

It was forty minutes later, and Maynard's sector-screen showed a dot moving along the A914. While around it digits showed speed, average speed, ETA, fuel-level, oil-levels and pressures.

'No, the thing is,' Maynard said, 'it's not tax-bother he's in, it's VAT.'

'What's the difference?' Renwick asked.

'Well, VAT's the bastard. You can't argue with those boys. They're Customs and Excise.'

'I never knew that.'

'No more did he,' Maynard said. 'But he found out soon enough, I mean after he went self-employed.'

Then he looked round. A light was flashing below screen two, police traffic data.

Maynard pressed PTD.

Display and logged print-out started at the same time.

24/11, 0948, Maynard read, Message 1: TRAFFIC INCIDENT COORDINATES . . .

Maynard turned to the third screen and punched up a sector. He built it up. Tiny twig-like roads became branches, became a single branch which sprouted a cluster of dots around it.

'Village,' Maynard said, 'name of Friar's Norton.'

He turned back to the PTD screen and read further down the message.

. . . SCAFFOLDING TRUCK PASSING PARKED VAN MOUNTED HIGH PAVEMENT AND . . .

Maynard went back to the sector-screen. He punched up full sector recall, and thought it out.

Then he looked up at the intercom. 'Problem,' he said.

Nanny heard him out. His voice rose. It rose higher.

'Listen, I told you,' Maynard said. 'There's this narrow street with a high pavement. And this scaffolding truck that spilled its load.'

'I don't care,' Nanny shouted. 'That's the second cut-off gone. The second in an *hour*.'

'Spilled its load right outside a *police-station*,' Maynard shouted back. 'I mean, what a diabolical criminal act. Real mastermind stuff.'

'All right.' Nanny's voice calmed. 'Just find me a route round. Anything.'

'Will do,' Maynard said. And then did nothing, nothing for a minute and a half by his watch. 'Sorry,' he said then. 'The only other route's Gurlay, and they've still got that pipe-laying going on.'

'I knew it,' Nanny said. 'It's Whycliffe. The shadow run.'

The intercom went silent.

Maynard raised his eyebrows at Renwick. 'Where were we?' he asked.

'Talking about your brother-in-law and his VAT,' Renwick said.

'Oh, yes,' Maynard said. 'Dead trouble he's in.'

'You mean it?'

''Course I mean it. He's spent the money. Spent a bloody fortune . . . Ford Ghia, speedboat, trips abroad.'

'Jesus,' Renwick said. 'What's he do to be earning money like that?'

'Loft-conversions,' Maynard said. 'He'll convert your loft into anything – micro-lite aircraft, anything.'

SIXTY

The latest message had the van coming into the outskirts of Whycliffe.

Haskell left the corner of the barn and walked out into the yard. He took two or three deep breaths. The air was cold, hurting his lungs. There was a hard blue sky above him, with high vapour trails. The day seemed huge.

But he saw only parts of it.

The Cathedral Square where Gummer and Dave Rowan would be in their big six-axle artic. The radio-phone link that would have them slowing in the traffic until the white van was behind them.

The lower roundabout where McIver, Jock McIver's son, would be keeping his eye out.

Nearer at hand, the London Road, where Bazzer and Jack Shannon would be parked. And Liney with them, who would be taking charge up there.

Nearer still, Trevor handling the radio-calls from the barn-roof.

And inside the barn, Mike Whitrow and his mate, standing by with their cutting-gear.

Cutting-gear.

Haskell didn't want to think about that. Not right now.

Instead he told himself the game was on. *On*. They were back to where they had been two and a half months ago.

SIXTY-ONE

The line of cathedral choristers came down the steps and on to the square. Towards their rear was Joffrey. He had his head back and was trying to catch a glimpse of the crane. But he couldn't, he was too close to the building, so he gave up and looked at the traffic. Then he saw it, the white van. And in spite of himself said, 'My God, there's that white van.'

The boys around him turned.

'Oh, what?'

'Is Joffrey starting on those crashing lies of his again?'

'No.' Joffrey bit his lip. 'That's over, finished with.'

'Well, what about this famous van?'

'It's just there,' Joffrey said. 'That's all.'

'Where?'

'Out in the road, behind that great big lorry.'

'And nothing else? No blood?'

'No,' Joffrey said.

'But there's *bound* to be blood,' Hallam said. 'And explosions. And arms and legs torn off.'

'*And* the rest,' Morpurgo said.

'What d'you mean, the rest?' Ralston came up and joined the group.

Morpurgo turned to him. 'Didn't you hear? Jackson got it from Haldane, the maths master, who got it from Gaf, who got it from the headmaster himself.'

'Got what?'

'Well, according to Joffrey, there's some hi-tech robbery going on.' Morpurgo raised his eyebrows. 'Some sort of radio-blackout, if you please, caused by all that metal stuff on the cathedral roof.'

'You're joking,' Ralston said.

'No, he's not,' Hallam said. 'And the really strange thing is, Haldane said it was all just about possible.'

'Oh, *Haldane*, he's weird,' Morpurgo said. 'He watches Coronation Street.'

'True.' Hallam nodded. 'Very true.'

'And anyway,' Morpurgo took up the story again, 'the fat boy went too far after that and spoiled it all. He said he saw *criminals* down in the valley. One of them dressed all in black.'

'Unbe*lievable*,' Hallam said.

'Black shoes, black suit, black-dyed hair,' Morpurgo went on. 'Like the very naughty man in the Rupert books.'

Ralston laughed. The choristers went on down the pavement. Except for one boy who stayed quite still.

Gillick.

Joffrey had other things on his mind. He was far enough from the cathedral now to see the crane. And he looked up, expecting to find the banner he'd put up there last night.

Only it wasn't there.

Instead, a group of men was swarming around just below the cab, the cog-and-wheel part, that moved the whole thing round.

Joffrey was amazed. And more amazed as Gillick ran up.

The boy came close. 'It's *true*,' he whispered. 'All of it.'

'All of what?'

'What the others were talking about just now. The robbery . . . *Everything*.'

'What?'

Gillick pointed. 'Look up there,' he whispered. 'Those men trying to mend the crane. And you going up there last night. And Zee—'

'Zee?' Joffrey shook him. 'What about Zee?'

Gillick slowed down. 'All right.' He bit his lip. 'You know it was meant to be Zee ringing you up yesterday?'

'*Meant* to be? What are you *talking* about?'

'It wasn't her. It was me.'

'*What*?'

'Me all the time.'

Behind Gillick's head the sky seemed to flicker. The cathedral swayed . . .

But the boy was going on. 'And not just me. There was someone else as well . . . I mean, you remember I talked to someone who knew about cranes? Well, it was this man, this *same* man with the black-dyed hair. *He* was the one who wanted you up on the crane. Wanted you to turn the red wheel-thing. And now . . . now it's all going to *happen*.'

The whole world was swaying. Pavement, cars, traffic . . .

Only one thing was still.

Away at the far end of the square.

The white van.

There were shouts from behind him, but Joffrey was running. Running hard the length of the square, and then turning into a narrow street. Because the van was stuck there, behind the great big lorry. And it had been stuck some time, was flashing its lights at the lorry's rear tyres.

For a moment Joffrey thought he could get there in time. But then he knew he couldn't. Because the driver's mate climbed down from the lorry. He signalled up to the cab. And with hissing air-brakes, the lorry crabbed its way up onto the pavement. Then the man signalled the van through – just the van – before he stopped the rest of the traffic and waved the lorry out again.

And Joffrey knew what he was seeing. A barrier that closed to clear the road ahead. And then opened to let the van through. On its own.

It was all going to *happen*, just as Gillick had said.

SIXTY-TWO

Inside the van Maynard had a blank sector-screen. Which meant they were in the area of shadow. Out of contact.

But they were moving again, and moving fast.

He turned to Renwick. 'You know,' he said, 'we're going to get through this town in record time.'

'Could be.'

'And I can't say I'm sorry. I mean, we all have a go at Nanny, don't we? But he's only right. Whycliffe gives me the creeps. All this gear we've got, and it's bloody useless.'

Renwick nodded.

'Different in the old days,' Renwick went on. 'You remember? When it was just a bog standard Transit for the bank-runs? Tin walls? And we used to duck down every time we saw a farmer with a shotgun?'

'Bloody hell.' Renwick grinned. 'And remember that driver? What was his name? O'Malley?'

'The one with the bird-whistles?'

'That's him. Remember how he used to arrange all these signals? How he used to park by the bank, get out, then come round to the back of the van and whistle like a curlew?'

'Yes,' Maynard said.

'And I used to say to him, don't be such a mad bloody Mick. Just tell me to open the bloody door.'

Maynard laughed. He'd been leaning sideways in his chair as the van went downhill. But now he had to hold on as they swung through the roundabout at the bottom.

The valley road, he thought. Another minute and they'd be back in radio-contact.

But Nanny's voice came through the intercom. 'Here,' he said. 'Listen, is there another of our lot out today?'

'What's that?' Maynard asked.

'Another of our mobiles? Out from the factory?'

'There's a peseta-run,' Maynard said.

Up in the cab, Nanny stared through the windscreen. It *could* be the peseta-run, he thought. It could have come this way for Heathrow.

The van that was parked some way ahead by the roadside.

The white van.

With the big recovery vehicle next to it.

Nanny slowed. 'Get me control,' he said into the intercom.

'Can't,' Maynard's voice came back. 'We're still in shadow.'

'Still?'

'Yes, it's been getting bigger recently. They reckon it's something to do with the work on the cathedral roof.'

Nanny slowed even more.

He saw a man leave the recovery vehicle, come out into the road, and flag him down.

Nanny stopped. Because the book said you could stop, provided you left the engine running, and kept the van secure.

He slipped the gear into neutral. He lifted his legs, slid over the transmission-bulge, and across to the passenger seat. He knew he couldn't make anyone hear him through the bullet-proof glass. He couldn't radio, as Maynard had just told him. All he could do was raise his thumb at the other driver, shake his head in a question, then put his thumb down.

The other driver put his thumb down too.

Which was when Nanny saw the recovery vehicle suddenly huge in his mirror. Heard the clang of the breakdown-hook against his rear axle. And, as he tried to scrabble his way back to his seat, he was jerked against the windscreen by the whole vehicle tipping.

Maynard was tipped out of his chair too. He picked himself up from the floor and clawed his way back to the console. He pressed unsecure and heard the wail of the siren starting.

By which time the whole van was being dragged backwards.

Downhill.

SIXTY-THREE

Joffrey was still running . . . over-running himself as he careered down the path.

The zig-zag path, the one that went down the cliff. Quicker this way, he'd thought, far quicker. And there was still the *chance* the van was caught in the traffic on the cliff road.

He reached the bottom, the river there and the cinder path. But he turned and ran to his right, towards the carpark and the roundabout just beyond it.

There was a flat-truck parked just short of the roundabout. It had garden tools in the back, and up in the cab a driver checking out a clip-board.

Joffrey ran to him. He could hardly get the words out. 'Has a – has a white – van come past you?'

'A what?' The man stared at him strangely.

'A white – van – big white van – coming out of – town.'

'No.' The man shook his head. 'Nothing like that.'

'You – sure?'

'Course I'm sure. What is this?'

Joffrey sighed his relief. The van had to be behind him, still up on the cliff road.

He ran round and banged on the passenger door.

The man frowned in surprise, but opened up.

Joffrey slid into the seat. 'Quick,' he said. 'Drive – drive out to the roundabout . . . Block the road.'

'Block it? What d'you sodding *mean*?'

'This *van*,' Joffrey said. 'There's going to be a . . . robbery.'

'*What*?'

'I've *seen* them,' Joffrey said. 'Two men. One with – black-dyed hair. They come – come from the Unicorn Hotel – in Bristol. They've got an Audi – blue Audi – CMX – 114E.'

The man started the van. But he didn't stop on the roundabout. He drove fast along the valley road, swung left down a track, bumped over a yard. Stopped by a barn.

There was another man there in a dirty white sheepskin. 'McIver?' he asked.

Then he saw Joffrey.

'Get me to Hask,' the man called McIver said. 'This kid has got him nailed. Down to his inside-sodding-*leg*!'

SIXTY-FOUR

Inside the barn it was weird.

There was this strange siren, the kind police cars had, like a snickering steel spring.

Joffrey put his hands over his ears. McIver had hold of him, but it wasn't necessary. His legs were like jelly. He couldn't move.

Weird.

That sound. That huge steel-spring sound hissing back off the walls.

And the lights, sort of searchlights, red and white. They came from somewhere high up on the white van. And they swung round. But not all together. There was a leap of light and then a gap. Round and round. Picking out the barn walls, and the other vehicles.

Because there were *two* white vans. One with the lights and the sirens. And the other parked ahead of it.

And the big crane-truck parked behind.

And the *men*. Heads like blobs of plasticine in their stocking-masks. Flat noses, flat eyes, in the whirling light.

Then they moved. And there was a different sound, a screeching machine-like sound. And there was some sort of big tool-thing, with cables and whirring blades.

It was being slid into the front of the van. The radiator.

Haskell stood just behind Whitty. He saw the big blades go in, saw the grey jet of lube-fluid spurt out as they bit. Saw Whitty's shoulders tauten.

Haskell's mouth, his nose, itched in the stocking-mask. But he kept his mind clear. He'd give Whitty time, he thought. He'd always reckoned to do that.

But, Jesus, the first bonnet-look took forty-five seconds.

And the second, as Whitty changed his stance, took longer.

Forty-five seconds.

Fifty.

Haskell reached round behind him and switched the generator off.

Whitty turned, amazed. And he was more amazed as Haskell took the cutters from him. Then got him moving round to the side of the van, and making a shoulder up.

'Get that jenny on again,' he shouted.

He was up on the van roof, above the red and white lights as they whirled round like some crazy fairground ride.

And close to the siren.

The shriek-shriek of it filled his brain. He didn't hear the generator start up again. But he felt the blades move.

And then he had those blades, those three contra-spinning chains, down against metal.

The ventilator.

He was cutting steadily through it. Grey lube-fluid was spilling out over the van-roof and into the lights – when suddenly Liney's head was close.

'The fuck's happening?' he shouted.

But he knew. He *knew*.

'Hask, you can't *do* it?'

And for one moment Haskell stopped.

'You want to get *home*?' he asked. 'I mean, *do* you?'

He cut on and on. He got through the stack of the ventilator and then started on the metal plate he could see below. The one they'd put in there since the last raid, as Larcombe had said.

In three minutes by his watch he was through.

He switched off the machine, pushed Liney to one side, and dropped down throught the lights to the barn-floor.

Nobody looked at him as he went to his duffel-bag and got out the Semtex plastic explosive, the quartz watch taped to its detonator.

He turned back to the cab of the van, the driver. He tucked the explosive under his arm and mimed a key turning, a door opening, with his hands.

Then he held up the Semtex and showed he was setting the watch.

He stuck three fingers up and mouthed 'three minutes', very clearly.

In the cab the driver was leaping around like a ferret.

Haskell went up to the van-roof again, and lobbed the explosive down the pipe.

Inside the van they both heard it, the clatter coming down the ventilator duct. The duct that wasn't steel but galvanised. And they'd seen photos of that other galvanised duct, after the explosion.

Nanny was screaming on the intercom. 'Three fucking minutes! Just *three*!'

'Didn't you fucking tell him?' Renwick screamed back.

'How could I tell him? From the fucking cab?'

'You've got fucking *over-ride*, Nanny! You could *open the cab*!'

'*Listen*! He just *showed* the fucking thing! He mimed three fucking minutes! And he was *away*!'

It was Maynard who moved. 'Come *on*!'

He saw Nanny had switched off unsecure. And he himself went through secure to unlock.

Renwick moved too. He was at the panel of buttons by the steel bars, stabbing his finger down a row.

The yellow disc-lights began to fade.

Maynard ran back to the inner door of the compartment, the switch of the magno-lock there. He tried to switch off. Nothing happened.

'No!' Renwick shouted. 'It's got to be done in *sequence*!'

And stood there.

Just stood there.

'What you fucking *doing*?' Maynard shouted.

Renwick pointed to the yellow discs. 'The pilots've got to cool! *Nothing* happens till then!'

And he watched the discs slowly darken.

'How long?' Maynard shouted. 'How long've we had?'

'A minute.' Renwick was shaking. 'More! A minute-fifteen!'

'And how long's it take? I mean, your all-time fucking best?'

'Never got it under four. Four minutes,' Renwick said. And then he swung round. 'But you know! You fucking *know*!'

Maynard's lungs were like footballs. There was a singing in his ears.

He looked at his watch.

A minute-thirty. Call it a minute forty-five to be safe.

And *still* Renwick stood by the panel.

The yellow discs went out.

Renwick hit the next row of buttons.

The red discs began to fade. And slowly . . . slowly . . . the heat-shields slid back across the racks.

Maynard's second-hand was racing. Forty more seconds had gone by. Which made it two minutes twenty-five.

Renwick started on the bars.

There was a click. The heavy steel began to move.

Took forever.

Two minutes fifty-five.

Three minutes ten.

Three minutes fucking twenty-five.

'*Leave* it!' Maynard shouted.

And he ran for the locker where the helmets were, the useless fucking helmets and the bullet-proofers. He snatched them out.

'Come *on*!' He shouted to Renwick.

But Renwick had the bars back, was down by the inner door. The magno-switch.

He turned it to off. Started swinging the massive safe-wheel.

But Maynard was looking at the ventilator-shaft, the thin metal.

'For fuck's sake!' he shouted. 'Get over *here*!'

And Renwick nodded. He came. He grabbed up his bullet-proofer, tangled his arms in the sleeves. Maynard, half in his, tried to help. They were sweating, screaming.

And then they turned to the toilet compartment. But they both knew. They'd known all along.

There was only room for one with the door shut.

Renwick's face was sick. Maynard nodded. 'Allow me,' he said.

The man was weak, slack, as Maynard pushed him in, shut the door. Then he crouched down outside. A tight ball. The collar of his bullet-proof waistcoat up round his helmet.

Outside, the siren and the lights had been out for some time. The van was still. Then there was a roar. A blast of air shot up through the ventilator-pipe. It smacked against the tin roof, buckled it. Brought down lengths of timber and thick black dust.

Joffrey didn't know how long he'd crouched there. All he knew was that the back door of the van was open. That men, men in stocking-masks, were coming out two by two. That they were carrying flat steel cases between them, like camera cases, only bigger, and heavier.

And that there was this noise. This tiny noise.

This sort of sucking, slurping noise that came from their shoes. And the soles of their shoes were sticky. Dark.

And then, he supposed, it had to be the last case. Because the men put it down. They opened it. They took something out from inside and held it up against the light. And they were crowing, happy.

It was a large white sheet of blank paper.

Joffrey's mind unzipped.

Unzipped.

Haskell was leaning against the white van. He turned as Liney came up.

'Anyone talking in there?' the man asked quietly.

'Yes,' Haskell said, 'one.'

'And the other?'

'Bad.'

Liney grabbed him. 'So why didn't they *open*?'

Haskell hesitated. 'Because the unlocking took four minutes,' he said.

'*Four*?'

'You think I'd've set it to three if I'd known that?' Haskell asked. 'Just one bloody minute on a quartz watch?'

Liney turned away.

Haskell moved round him. He spoke quietly. 'Just get it out of your mind. Just remember we took twenty-five minutes here, start to finish. And there's *still* another ten minutes to go before anyone presses the alarm-button.'

'Yes,' Liney said. And he walked away to one of the two remaining vehicles in the barn. It was a two-ton truck. There were men waiting inside, sitting on the steel cases.

Liney joined them. And he turned once again to Haskell before he pulled down the rear shutter.

'What about the kid?' he asked.

'I'm taking him with me,' Haskell said.

'Where?'

'Where I was always going. Where our good mate Larcombe's waiting with his cases packed,' Haskell said. 'Nothing changes.'

The rear shutter closed. The truck reversed away. Haskell went over to where McIver was waiting with the kid.

By the last remaining vehicle. A black Merc 190E.

Quality car, Haskell thought, fitted extras.

He opened each door in turn and put on the child-locks.

SIXTY-FIVE

Haskell drove east along the motorway, east, the opposite way the others had gone. He kept the needle just below seventy, and he watched the kid on his left.

It was the fat kid, he knew, the one he'd seen in the cathedral last night, coming for the key.

But the rest of it, all that stuff McIver had told him . . . the description that fitted, the car-number that fitted, the Unicorn Hotel *and* the radio-shadow . . . he just didn't understand.

Forget it for the moment, he thought. Keep everything in its separate compartment, just like always. Stick with the *now*.

And the now was getting eleven miles down the motorway to the first turn-off.

Should be okay, he thought. The white van was still in shadow. Control would still have the Whycliffe traffic-jam on their screens. Only thirty-five minutes had passed.

Should be okay.

The first warning for the junction came up. Haskell moved into the inside lane without signalling.

The second warning. He slowed. Slowed more. But there was no sign of John Law up on the roundabout. He took the turn-off.

And was through. Simple as that.

He was on a broad three-lane road in open country. There was stubble on one side, and winter wheat on the other. And then a signpost, Lodwick 3 miles.

Haskell breathed more easily. He remembered the thought he'd had a week or two back, the good thought. And the phone-call he'd made.

To Landon-Higgins. The man with the jowl, and the gut, and the tent-like suit.

'The hell you after, feller?' the man had asked.

'Just a social call, a little favour,' Haskell had said. 'I'm looking for some pigeon-shooting.'

'Pigeon-shooting?'

'Put it like this,' Haskell said. 'You must have got mates with a bit of land. Mates with a few fields of winter wheat, and a problem with pigeons.'

'No,' Landon-Higgins said.

'What I was thinking about,' Haskell said, 'was somewhere out Bristol way. Somewhere with a sizeable estate, and maybe a cottage tucked away that could be used by shooting friends.'

'*No*.'

It had taken Haskell a little time, but he'd got there in the end.

Just short of Lodwick there was a driveway leading off to the right. It broke high ground between black thorn bushes, and then sunk down into a dip. Until, maybe a mile further on, there was a chestnut tree standing up from a scattering of brown leaves, and a small stone cottage.

Haskell parked. The garden was overgrown, he saw, but the house had been looked after. The roof was new, the guttering was grey plastic, and the windows were white-painted. Then, at a downstairs window, he saw a face. Larcombe's face.

Haskell got out. He went round, unlocked the passenger door, and got hold of the fat kid by his blazer. He took him up the path and in through the front door.

Larcombe stood back in the narrow hall, his face amazed, as the two of them passed. Their feet were loud on bare wooden stairs, and louder still on the narrow landing. Haskell chose a room. He checked that the door had a lock and a key, and he took the fat kid inside.

There was the smell of new white paint, and bright light came in through the uncurtained window. Haskell nodded the kid over to the bed in the corner, and started asking him questions. The kid was too afraid not to answer. And gradually, as the talk went on, Haskell began to understand.

* * *

Larcombe was waiting for him down in the shadowy hall. His face was a dark blue, just as it had been in the dawn-light this morning. And he was still shivering. 'How the hell does he come to be here?' he asked. 'The kid?'

'He got involved,' Haskell said. 'There was nothing we could do about it. He saw.'

'Saw?'

'That's right. He was out on the roundabout, the one below the town.'

'But what . . . what could he see from there?'

'Enough,' Haskell said. 'McIver brought him in.'

But Larcombe shook his head. 'I don't get it,' he said. 'I mean, that's one of the kids from the choir school. Why was he out there? Why wasn't he in school?'

'I don't know.'

The man's shivering grew worse. There was a wildness about him, a crackling in his throat. 'For Christ's sake,' he said, 'if he only *saw*, like you said. I mean, the crew of that shipment van *saw* too. Why didn't you leave him with them?'

Haskell sidestepped. 'Look, you're upset,' he said. 'You've been here all morning on your own.'

'Sure I'm upset.' Larcombe's voice rose. 'Because you don't *answer*. This kid, you talk to him for hours. You lock him in a room. What's going on? What are you going to *do* with him?'

Haskell hesitated. 'Leave him here,' he said.

'Leave him?'

'When we go away tomorrow or Sunday. When it's safe.'

'No,' Larcombe said.

'What d'you mean, no? I'll phone the Law when we're clear. When all of us are clear.'

But the man came closer. 'No,' he said again, 'there's more. A *lot* more to it than that.'

'No more,' Haskell said.

And he eased his way past Larcombe. He went out to the car, opened the boot, and got out the Mercedes toolkit. He found a screw-driver and started unscrewing the window winder-handles from the doors.

He was just finishing the last one when he heard it, the man talking inside. Talking softly.

Haskell ran in. He crossed the hall to the front room, white-painted like the room upstairs.

And he should've bloody *known*. The house with its new roof, new windows, new white paint . . .

There was a phone.

And Larcombe was sitting on the floor, talking.

Haskell grabbed it from him. He heard a woman's voice, a voice he recognised. He slammed the phone down.

'It's her, isn't it?' he asked. 'That bit you had back at the hotel? What was her name? . . . Julie?'

Larcombe shrugged.

'For Christ's sake, why?'

The man looked up at him. 'I've been talking to her all morning. I've been feeling bad. Very bad.'

And now suddenly, in the bright white room, away from the shadows of the hall, Haskell understood. That crackling in the man's throat . . . the shivering, and the blueness of his face.

The things that London specialist had said to look out for.

Haskell took his time. 'Okay,' he said, 'you're feeling rough, more than rough. But I'll have you away from here in two days' time. I'll have you on that cruise ship, like I said . . . Just see things my way.'

The man shook his head.

Haskell went towards him. 'My way,' he repeated. 'I mean, I have to know. That woman, what did you say to her just now?'

No answer.

Haskell bent close.

'I told her,' Larcombe said slowly. 'I told her what you're going to do with that kid. What I *know* you're going to do.'

'You *what*?'

'And she,' the man started to get up, 'she said she'd ring the police.'

'Jesus,' Haskell said. He started for the door.

Still crouching, Larcombe came after him, grabbed him. He rasped in breath and pulled his arm back. He hit soft as a child.

Haskell held him away. 'Now, listen . . . Listen . . .'

But Larcombe pulled his arm back again. And Haskell pushed him away. The man toppled, hit the floor.

He made a huge effort, got up again. Fast. There was a crack inside him. His face turned dark, mottled. He fought for breath. And then he shot, *shot* four feet across the room.

Haskell went to him, bent down. The man came up again, got breath, hauled his arm back a third time. But motors inside him took over. Terrible motors. Jerked up his legs, his dark face.

He fell back. And in a few moments it was over.

Haskell stood up. There was just his breathing in the room. It seemed very white. And through the window the land was white and flat. He looked out at it, shooting country, good shooting country. And gradually it got through to him. The copse of beeches, the kale on the slope above, the really classy high shot there'd be for the guns on the right, and the hedge they'd grubbed out to stop the birds running left.

It cleared his mind.

He undid his belt from his trousers, coiled it, put it in his jacket pocket.

And went upstairs for the kid.

SIXTY-SIX

Joffrey sat in the front passenger seat. The man sat next to him, black and hard-edged against the light. He started the engine.

And Joffrey looked away. Something had changed, he thought. Something was different in the car. And then he understood. The window winder-handles were missing.

They started off along the driveway, past the tree with the dead brown leaves around it. Along the straight. Then down towards the slight dip.

Joffrey knew the man was going to slow. Knew he was going to stop. Down in that dip. Where nobody could see.

The man pulled on the handbrake. He turned.

'Better put your seat-belt on, kid, before we get to the road.'

Joffrey nodded. But inside he was beginning to feel panic. It was made up of the missing winder-handles, the dip in the road, and the seat-belt. A fat boy's panic, that put things together like that.

Think *thin*, he thought.

'Better do it, kid. It's in the Highway Code.'

Again Joffrey nodded. With one hand he reached up and to his left. He got hold of the metal end of the belt.

Then he stopped. The fat boy's panic told him the man was doing something. Was feeling in his jacket pocket.

'What's the matter, kid?'

'Nothing.'

'Is it a bit stiff? The seat-belt?'

'No.'

'Sometimes it is. It sticks.'

Joffrey pulled it down a few inches. Just a few inches. The belt came out quite smoothly.

'Here, let me try.' The man reached over with his left hand, took the belt-end. He pulled it further down. Then he stopped.

'Sticking,' he said. 'I told you it sticks.'

And then:

'Give it a good tug, kid. Both hands. Up at the top.'

Joffrey froze. The belt wasn't sticking. The man wasn't pulling at all. And his right hand was still hidden inside his pocket.

'Go on.'

Panic made Joffrey squirm. His knee came up and brushed the dashboard. There was a click.

Think *thin*.

But he was shaking. He knew the man wanted him to raise both hands up to the belt-fastening. Up and away from his face. He didn't know why.

Then something caught his eye. He saw what had made that click. The cigarette-lighter was lit on the dashboard. He'd pushed it in with his knee.

Thin.

He snaked down past the man's arm. Grabbed up the lighter. Stuffed it straight into his eye.

There was a scream. The man batted the lighter away. He doubled forward.

And, fast, Joffrey threw himself behind him, head-forward to the driver's door. The handle. It moved. He fell on his shoulders on the gravel.

And was running.

The man was running behind him, one hand pressed against his eye.

Was catching him.

Until, from the slope ahead, and the gap in the thorn-bushes—

Sirens. Those sounds like springing steel.

And flashing lights.

Not red this time, but blue.

SIXTY-SEVEN

Things were strange then. They happened quickly, and became telescoped together.

There were the hours in the police station with the CID men, Joffrey answering their questions, answering them a second time, and all the while thinking about those other men with stocking-masks. How they would come for him. At school.

'Don't worry about it,' the CID men said. 'We'll lift the lot of them. Just keep talking.'

There was the going away from the police station in the Telecom van, to avoid the press.

There was the changing over from the van to the headmaster's car. Then, in Melchior's study, the man giving him cocoa, putting his arm around him, and talking with ever more watering eyes.

And then the strangest thing of all.

It didn't happen all at once, but over a few days.

Joffrey gradually realising that people were repeating what they said. That he himself wasn't answering. Not in fact saying very much.

Then nothing at all.

Not one word.

His mother came and fetched him from school in her car. It was the small new Fiat she'd bought. It smelled of her new scent. And of course they went back to the new house.

The house in the Midlands that was tiny. That was filled with the large furniture of the past. Where every room was a corridor, his mother walking with her hands held out to ward off chairs.

She smiled and hugged him a lot, but she'd been crying.

And what he hadn't expected was that he couldn't talk to her either, except for Yes and No.

But he felt black, this hard blackness inside him. His mother's arms were like sticks, there were the crying-marks under her eyes. And never again would there be that calm, heart-clutching *delight* in her face. The face of the photographs.

He was appalled by himself as he sat in her arms, her sticks. As he felt the blackness push out to the edge of his skin, his shirt. As he said Yes and No.

He was helped . . . both of them were . . . by the Christmas present she gave him early. The mini-stack of tape and amplifier and stereo radio. There were blank tapes too, and he recorded A-Ha and Simple Minds. He sat with his ear to one of the speakers, and the days grew dark, then dark again.

She let him off church on the first Sunday.

She let him off everything.

He expanded Yes to Yes, I'm All Right.

But he wasn't.

Even when the new stereo radio told him the men in the stocking-masks had been caught.

And the paper found.

The paper.

Those strange sucking, slurping noises coming from the shoes.
And the strange thought he'd had at that moment.
His mind *unzipping*.
He sat and thought about a mind unzipping with an unzipping mind.
And the blackness inside him changed. He began to wake up at night screaming, filled with people.
Gillick inside him, phoning and saying he was Zee.
The man with the dyed hair standing beside Gillick and saying, now tell him about *lax*. Now tell him you'll *show* him lax.
And beside the man standing beside Gillick stood Zee.
But he couldn't think about Zee.
He knew if he unzipped himself that far back.
Found out how deep they'd got inside him.
He'd be split apart.

He was having pills now. And the doctor said he should go out, out of the house.
His mother said it too.
He said No.
But on the second Sunday she made him get ready for church.
He got his best suit down from the wardrobe.
He put it on.
And felt . . . felt in his right-hand pocket something hard. Hard and round.
He got it out, a small green pebble.
And he remembered. The three coloured pebbles. The first one he'd thrown, and been given very high marks for.
Five-point-*nine*.
Five-*nine*.
The second one he'd thrown, hit the self-same spot, and been given three-point-two.
And the third one he'd kept. In the pocket of his best suit.
Real, real, *real*, he thought.
It had happened.
They'd played that game.

And afterwards Zee had stood there by the pool.
Alone with him. Close.
And she'd said . . .

On the Sunday afternoon, after church and lunch, his mother fell asleep by the fire.

He went upstairs and searched through her cupboards.

He didn't know why.

But then he found letters on thin prison paper.

From his father.

And he was amazed. The word love kept cropping up. Love . . . love . . . love . . . Three times on a page.

And the words, I can't wait to see you next visiting day.

And, only eight more *months*!

His mother was awake.

And he hated himself. He still couldn't go near her, hug her.

But he could say more.

'I want to go back,' he said.

'Back?'

'To school.'

'Now?' She frowned. 'But there are only two days left. The last day, and then the carol service.'

'I want to be near,' he said.

SIXTY-EIGHT

Outside the headmaster's study was the darkness of the court. Inside were Melchior, Sorley, and the grey-suited figure of Maunder the organist.

'But, you have to admit it's awkward,' Maunder said.

'Yes,' Melchior said.

'More than awkward,' Maunder insisted. 'It could even be foolhardy.'

Melchior frowned.

'Agreed, agreed, this boy has had an extremely disturbing experience,' Maunder went on. 'But the fact remains he *is* disturbed. He said nothing, absolutely nothing, during the time before he went home. And at home, according to his mother, he said very little . . . So how is he now? Talking away normally?'

'Not really,' Melchior said. 'In fact hardly at all.'

Maunder adjusted the fall of his suit. 'You see what I mean,' he said. 'If he won't talk, will he sing?'

Melchior shifted. 'I'm not very good at psychology,' he said. Then he turned to Sorley. 'But, about his singing? I mean, did he pull his weight at choir practice yesterday?'

'Well, he sang,' Sorley said, 'the parts he knew well. The parts that were safe.'

But Maunder cut in between them. 'Safe?' he asked. 'What's *safe* about a boy singing a solo? One that starts the entire carol service off? Unaccompanied? With only a pitch-pipe to give him his note?'

Sorley flushed. 'Well, as for the solo,' he said, 'I didn't rehearse it with him yesterday. I intended to go through it in a few minutes' time.'

'Did you now?'

'Yes,' Sorley said. 'And if it works, as I'm sure it will, I really think we should give it a try.'

'A try, Mr Sorley?' Maunder moved closer. 'Can I remind you that we have the reputation of the choir to think of? Not to mention my own?'

Sorley was angry.

Melchior saw it, and he knew it was time to intervene. 'Just now we were talking about the boy speaking and the boy singing,' he said. 'I mentioned I wasn't very good at psychology . . . And perhaps that's the whole problem.'

Maunder turned.

'It occurs to me,' Melchior went on, 'that in this choir school of ours we have very few words for the twentieth century. We never say boys are adjusted or disturbed. We say they are on good form or under the weather. It's an easy, ritualised way of talking.'

Maunder smiled coldly. 'An interesting observation,' he said, 'but I don't see how it helps.'

'Ritual.' Melchior found he was angry too. He waved a hand at Sorley. 'This man,' he said, 'once came here, into this study, and accused me of ritual.'

Sorley looked up, surprised.

'As it happens, he was right,' Melchior continued. 'And as it happens, it was about this self-same boy, Joffrey. I punished him unjustly. To my shame I didn't see what was in front of my eyes.'

Maunder came forward. He was conciliatory. 'There are many difficulties in looking after young boys nowadays,' he said. 'My only concern is where they spill over into the choir.'

Melchior raised his voice. 'A young boy has come back to this school, a place that has caused him untold distress. He has come back to sing a solo in the carol service. He wants to sing that solo. There is a part of him that is greatly talented, and we must allow it to develop. What I'm trying to explain to you, Mr Maunder, is that there's a *greater* form of ritual this school has to offer. It comes from a thousand people waiting in a darkened cathedral, for a single voice to begin. It's a sense of expectation, of mystery . . . And if Joffrey fails, there'll be a slight hiccup in your service. But if he succeeds, with God's help we can start to win back a soul.'

SIXTY-NINE

Along the west front of the cathedral, on the paving-stones, there were candles. Candles in jam-jars, gusting in the wind. There were candles too inside the portico. And through the open west door the great nave was flickering, smoky, lit by more candles, hundreds of them, on the capitals of pillars, along the nave walls, and on two huge chandeliers above the aisle.

Joffrey stood there, in the open doorway, alone. To his right was Sorley. And further to his right, Morpurgo, who had been brought along in case Joffrey failed.

There was coughing. There was clearing of throats from the vast congregation. Then, gradually, silence.

'Once in Royal,' Sorley said.

But Joffrey ignored him. He was still staring ahead, at the chandeliers above the aisle. And it had to be his nerves, but they were pumping up and down.

Sorley came forward. He touched Joffrey's shoulder briefly. He had a pen-torch in one hand, to beat time. And in the other, a pitch-pipe.

He blew a D.

Then he helped Joffrey further. He hummed the same D, and also the F sharp above.

He raised his pen-torch, beat two-and-in.

Joffrey had breath. He opened his mouth. Not a sound came out.

Sorley smiled.

He hummed D and F sharp again. Again beat two-and-in.

Joffrey sang.

It was quite simple. His voice was not part of him but a separate thing, a pencil or a ruler, which he used. Pressing harder on the upward lines, and softer as he came down. And not, when he came to it, pressing too hard on the high E, the Mary was. Just thinking Mary was.

The torch beat on. Then it stopped. The echo of his voice hung for a moment in the cathedral. Until, from far away, the choir came in with the second verse.

Sorley touched Joffrey's shoulder again. He led him out along the aisle. The whole length of it. And as they walked, the lights above each archway came on, keeping pace with them, until the nave was full of light.

Then they were through the rood-screen and passing the choir, decani and cantoris, halfway into the third verse. They walked on beyond them to the altar rail, and the great reredos in the smoke.

Sorley bowed first. And he thought of a voice that came once in a person's lifetime.

And, from his headmaster's stall, Melchior bowed slightly too. In gratitude. To the God who was always, always there in the shadow.

Then Joffrey, gripping the altar rail, bowed in his turn. And looked slowly up at the great reredos, at the latticework of stone, the statues of the saints, and Jesus high above.

But he didn't see saints. He saw women with bright dresses and mysteriously smiling faces. Women who seemed to move in the smoke, dance with great happiness, holding hands.

Nor did he see Jesus. Instead he saw a girl by a diving-board in a pure white costume. Her face coming closer, pouring out light.

The cathedral organ broke in. The choir were now starting on the fourth verse, accompanied. While he, Joffrey, was repeating the words of the first.

He had been Once in Royal.

He knew that.

Just as he knew there were other Royals waiting for him.

Knew it from his father's letters.

There would be summer. There would be delight. A chain of glittering islands.

And if he hurried he would get to them.

Also available from Mandarin Paperbacks

Ed McBain

DOWNTOWN

The Big Bad Apple on Christmas Eve is no place for an orange grower from Florida. Especially when a blue-eyed blonde accuses him of stealing her diamond ring, a phoney detective rifles his wallet and a casual Good Samaritan makes off with his hire car.

For Michael Barnes, that is just the beginning of a nightmarish caper through the concrete jungle of downtown Manhattan. Not even Vietnam was this bad. Crazy killers, cops, actors, bimbos and million-dollar crack dealers are all out for his blood. Even the corpses can't be trusted.

But for an unexpected ally in the shape of Connie Kee, a beautiful and streetwise Chinese girl, Barnes stands next to no chance in these unfriendly precincts. He can guess the answers to every question but the one that might save his skin. Who the hell is Mama, and why does she so badly need him dead?

Downtown is a page-flashing Christmas cracker of a novel that sparkles with all the wit and tension that fans of Ed McBain have come to expect.

'McBain has a great approach, great attitude, terrific style, strong plots, excellent dialogue, sense of place and sense of reality. He's right where he belongs – at the top.' *Elmore Leonard*

Shizuko Natsuki

MURDER AT MT. FUJI

In their luxurious country villa, the large and wealthy Wada family have gathered as usual to celebrate New Year. This time, however, they have another guest, for Chiyo, the family favourite, has invited her American friend and part-time tutor to join them and help her with her studies.

At first a little awed by the family whose name is a household word, Jane Prescott has barely settled in when a distraught Chiyo bursts into the living room claiming to have stabbed her grandfather to death.

The old man, it seems, has in fact died by accident and so the family are quick to club together to protect Chiyo and their reputation. They weave a complex web of alibis and deceits to fool police and blame an outsider.

But no sooner have they all joined the conspiracy, when it dawns on Jane that one of their number has a reason to see that it fails . . .

Through the eyes of an American, Shizuko Natsuki has contrived a deceptive Japanese conjuring trick which is as refreshing as it is ingenious.